The
DRAGON UNKNOWN
PART I

KENNETH KAPPELMANN

The DRAGON UNKNOWN PART I

HIDDEN MAGIC VOLUME II

TATE PUBLISHING
AND ENTERPRISES, LLC

The Dragon Unknown - Part I
Copyright © 2014 by Kenneth Kappelmann. All rights reserved.

No part of this publication may be reproduced, stored in a retrieval system or transmitted in any way by any means, electronic, mechanical, photocopy, recording or otherwise without the prior permission of the author except as provided by USA copyright law.

This novel is a work of fiction. Names, descriptions, entities, and incidents included in the story are products of the author's imagination. Any resemblance to actual persons, events, and entities is entirely coincidental.

The opinions expressed by the author are not necessarily those of Tate Publishing, LLC.

Published by Tate Publishing & Enterprises, LLC
127 E. Trade Center Terrace | Mustang, Oklahoma 73064 USA
1.888.361.9473 | www.tatepublishing.com

Tate Publishing is committed to excellence in the publishing industry. The company reflects the philosophy established by the founders, based on Psalm 68:11,
"The Lord gave the word and great was the company of those who published it."

Book design copyright © 2014 by Tate Publishing, LLC. All rights reserved.
Cover design by Samson Lim
Interior design by Mary Jean Archival

Published in the United States of America
ISBN: 978-1-63306-508-6
Fiction / Fairy Tales, Folk Tales, Legends & Mythology
14.10.07

For

Keith Kappelmann

and

in loving memory of

Carol Kappelmann

Contents

Prologue 9
The Masquerade 11
The Separation 29
A New Direction 48
Gnausanne: The River 66
Captured: The Boat 82
The Reunion 102
Kapmann Captured 126
Hawthorne 144
Slayne's Plan 160
Cindif 177
Fehr and Maldor 195
Trees of Death San-Deene 210
The Next Attack 229
Characters 241

Prologue

Schram Starland, prince of the human city of Toopek, thought about the last three years of his life. He had gone from a human youth walking with his canok friend to an elf-human magician providing leadership over the world. He had lost much—his lifelong friend Kirven, his mother and father; new friends had died and new relationships made. He had married his love and seen love grow in those around him.

Their trek to save Troyf had been successful for now. The prophecy Kirven had created had been fulfilled by what Schram believed was how his friend had designed it. Schram was tall, strong, and powerful, but was he powerful enough to defeat the black dragon, Slayne, and his magical wrath? With his companions, Stepha, Princess of the Flyer Elves and wife to Schram; Maldor, the young human-built maneth (large creatures with a lion mane) thrown into Batt Line Leadership and currently captured by Slayne; Jermys, the dwarf who lost his twin brother in the final battle with Kirven; Krirtie, the fiery human girl who was in love with Maldor; and Fehr, the bandicoot rat with a habit of getting into trouble but a critical piece nonetheless. They had found the source of the evil and struck hard against its offensive.

However, Slayne, the evil black dragon believed to be behind this dragon offensive still lived. He has captured Maldor in their pursuit to obtain the weapons of the Ring of Ku. The maneths and elves have moved to support Toopek, for they all know if Toopek falls, their chance of winning this war is low. Geoff, King of the Maneths, is overseeing Toopek while Madeiris, King of the Elves is supporting both the maneth homeland and Toopek while still holding Elvinott against all forces as Schram and his companions still try to find the solution to defeat Slayne.

Fate has taken them far, but what does fate have to do with the future? What has happened to Schram's mother, not seen since Toopek was originally attacked so long ago? How can they save Maldor and how can they obtain and harness the powers of the weapons of the Ring and the Staff of Anbari? They have only begun to understand the powers held deep within Krirtie's scimitar, Jermys's hatchet, Stepha's bow, and the hammer that had become affixed into Maldor's arm, perhaps protecting them both from the evil clutches of the black dragon. Where should Schram begin, and who can he trust in these very dangerous times, and how can he learn about the powers of his staff, the simple branch obtained in Anbari's Dominion? What does it mean, and who can teach him? All these questions must be answered before the hidden magic may finally be revealed.

The Masquerade

Schram did not know exactly what to expect as he approached his longtime friend's door. They had only been back in Toopek just over a week and already all of the companions, except Krirtie and himself, had departed to prepare for the first unified offensive against the dragon forces. Since their return, Krirtie had remained in her family's old house, spending her free time by herself as she fought to work through her hardships, giving her presence only to bid farewell to those she had fought beside for so long. Schram only hoped the news he brought could break down some of the shell she had built around herself, for he did not want to leave her in this state. However, the time to act was soon approaching, and it was his job to lead the maneth troops through Elvinott. He knew that he must speak with her today.

Slowly, he raised his hand and began to knock, gripping his magical staff, the Staff of Anbari, tightly with his other. He was greeted with silence and proceeded to pound harder, although he knew the first had been heard clearly. Again, no sound was returned, and giving a slight sigh, the human-turned-elf magician said in a raised but gentle tone, "Krirtie, it is Schram. Please open the door."

He waited patiently as he heard the shuffling of various papers depicting of someone rising from a seat, knocking whatever they had been working on to the floor. His elven ears heard footsteps slowly walking toward the door, then the soft, cracked voice of his lifelong friend. "Go away, Schram! I do not wish to speak to anyone, including you."

His head dropped, letting his long black hair fall about his shoulders. "Please, Krirtie, I bring news which I think you might find valuable. Besides, if you don't open the door, I shall enter by my own resources, and you know what a mess I can make going that route," although they both knew in moments Schram could have the door swing harmlessly open with only a short incantation.

With a loud snap, the bolt holding it closed popped back, and slowly the large wooden door swung ajar. A deep musty odor bit Schram's acute elven sensing nose causing the magician to take a step back while the stale air from inside was quickly replaced with that from the summer afternoon. He wore a broad smile in spite of the smell and the worn expression of his friend. Her hair was tangled and not well kept, with as much dirt spread across her face as appeared to be in the front room of her house. The armor she had worn so proudly for nearly the past two years remained stacked beside the door while her brilliantly curved and glistening scimitar sat against a chair Schram assumed she had just come from.

Her voice was dry and spoke of many sleepless nights. "Come on in. I suppose you would only make more of a mess if you used your *other resources* to force entry."

"I don't think more of a mess is possible."

She shot a daggered stare back toward him questionably. "What?"

Schram smiled in return but did not repeat himself. She already gave the distinct impression she was not pleased to see him, and he did not wish to make matters worse. He opened his arms and replied, "Are you not even interested in my news?"

She returned with a quick hug of her own. "If you brought the news I desire, you would have kicked the door in to tell me. I know you well enough to know that you cannot keep good news a secret too long. I suspect you are here to bid me farewell and give your love as the others have already done."

Schram frowned as he felt the pain she was still feeling over her losses. She made her way over all the rubble to again sit in the chair next to her sword and pick up a book that had remained open to where she had left off when he had knocked. Schram glanced around the small room to see that his first impression was correct—this house was in shambles. Books and papers lay scattered anywhere they could find a spot to rest, along with enough other garbage to keep a wandering bandicoot busy for weeks. His expression must have told his feelings, as Krirtie added, "I haven't had a chance to clean in a while."

The magician smiled. "Pay it no mind. I am used to it when I come to visit here." He paused to let his comment sink in. Then he added, shaking his head, "Yes, the Waywards were never known for their cleanliness."

Krirtie's frown began to turn slightly upward as she heaved her book at him. "Watch your mouth, Schram, or so help me I shall make you clean this place on your hands and knees."

Schram caught the book before it struck him in the stomach, laughing slightly when he saw the redness in his friend's face. "There, I told Jermys I could make you smile. That dwarf is buying the first round of ales." His speech stopped when he began to inspect the book she had been reading. "*The Legend of Draag?* This book is nothing more than a fable. It is based more on one elf's mystic dreams than true reality. What is going through that mind of yours now, Krirtie?"

His tone had become much more serious, and the smile that had begun to form on Krirtie's face as quickly vanished. "In less than two years, I learned to love another like I have never loved before. I always believed you would be the one who would capture my heart for good, but when I met Maldor, my whole life changed." Schram set his staff to the side and moved over to sit next to the girl who had a large tear forming in her eye. Her voice cracked slightly as she continued. "More than once he risked everything to save me, and for what? To end up prisoner in some forgotten caverns facing the wrath of a crazed dragon magi." She put her hands on Schram's knee and her voice became much stronger. "I have taken every book from our libraries regarding the subject, whether fiction or fact. I will find a way to help him, for he is all I have left."

Schram put his hands over the girl's, and his expression told her he understood. Gently he pulled her close. "Krirtie, I know of the feelings you hold for Maldor, and I carry similar feelings for Stepha. However, to attempt to help him on your own would be foolish, only resulting in your capture or even worse, death. How do you think that would make Maldor feel? Also, you are by no means alone. When Maldor was taken from us, our entire group was struck deeply. None have forgotten what that maneth did for us, and in time, we will all go back to help him, that much I promise."

Krirtie looked up, still crying. "But Maldor doesn't have any time. Each day more of his life fades as Slayne slowly wins over his plight for the hammer. If we don't act soon, Maldor will die."

He sighed deeply, then continued in a voice that hinted at pleading. "How about this? I will take care of my business at the canok homeland, then return to meet you at Elvinott, and we will discuss a possible rescue effort."

Her face showed surprise when she said, "You wish me to accompany you to Elvinott to aid in the elves' attempt to retake their forests?"

"I wouldn't think of going without you. Besides, your mother is not comfortable around the elves and dwarves. I think she would prefer your company."

"My mother! Where is she?"

Schram smiled broadly as the now-excited woman was on her feet and standing over him. "Jermys and Madeiris happened upon a small group of renegade humans trying to make it back to Toopek. They had fled at various times and subsequently been captured by goblin armies. All the men had been killed, but some of the women were spared. This group broke free from their captors sometime ago and has since been wandering aimlessly, trying to avoid recapture. Your mother saw the elven party traveling through the forest and made her presence known, speaking to the two she recognized, Stepha and Madeiris. They felt it better to take her on to Feldschlosschen rather than let her party risk returning to

Toopek. Although our surrounding forests are fairly safe, you can never be sure."

"Oh, Schram," she exclaimed, falling into his arms. "Thank you. Thank you very much. This is the best news I have heard in longer than I can remember."

He pushed the woman back a little and added softly, "Now, I haven't seen her, of course, but remember all she has been through. I am sure much has happened to her in the past eighteen months, and I don't want you to have false expectations."

Her smile faded. "I know, Schram, but the point is, she lives. I still do have a family."

He lifted her aside and then rose, retrieving his magical staff in the process. "I trust you will be ready to leave at first light tomorrow?"

She stood on her toes and kissed her childhood friend on his cheek. "I am ready now, you fool magician."

He shrugged a little, pressing his lips into an odd smirk before adding, "I would not want my mother returning to this mess, but I guess for Waywards, this is clean."

He shut the door quickly before hearing another large book strike hard behind him. He briefly twisted his lips into a smile, as he knew he could clean that mess in only seconds with a simple spell, but also feeling it would do Krirtie good to do it herself. He hurried off, remembering he too had much to do before tomorrow, including talking to Geoff and Alan regarding the safety of Toopek.

"I can't believe you are erecting a second wall around the entire city," said Schram, looking over the top view drawing of Toopek that Geoff had prepared.

The maneth appeared concerned. "It's all right, isn't it? I mean, this is a human city. It is not really my place to enforce—"

He was cut off by Schram's raised hand. "You have guarded this city better than anyone else could have hoped to do. It is our city, and if you feel this will help protect it, then by all means, do it."

Geoff smiled. "Good, it should be completed in less than a month. And look here"—he pointed to another spot on the map—"all the buildings that remain standing are reinforced and in key positions to defend, in the unlikely event both the walls are breached. I think by hiding bowmen on the rooftops, we will be able to hold against any ground assault the goblin and dark dwarf armies can throw at us."

"The problem lies with them damn flying beasts," echoed Captain Maximus Pete's rough voice from the side as he guzzled a mug of ale. "Those dragons ol rip this town apart sure as I'm the ugliest captain in the Toopekian fleet."

"Aye," said Geoff, "the dragons present a problem."

Schram stepped forward. "I will create a magical barrier over the city, but it will, by no means, be safe from penetration. The dark magic the young dragons wield will break through soon after encountering it. However, if there is an all-out attack, it might give you a little extra time to create a possible defense, or if necessary, provide the time to gain a retreat for some."

There was a brief silence as the assembled leaders thought about the prince's talk of retreat. Geoff then smiled and said, "Don't you worry, Schram. We'll hold this city." He slapped Alan Grove, the third lieutenant who now was leader over the human forces, on the back, and in a strong and defiant voice continued. "This human and his men fight like none I have ever seen before, and besides, we don't have anywhere to run. Assuming the attack strikes here first, we could fall back to Empor and then Drynak, but after that, where do we run to? Furthermore, what kind of defense could we put forward at Drynak? It's nothing more than a desert town as it is. We'd be no more than targets on an open pond in that pathetic city. No, we will fight to the end here and possibly take a good number of them bastards with us."

Pete gave an affirmative nod, filling another ale for himself in the process. Schram's face did not show the enthusiasm that the pirate's did, as he contemplated the thought of Toopek being a city under constant war and possibly becoming the first of the fronts to reach a point that it must fight to the death. His thoughts showed clearly in the lines on his face, but he spoke with the energy of one confident and sure. "Assuming our troops with the elven and dwarven armies are successful, Elvinott will again be in our hands and another possible escape route if the situation dictates as such. Also, perhaps I can come up with some other defense against the dragons when I consult with the canoks. Their knowledge is much more extensive than mine. If there are other possibilities, they will know them."

"Are you sure they'll help you?" asked the huge maneth, now joining Pete with a drink. "The canoks are still not considered survivors from the first dragon attacks 200 years ago."

"I am sure, for I bring them an offer they cannot refuse."

Geoff smiled and passed an ale over to the human. "I hope you are right, for Toopek's sake."

The plans were clear. March a direct course toward Elvinott. If they met with any goblin interference, they were to be killed on the spot. Word of their movement behind the force holding the elves and dwarves at bay in Feldschlosschen had to be kept secret. Schram had assembled about 200 humans and maneths to tip the scales against the dragon armies at Elvinott, but if it was going to be enough, he did not know.

He had chosen a route to take them deep into the mountains, well around the goblin-held town of Lawren. He toyed with the idea of going through the small outpost in an attempt to put it back under human rule, but he could not afford the time or the risk should a warning of their movements spread. All reports from the town was that it was business as usual there, regardless of who claimed leadership. And of what Schram knew about Lawren from his past visits, he could only assume this to be true.

It was still hours before dawn, and even leaving at this hour, the best time they could hope to arrive in Elvinott would be late tomorrow. Schram greeted Krirtie pleasantly as she appeared next to him in her full armor with her magnificent curved scimitar at her side. She returned with a smile, though most of her attention was drawn to the farewells from various friends and, of course, Geoff. He added a few extra words meant only for Krirtie's ears, and Schram assumed they had been in reference to their mutual friend, Maldor.

The large King of the Maneths and now leader of Toopek moved over and faced the human prince. The two did not speak but only gripped each other in a powerful embrace, their words spoken clearly with their eyes. The two parted, and Schram gave the motion with his staff to depart, followed by an echoing roar and cheer from the accompanying maneth and human guards respectively. As they reached the first glade just outside the city boundaries, Schram turned around with Krirtie to take a final look at their homeland before it drifted out of their sight. A slight red haze showed like a shell stretching from city wall to city wall but only apparent to the magician who had created it. Schram pulled his human friend close. "I wonder when we shall return this time?"

She sighed slightly. "I hope when it is all over." There was a pause before she added, "And I hope we will not be alone."

Schram smiled as they turned and moved to again walk at the lead, but the frown, which slowly grew on his face, told that he believed Krirtie's statement would not become true. He did not know from where it originated or what exactly it meant, but he had an overwhelming fear that his lifelong friend would never see her homeland again.

They walked steadily for a long time, completely free of any interference. Schram pushed his party onward, but his instincts were telling him that something was not right. It was just past noon when they stopped. "What do you think, Krirtie?"

"I don't know, Schram," she replied, looking around. "If these are all there are, it will not be a problem. We could silence these twenty trolls in only moments. However, it's more likely that they are not alone, and if a search party should wander back to a slaughtered camp, our presence and movements would definitely become common knowledge."

"I agree," he replied, motioning to a nearby maneth guard. "Meris, spread the word for everyone to sit down tight and keep their ears open. If fighting breaks out, tell the company to sweep the forest looking for strays."

The maneth, who is actually the current head of the Dimat line, though all are fighters now, nodded and began to relay the orders when Schram caught him again. "Also, take a small party out and see if there is a way around this camp."

Again he gave an affirmative nod and quickly departed. Schram knelt next to Krirtie as they both peered through some tree cover at the trolls camped before them. Krirtie whispered, "It is funny that they sit so calmly while a force ten times their size watches them unnoticed."

"*Unnerving* is the word I would have chosen. Trolls are by no means the dragon army's finest, but they are also not ones to have an isolated party of this size alone in the woods. I don't like this at all."

The entire party sat motionless for several hours as they waited for the search party to report. It had taken much longer than Schram had expected, but since there was no change in the troll camp in front of them, he decided to hold his position until he was forced to act. There was some commotion at the back of the lines that drew his attention, and he quickly moved to investigate. His run was greeted by Meris coming at a full sprint back to him. The maneth was white as a ghost and panting heavily by the time they reached each other, and after he took a brief drink of water, he said, "Trouble, sir. We made a path southerly through the mountains thinking we had found a new line to take to Elvinott. However, after about a mile, we came across another group similar to this one in size. We continued southerly and then came upon our worst fear—a huge troll outpost. It is well hidden in the trees, which is probably why none of our scouts or flyers have come across it before, but trust in the knowledge that it is there, and their numbers are great. These forests are thick back here."

Schram looked disturbed as Krirtie joined his side. "How many?"

"We couldn't be sure, at least 400, not counting those camped in the smaller parties."

The magician slumped. "Damn! I knew it just didn't feel right not running into any resistance until now. Slayne probably has these mountains planted thick with these parties, guessing what our plans would be. He found the perfect use for his near-useless troops—an alarm."

Meris raised a hand so he could continue. "There is more, which is why we had to return at such a quick pace." Schram's frown became even more grave as he knew what was coming next. "A group of about five trolls snuck up behind us as we looked over the camp. We were caught by surprise, but their inferior fighting abilities proved no match for ours. However, none were sure, but I think one could have fled. We might have set off their"—he paused then added—"alarm, as you call it."

Krirtie interrupted. "Now we have no choice, Schram. We have to go through them here or return to Toopek and get word to Feldschlosschen that we could not make it."

His expression did not change. "No, we won't retreat. We will never have a better opportunity to retake Elvinott. Some of us have to get through." He turned to Meris. "How far is the outpost?"

Meris replaced his maneth club he had been carrying since his return, then replied, "One mile to the first camp and another to the main outpost."

"Good, then we might have enough time." He turned back to Krirtie. "Gather up the eighteen best human fighters we have with us. Meris, lead a group of about five maneths back to the nearest troll camp and keep watch over it, for I believe if the main camp does know of our presence, they will continue backtracking in pursuit, alerting that camp rather than following your trail exactly. Keep a close eye over them, because this is what I have planned."

"They never knew what hit 'em," said Krirtie, pulling her troll armor over her head.

Schram motioned to the other humans Krirtie had selected to join her in changing armor. "Help move these bodies into the trees, and I will prepare them as is required," he shouted as he hurriedly ripped the dead troll's armor free and launched his bloodied body into some nearby brush."

One of the humans approached him. "Prince Schram, this troll's armor is too damaged to even think about wearing."

Schram frowned, both from his address as "prince" and the news the man brought. "Here, our numbers are already too thin. Use this armor and I will find another answer."

The human busily switched into the troll gear Schram had recovered and joined the other humans, all now almost completely "trolled" over. Schram caught Krirtie's worried gaze and then began chanting softly to himself. The woman stared at her longtime friend, watching alongside the frozen gazes of the other guards as Schram's face suddenly began to lose its shape and character. His body began to shorten and become fatter, with his green-brown elven skin turning a deep black. His nose grew long and bent downward at its tip while most of his muscles moved to better position themselves as rolls of fat folding over his troll-like boots. His armor lost its elven shine to be replaced with the dull, black dents common to the other trolls. Schram fell to his knees. The only feature depicting that he was the Prince of Toopek was his long jet black hair pushing from beneath his helmet, and the long wooden staff he had become known to carry held tightly by his side.

"Schram," hollered Krirtie while she watched the magician collapse to the ground.

He looked hazily toward the girl. "Quiet please, I am all right. I just did not realize how much it would take out of me, or even if I could do it. Tell the others we are in position. If we have been discovered, Meris will be returning shortly, and stopping to chat will not be an option. We must be prepared."

Krirtie moved to relay the message, clanging uncomfortably as she fought to adjust to her new armor. Schram groggily rose to his feet, and he knew if what he had planned was to work, he would have to fight through his weariness and act like a troll in pursuit. He gave one more incantation, and his staff took the form of a curved, black sword.

Maneths and humans, 170 of them, sat patiently about 500 yards northwest of the masqueraded troll party, while two parties of five maneths each had left on their own. One was Meris's group, who went to watch the troll camp to the south, whereas the other took off at the fastest pace possible to warn Geoff that a force of over 500 trolls could be closing in on Toopek—that is, if Schram's plan was successful.

An uneasy silence seduced the entire forest before the loud maneth roar burst through the air.

"That's the signal!" Schram hollered. "You all know what to do, and remember, we are trolls, so hide your faces. If discovered, you are on your own."

There were mixed sounds through the group when Schram waved his sword, and the twenty humans fell into the trees behind him. They shouted and cursed in the best troll voices they could muster with the few key phrases Schram had taught them as they fell into pursuit behind the thunder of maneth and human footfalls tearing a mean path through the underbrush toward Toopek.

They had gone less than half a mile when Schram could see their party growing larger from the other trolls joining in the chase. In all the wild confusion, he could not tell his party from the real ones. He only hoped that feeling would be equal in reverse. Furthermore, he hoped all would be able to stay near the rear guard and turn around when the time was right.

"You there," echoed a raspy troll voice from behind. "Were you the leader at the north point that alerted them?"

Schram had trouble understanding all the linguistics, but he thought he had gotten the main idea. He stopped his slow pursuit to turn and face the troll who had spoken. "Aye, do you have a problem with my actions?" he asked in return, raising his sword slightly to show displeasure at being questioned.

His tone was condescending and hard, trying to equal the other troll's displeasure with the situation. Thankfully his voice had become altered with his physique, so the approaching troll was completely fooled by Schram's appearance. However, since the troll had his sword drawn and his eyes locked in a displeasing stare, Schram knew his effective magic would help him little except to die looking and sounding like a troll. If not for his quick reflexes, his head would have been removed without another word spoken. The surprised look from the troll that had attacked turned to that of fear when he was on his back with Schram's sword tip to his throat.

Fire beat down from his eyes as he roared at the now-humbled troll leader. "Attack me, you swine! I shall slit your throat for having the thought."

The fear in the troll's eyes was matched only by that in his voice. "I am Garschmidt. Highest ranking troll. Why do I not recognize you?" He paused for Schram to answer, then added, "You know I was only following our master's orders. You know he said only to keep any troops back, not pursue."

Schram smiled, letting a ball of saliva drip between his lips to strike the troll in his forebrow. "My men saw the party and knew with your aid, we could easily smother them." He pressed his foot deeply into the captive's chest, causing him to gargle up some slop. "They numbered less than one hundred. Think how pleased our master will be when we tell him we single-handedly crushed the offensive."

The troll's eyes seemed to brighten as Schram's plan for bettering their position with their master appealed to him. He pushed Schram's foot aside and sharing a crooked smile, adding, "Yes, I believe you are right. We will crush the rebels then return to our post and send word to Slayne himself." He laughed deeply and leaned closer. "We will be well rewarded."

Garschmidt was now on his feet hollering at any guards around him to follow. Schram suggested he scout the area to gather more troops, but the lead troll would hear nothing of it, grabbing the human and pulling him along beside him.

They ran for some time, and although Schram tried to keep an eye out for any of his camouflaged friends, he found locating them an impossible task. The longer he remained with the trolls, the more danger he was in, as Toopek may be poised for a defense that would include defending against who he appeared to be. Suddenly, a scuffle broke out between two trolls that had bumped each other during the chase. The commotion grew drawing Garschmidt's attention. The troll approached the two fighting and in one swift motion beheaded them both. He turned back to Schram for approval and saw that Schram was gone.

⁂

"I hear something coming," said Krirtie softly.

"I told you we should have left while we had the chance," replied one of the guards. "Now the troops have started to return."

"Be quiet!" she exclaimed as they all now heard a twig snap, followed by the worst chirp of a yellow-bellied ingle fly any had ever heard.

"Schram?" she whispered outwardly toward the sound.

The magician burst through the trees, almost knocking his friend over as he came. "Krirtie, what are you doing saying my name? What if I had been a stray troll party? With that comment, you could have alerted the whole forest to your presence."

The girl appeared stung. "Well, what the hell kind of call signal was that? You sounded like a female bandicoot giving birth."

"As if you couldn't tell, whistling through these god-awful troll lips is not the easiest thing I have ever tried to do."

Both seemed to be growing in anger and defensiveness until one of the other guards interjected. "You know, you both are making enough noise now to wake the dead, let alone alert a nearby troll detachment."

Schram froze on the guard and then his look gradually softened. "You are correct." He turned to Krirtie. "How many more of our team still need to return?"

She glared. "Including you, that makes twenty here." There was a moment of silence, then she added sarcastically, "Some of us felt that hurrying back to the rendezvous point was important."

Schram recognized her tone and gave a quick smile. "I am sorry for everything. However, I was, shall I say, unavoidably detained."

She grinned in return. "I saw you get stopped by that other troll, but I couldn't help as I was pushed along with the troll assault. It took all my strength just to work my way to the side and slowly drift back."

Schram threw his blubbery black arm around the girl. "Tell me about it." He turned to the group. "Come on, we should hopefully now have a clear path to Elvinott. If we move through the night without making camp, then we should be able to reach the safety of its forests by early afternoon."

There were mixed emotions stirring among the men, and it brought about a comment from Dolf Stollman, the largest of the humans chosen. He stood nearly Schram's size and build before the magician's magical metamorphosis to the troll, and now the human appeared completely out of place as his troll armor did not nearly cover his body. Dolf said, "I do not feel any pleasure in the idea of running through this jungle throughout the night, but compared to the choice of mixing with the troll parties again, I shall run for a week. I now understand why you wanted only humans for this part of the task. I am over a foot shorter than most of the maneths, and I still stuck out like a stray bandicoot at a tigon banquet when we mixed with the trolls. Several glanced at me questionably when they passed by, and I can only imagine how they would have treated a maneth. However, coming to the point of my comments, would it be all right to ditch this garb now, for the discomfort is unforgiving?"

Schram smiled. "Relax, friends. We only have to wear this armor another day, and we shouldn't have any more troll entanglements. However, just in case, I will take the lead, as I believe I would be more convincing in a confrontation, but if weapons are drawn, no troll can be allowed to escape. We are only twenty, and we have to make it through. Even in these small numbers, we will be a major force against the goblin armies at Feldschlosschen. Let's move."

There was a scattering of waving swords and cheers when Krirtie grabbed Schram's arm. "I will take the rear and try to cover some of our trail." Schram nodded affirmatively and she added, "Oh, and Schram, is there any customary procedures for elves to break a joining?"

He raised one of his thick eyebrows. "A separation? It is written, but never has one occurred. Why do you ask?"

"I just wanted to know if Stepha would have something to fall back on when she sees you." She laughed heartily. "I used to think how bizarre your ears looked after you began to become more elf-like." She paused while her smile grew even greater. "But that troll nose?"

She continued laughing now, with several of those nearby not hiding that they had overheard and were finding the same humor. Her laughter did not cease or even lessen as she headed to take her place at the rear, snickers from each guard echoing as her comments were passed. Schram glared momentarily and then smiled as he too thought about the reaction of the Princess of the Flyer Elves if she was to see her husband looking as such. With a slight chuckle of his own, he disappeared into the brush with a line of human trolls at his heels.

***

They traveled throughout the night, and as Schram had hoped, they had not encountered any troll resistance. By the time they reached Elvinott, most of the magical physique Schram had induced upon himself had been worn away by the enchantment of the wood. He turned to his weary companion now standing next to him and said, "You see, now there is nothing for Stepha to see."

Krirtie grinned briefly, but her attention was drawn to the faces of those they traveled with. She pointed, "Look at their eyes as they behold the beauty captured with this forest. They look like children looking upon a mound of the sweetest chocolates Gnausanne has to offer."

"Don't laugh too hard," replied Schram as he reached his hand into the wondrous fountain of the princess to scoop up a mouthful of water. "It was not so long ago that the young woman standing before me now wore that same look of amazement. It is said that to look upon the trees of Elvinott, any evil mind would turn good. If their expressions"—he motioned to the eighteen humans still dressed as trolls—"are any example, then it must be true, and those trolls are on our side."

She smiled again. "I will always believe this to be the most beautiful place on all of Troyf."

"Then you feel as I do." The two hugged, and then Schram turned to speak to the spellbound men behind him. His speech momentarily broke them from their trance. "Men, please deposit your armor into the waters of the fountain. You will be given more when we continue after we eat and rest."

With that, he turned and headed toward the king's castle, the most magnificent oak in the forest with a huge castle carved into its base. The men behind were stunned, both from the idea of depositing their black and dented armor in such a beautiful fountain and from the idea of continuing their trek after dinner; but when they witnessed Krirtie's armor splash briefly into the water to be replaced with brilliant flashes of all colors on the spectrum and appear on its surface as shiny, newly forged armor bearing the crest of Toopek, all concerns for the journey were quickly forgotten.

Each man was proudly wearing their new armor when Schram returned, himself carrying only a shield bearing the colors and markings of Elvinott and his marvelous wooden staff. The chatter and conversation that had been taking place quickly dissolved, leaving the large human-elf looking down over his resting army of twenty. He gazed up into the dark sky and peered at the explosion of stars across the forest's roof, absorbing the silence and peace he heard as if it was a song. The calmness in his eyes seemed to be a drug affecting those around as all reveled in this moment of pure serenity.

Softly, Schram turned his head downward and spoke. "My friends, let me extend my apologies for having to push you so hard these last two days, and my appreciation for how well you performed. However, even as I speak now, I can only assume Slayne is moving what troops he can over to reinforce his barrier between here and Feldschlosschen. With this in mind, we have to continue on tonight so we will be in position for an early strike tomorrow morning. I know we are all tired, but since only twenty of us were able to make it through, we must attack before the reinforcements arrive. If we make good time through the forest, we can still catch five or six hours of sleep before dawn, and also, there is safety in these forests, so we will have nothing to fear as we travel."

His last statements seemed to pacify those on the verge of falling off as he spoke, and gradually the entire group stood and continued behind their leader.

The Separation

Even leaving at dawn from the Elvinott forest border, they still had over three hours of traveling to reach where Madeiris had said the goblin armies were massed, and that was assuming they would not meet with any other resistance. Since they were no longer under the elves' protective enchantment, dragon troops could be placed anywhere along their path, which would slow their journey.

However, Schram felt lucky to have made it this far only running into two small goblin parties, which were both possibly considered deserters. He looked across the large glade that nearly six months ago had been the sight of a fierce battle when the fleeing elves had met a battalion of dragon forces being led by one large blue dragon. Schram looked to where the blue had fallen beneath the wrath of Jermys Ironshield's fierce hatchet, and a deep sadness fell over him. He thought of Draketon, the large red dragon that helped them in the Black Pool of the South Sea, and the promise he made to him. Hopefully Schram could keep that promise and only a very few more dragons would be needlessly killed in this war, though he knew one which must. Yet, as he looked across the now-busy and -filled glade, he did not see how this situation would allow it. Whether all three dragons had been there the whole time was now beside the point. The fact was that now they not only were facing nearly a thousand goblin and troll armies, but they had the support of three large and seemingly mature and very powerful dragons. Schram saw the confident expressions of his twenty soldiers quickly begin to fade as they too witnessed what stood before them.

Schram gathered his troops into a small semicircle as he quietly spoke. "I know it does not seem likely as you look across this glade that our mission has any chance of success. However, remember that the elves and dwarves have nearly twice that number ready to tear down upon them at our signal." He paused while he prayed in his mind that this really was the case, and the dwarves and elves really were there waiting. "Furthermore, I will make it appear with a display to make the gods proud that we are in much greater numbers than we actually are. But once again, I am not a fool or a leader to force any man to his death. The chance of success is not great, and if anyone would rather retreat to Elvinott, then I will harbor no bad feelings and apologize for not being able to accompany them in their return." There was an ominous silence as each turned their heads to see the other's reactions. He waited several moments before continuing. "Fine, and thank you all, and may all our gods be with us. On my signal, we attack."

Several dropped their heads in final prayers while Schram moved back to where he could watch what was occurring across the clearing. Krirtie came over to join him. Softly, she said, "Schram, I just wanted you to know that I have always loved you and regardless of what happens, you will always be my greatest friend."

The human magician was quite taken by the words and rose to face the hard but sensitive girl before him. Her eyes spoke of confidence, but Schram could feel the fear within her. Placing a hand on her shoulder, he replied, "Krirtie, you know I feel the same toward you. You were my only human friend in Toopek when nobody else would even talk to me. You were the first human who did not look at me as some sort of alien from the elves. I was young, and I did not know at the time exactly how important your actions would prove to be to me, but know this, they were more important than I could ever put into words." They embraced tightly, and he knew they needed to clear their heads before they could effectively mount an attack.

When they separated, Schram stared into Krirtie's eyes and added, "An old friend used to say the same thing to me every time I left his homeland—'Schram, don't lose your head, and you won't lose your head.' He meant it to be funny, but as with most of what he said, there was a great deal of wisdom behind his words." He smiled. "You are a powerful woman and a great warrior. Trust in your actions and the sword by your side, for I know then that you will act bravely and always be victorious. Don't fall into simple traps because they appear the easy answer, for usually the easy way is the wrong way."

He removed his hand and looked over his small army, motioning for her to go to the far side away from the dragons. As she positioned herself, she thought about all she had heard and knew that his message was meant for a time other than the present. She made herself a mental note to explore his words later as all the explosions and noise taking place now brought reality upon the whole group. Schram had given his signal.

He had sent a barrage of energy pulses throughout the group, ending with his total force being directed toward the three dragons. Commotion ensued everywhere as his tiny force attacked from the trees, screaming and ranting as if they brought several thousand soldiers. The goblin armies that had been focused toward the dwarven mines spun to greet the onslaught of attackers, and as the humans drew near, none knew if the elf and dwarven cavalry were going to be present or not; and if you could read anything from their fierce attack, they didn't care. Suddenly, the sky erupted with elven arrows, and the lines of goblins preparing to meet the human force fell face down, arrows protruding from their backs.

Schram sent bolt after bolt toward the dragons, but as he had feared, these beasts were stronger than those he had faced in the past, and quickly two moved from his attack, leaving only one faced off against the magician, essentially buying the magician's time so the others could defend and attack those around. Schram created a barrier of energy around him, which allowed all attacks upon him to be easily discarded so he could concentrate on the dragons. The one he now faced had created a similar shell around itself, and the two locked magic as each attempted to break through the other's defenses. An overpowering screech was heard to his side, but Schram could not turn his head to see what had happened. All he knew was one of the other dragons was screaming its wicked roar in anger, the source driving it to that being unknown.

Stepha lay on the ground, her magical bow knocked to her side as the beast she had just wounded deeply howled at her, swinging its talons, trying to grab the elf who had inflicted so much pain, but being met with a human woman's sword between them. This dragon, though younger, had a similar barrier surrounding his blue body, but it seemed nonexistent to the blade of Krirtie's scimitar and the arrows from Stepha's bow. Krirtie stood strong between the two, swinging her sword wildly, trying to give the elf princess enough time to recover. She could feel her arms starting to tire when another screech broke through the glade, and blue blood flowed profusely around the arrow lodged fatally in the dragon's breast. Krirtie began to fall to her knees only to be grabbed by Stepha, who drew her sword to block a goblin attacking the human from her side. Krirtie quickly recovered from her momentary lapse, and the goblin attacker was almost as soon dead.

Everywhere they turned, another goblin party was preparing to attack. "They seem to be coming out of the cracks in the soil," hollered one human before feeling the point of a goblin dagger break through his armor, striking a death blow to his back. The other dragon, a huge green, which was the largest of the three, had moved to battle a party of dwarves, who were being savagely slaughtered by the beast. Flames erupted across the glade as elves, dwarves, and goblins alike screamed helplessly while their bodies were engulfed by fire. Elves sent repeated bowfire into the dragon's belly, but the arrows only seemed to strike and then bounce aside, only harming whom they fell toward. More fire blew in waves, flooding the clearing with enough heat and smoke to melt the strongest of steel.

The dragon became entranced by the screams and pain he was causing to those he had been taught were his enemy. Jermys spotted his opportunity and attacked, swinging his magical Hatchet of Claude at the green's glowing enchanted barrier. There was a flash of brilliant light as the two forces met, and the strike caused the dragon to roar in pain, though his armor he called skin was not broken. His magical barrier shifted in intensity, becoming thick in the area where the dwarf was madly striking him. The dragon arched his head downward, bellowing a deep laugh, which rocked the dwarf back nearly pushing him to the ground.

Fear filled Jermys's eyes. For the first time, his hatchet was not powerful enough to strike the beasts he had so often been able to bring down at will. Fire dripped from the green dragon's nostrils, dropping like balls of lava scorching whatever they struck. The beast arched his neck and sent a sheet of fire point blank upon Jermys, who stood with his hatchet raised. There was a roar louder than any clap of thunder Troyf had ever heard when the beast felt the point of Stepha's arrow into its back and Krirtie's sword cutting deep into its neck. The dragon shifted its protective barrier to face Krirtie and Stepha as green blood flowed across the scorched ground. He was totally lost when the hatchet bit his neck. Jermys' last thought was how he was not cooked with the ground around him, but the problem was, he had no answer. Krirtie stepped forward and swung her blade downward, silencing the dragon for good.

The fighting across the glade remained fierce, with heavy losses occurring on both sides. Schram and the remaining dragon, a brilliant red, were held locked tightly in their battles of wills. Several large parties of elves had been moved through the lines, and it became apparent to Stepha and Krirtie that the plan was beginning to turn successful. The noise of the fighting grew to an apex until the last dragon let out a roar, as if something had opened its chest and pulled its heart out while it remained beating. Many in the glade swung their heads to where the beast was struggling to stand. All fighting halted when they witnessed what had happened and what was approaching. Stepha ran over to help Schram make it back to his feet from where he had been thrown when his opponent had been struck. Both their eyes grew wide when the huge blue landed next to the red and its rider climbed from its back.

"Greetings, Schram, my son. It has been a while."

"Yes it has, man who was once my father," responded Schram as he took a step toward the dragon lord.

The dragon lord's laughter seemed to strike Schram deeply as it pierced the silence that had seduced the glade. All waited patiently to see what this new encounter could mean, except Jermys, who motioned for more elves to seize this opportunity and slip through the lines. The dragon lord looked around, his ever-present robe still in place, but his hood was absent and the reptilian tail showed clearly from his back.

His eyes burned ice into each individual but froze on Krirtie like fire. His voice was raspy and completely foreign from the man he used to be. "I am pleased we meet again, Krirtie. I was deeply angered when you murdered my comrade, your father."

The human woman stood strong, though the memory of killing her father at the confrontation at Eltak struck her deeply, as was intended. Schram spoke, trying to bring the attention back upon him. "Her father has found peace and been welcomed to the afterlife—something you may never find yourself."

The once King of Toopek ignored his son's statement and moved to stand in front of the girl. "The one you know as Maldor is close to meeting your father." Krirtie's eyes swung to greet Keith Starland's, and they met like two fireballs colliding at the speed of light. "Yes, girl," he added slowly, "soon he will die, even possibly before my return."

The pain and anger was clear as it boiled within her, but Krirtie surprised even Schram when she replied, "What makes you so sure you are going to leave this glade?"

The dragon lord laughed and turned, pointing his finger toward the human known as Dolf Stollman. A beam of light shot at the bewildered man and suddenly the spot he stood was empty. He turned back to Krirtie. "Because nobody will ever be able to defeat me or those who stand at my side."

Schram immediately pointed his staff toward his father but then suddenly swung it back to the dragon he had previously fought that now seemed fully recovered. With a similar flash of light, the large red vanished. The magician swung to face the deep, angered expression of his former father. "He was a fool to keep his guard lowered. He should have known I would have realized you would be prepared for my attack."

Isolated scuffles began breaking out as elven arrows began dropping goblins who also had dropped their guard during this unique break in fighting. The dragon lord's stare bit through Schram with hatred. Suddenly, his face dropped, and Schram could feel the presence of magical hands prying into his mind before protection could be erected. Schram's father wore an expression of complete disbelief, which seemed to be shared by the dragon he had previously ridden. Schram had quickly blocked the mind search, but whatever he had exposed to the ones before him put extreme fear and amazement in their eyes.

The dragon lord moved over to stand beside his mount while sending telepathic messages to his dragon troops. The goblins quickly began backing away from the fighting, many fleeing in whatever direction they could. The stunned gazes of the allied forces only remained frozen, completely confused about what was taking place. However, none of their looks compared to that which Schram wore.

The dragon lord leaped onto his dragon's back. "You are full of surprises, my son, though I no longer am sure that is the case. We give you Elvinott, for I must talk with Slayne. I don't think even he has considered this." With that, the dragon spread its huge wings and lifted them into the air, quickly disappearing over the horizon.

Many dwarves and elves gave a slight pursuit behind the fleeing goblins, but the more important matters of moving the elves back to their home took precedence, making any pursuits short-lived chases serving only to assure the goblins were indeed retreating.

"What the hell was that?" asked Fehr. "Why did they leave?"

All eyes fell to Schram. "I don't know, my friends. I don't know."

Though the answer was not what they wanted to hear, they all accepted it for the time. Krirtie seemed the most disturbed but held her tongue.

Schram and Krirtie joined Stepha in the elves' return to their homeland. Jermys remained in Feldschlosschen to help restore order to the dwarven lands, but not before he had a chance to greet those and bid them farewell and safety for their journeys ahead. Also, he again extended the welcome arms of Feldschlosschen and Antaag, should their paths ever bring them near, and added his support if his help was ever desired.

Schram knew Jermys to be as honorable as any on Troyf. If he was needed, he would be there, no questions asked. He was one of the companions who had done it all, and now he proudly carried one of the weapons of the Ring of Ku—the Hatchet of Claude. Like the scimitar by Krirtie's side and the magical bow on Stepha's back, Schram knew the weapons of the ring were key to their success. He only worried about the remaining one, the one tightly tied to their lost maneth friend.

Schram bid Jermys farewell and sent his best to Fehr, to the grumbles from the dwarf who said the rat had been tearing up his mines worse than any of the goblin attacks could dream to. Schram smiled and waved but once again felt sad about leaving his friends behind.

"Really, Krirtie, I don't know," he shouted. "Believe me, I wish I did, but I am as much at a loss as you."

Krirtie frowned. "You better not be holding out on us, Schram Starland, or so help me, I'll…"

Stepha raised a hand, halting the girl before she could continue. "Really, Krirtie, the look in his eye should tell you he does not know what the dragon lord meant. Let him be for a while, it has been too long a day to end it fighting." She turned to Schram. "Clear your mind, my husband. I know he searched your mind and more than that, I know he found something within you that scared him. Try to find it, for I am certain it is important."

Krirtie quickly calmed and added to both of them. "I'm sorry. I should have known better." Both nodded appreciatively as she turned to Stepha to continue. "I never had a chance to thank you for saving me from the dragon and then the goblin attack that followed."

Stepha looked surprised. "It is I who should be thanking you. If you had not acted so quickly, the dragon would have snared me quick as anything. You saved my life, and I hope someday I can repay the favor."

Krirtie only bowed her head slightly while Schram sat up, both stunned and worried about the discussion of events he had just heard. He started to speak, but the elf princess cut him off. "This is not the time for painful discussions of war. Though many lost their lives, and this saddens us all deeply, we were victorious and my—our people are home. We will have celebrations this night."

Schram pulled his beloved close and held her tightly as the door to the great hall of the king's castle slowly was pushed ajar. A tall muscular figure broke through the opening to stand before the small group. "I have been looking all over for you three!"

"Madeiris!" cried Stepha with tears filling her eyes as she leaped to her brother's arms.

"Greetings, King," said Schram, also rising to stand beside the elf.

Madeiris grinned. "*King* sounds as proper from your mouth as it would from mine in reference to you."

Schram smiled as he too hugged the elf. "Well said, brother, well said."

"And you," Madeiris began looking toward Krirtie, who had moved closer. "I have someone I think you might be interested in seeing." He motioned to a guard in the hallway, and in a moment the guard and another figure entered.

"Mother!" cried Krirtie, tears now filling her eyes as they met each other in a tight embrace.

The festivities, though clouded with the thoughts of those who gave everything to make this plight possible, continued, and an essence of cheer was carried to all of their hearts. It was late in the night when all finally retired, but that night carried something with it that none in the forest had felt for a long, long time. All slept with a calming peace surrounding them and the ones they loved.

"Damn, Schram, I swear you can move giving less sound than the most gentle of elves."

"From you, Madeiris, I take that as the greatest compliment." He looked across the peaceful glade where the elf king sat alone. "What brings you out so early this morn?"

Madeiris leaned back and said, "For the first time in too long I was allowed to sleep in our forests, a feat my father—and you—made possible. I could sleep here every night if given the opportunity."

The human smiled and sat down beside his friend. "Don't leave yourself or any of the elves out of your memory. Many died in this most wondrous effort, and its success is attributed to what everyone gave for it."

"Trust in the knowledge that I will never forget what the humans, maneths, dwarves, and the elves gave of themselves…" His voice trailed off then he added, "But just looking at the faces of those throughout Elvinott last night"—he paused as he fought for the proper thought and finally added—"I know my father would be proud."

"Aye," replied Schram with a sigh. "That much is certain. You returned the elves to their home." He put his hand on Madeiris's shoulder. "You should be proud as well."

The elf smiled in return, but his eyes told that he knew why the magician had searched for him so early this morning. Softly, he added, "Do you leave today, my friend?"

Schram sat back, letting his long black hair fall down below his shoulders, revealing the tips of his brownish-green pointed elven ears that had begun to develop during his training of the Ring of Ku. His look was long and distant, and all he answered was, "Yes, I must."

There was a long silence as both individuals seemed to be trying to gather up all the peace and serenity they could before they shuffled back to the reality of the period. Madeiris finally rose and brushed himself off. "I assumed last night that you would be leaving soon. After our discussions last week in Toopek, your plans have been completely clear, although my stubborn-headed sister has been prying at me since then to try to convince you to take her with you." Schram smiled as he knew what the elf king had been going through regarding his sister. However, his decisions had not changed, although Stepha had not kept her desires to join him a secret. Schram wondered if his ears were still red from her verbal assault.

Madeiris grinned slightly as he seemed to read his friend's thoughts. "I told her it would be your decision, and I see in your face that she did not agree with it."

He put his arm around the king's shoulder as they began to walk back. Softly, almost to himself, he added, "To say the least, old friend."

"Yes, go," replied the king, sending an elven guard running to the forest.

"What is it?" asked Stepha as she and Schram approached, the human well packed with provisions Madeiris had ordered prepared for him.

"It is nothing much," replied the king. "I sent scouts out last night to investigate the trails between here and Toopek. The first flyers just returned saying that trolls were scattered in small bands throughout the Toopekian mountain forests. It seems Geoff had a surprise waiting for them as you hoped he would."

Schram replied, "That is the best news I have heard today. I knew he would be ready for them. I only hope Slayne doesn't wish to retaliate against the city right away, for I am not sure he could handle an all-out offensive against him yet." He paused, thought a bit more, then added, "But if anyone could, Geoff would be the one."

"Aye," added Madeiris, "but don't worry too much about Toopek. My elven reinforcements will be there in another day. Any attack will be met with a strong defense."

He smiled broadly now as he took the elf king's hand. "Thank you, my friend and brother."

The king bowed his head, followed by a strong embrace. "I will leave you now and let others bid their leave, but know that my thoughts go with you, wherever your path takes you. Take care, Schramilis, and know that you always have a home among the trees."

"You take care as well, Madeiritilantilis Malis, and thank you."

The king left, leaving Schram beside Krirtie and Stepha, the elf moving aside to let the human woman have her old friend for a time.

"Hurry back, Schram. We all need you with us."

"I will, Krirtie, but like I said before, trust in yourself and you will always do fine. Also, tell your mother I send my love. It was nice to see her again, especially since she seemed so well."

"I will tell her." She smiled, and before departing added, "And don't worry, I shall keep my head about me."

Schram smiled briefly and then turned to Stepha. He could already see tears forming in her large green elven eyes. The two said nothing at first and only fell into each other's arms. Schram set his pack down upon the only piece of armor he was going to carry—a delicately shaped shield with intricate artwork etched into it depicting both his Toopekian crest and the colors and symbols recognizable only to elves. It was a gift from the elf he now held tightly. Next to it, he rested his magical staff, though it looked to be nothing more than a fallen branch from one of the magnificent trees they now stood beneath.

Schram gently pushed the woman back, letting his hand fall into hers, matching their elven Rings of Joining to cross backs. "I love you, Stephanatilantilis, now as much as ever. No matter what distances separate us, we will always be together, and soon no distances will remain."

I love you too, Schramilis, and I understand what you do and why you must go alone, but that does not make it easier. I shall wait for your return, standing by my brother as princess over Elvinott."

The two gripped each other once more and then parted, Schram slowly moving to gather that which he was carrying with him. Giving one more kiss to Stepha and wave to those who looked on from the city, he disappeared into the trees.

Large rolling tears now streaked the elf's cheeks as she turned to head back to the city. Nearly halfway back, she was greeted by Krirtie, who said, "Stepha, I know this is not a good time, but we have to talk, for it is a matter of life and death."

"You sap-bellied dragon lover, this is preposterous!"

"Then stay here, you no-good flee blanket!" answered Jermys.

"Use your head, Jermys. We need help if we are going to help Maldor. Damn, you need help for even thinking about it. Let's get Schram and Stepha. They will give aid, and you know Krirtie would be willing to try, assuming she hasn't already left." He paused as a fearsome frown grew across his face, sending a tight, beaten edge to his words. "Damn it, put that hideous pipe away and listen to me!"

Fehr was now yelling, and the agitation building on the dwarf's face was not hidden. "No! You listen to me, gar bait! King Kapmann at Antaag has a ship leaving tomorrow for Gnausanne. He said we could take it on as far as we needed to. If the currents and winds are in our favor, that means we could conceivably go all the way to Draag in only days. Schram himself said Slayne had some new plan cooking. He definitely would not expect a rescue attempt to take place at his stronghold. With only two of us, we have a better chance of slipping in unnoticed, and who knows, maybe when Maldor is with us, we will be able to do some real damage at the heart of the enemy." He paused and then added, more softly, "And think of the story it would make."

The rat's eyes began to glow but quickly faded as he contemplated the entire plan. "You mean you want to just sail down the Draag River completely unnoticed, then go walking randomly through the caverns and save Maldor, and then complete the journey with a surprise attack?"

Jermys grinned. "Yes!"

Fehr began cursing irately in every language he knew, ending with some choice words of ancient dwarven. Jermys now smiled even more broadly. "So you will be joining me then?"

"Yes, someone has to keep you out of trouble." The rat went mumbling off, still cursing every other word.

The dwarf yelled to his back. "Hurry, friend. We'll leave as soon as you are ready. And the correct pronunciation is 'hevenslen.'"

"'Asshole' is how Schram says it."

⁂

"This will truly prove to be a first," said Fehr as the two traveled through the mine tunnel under the river connecting the two dwarven cities of Feldschlosschen and Antaag.

"What's that, a dwarf teaming with a vile rat?" asked Jermys, smiling.

Fehr's lips formed a tight frown. "No, a rat joining with Jermys Ironshield, Great Sea Captain of the South. What color was it you turned when we were sailing the South Sea with Captain Pete? Green? Blue? Or was it a mixture of both? Did you turn elven on us?"

The dwarf's face was devoid of pleasure as he thought about the past journeys he had taken by boat. He glared at Fehr. "King Kapmann has assured me this boat is quite large and will sail the roughest waters as if it were a spring day."

"What difference does that make?" chattered the rat, his face blushing beneath his fur. "Even if we sink, it wouldn't matter because you are such an excellent swimmer." His laughs began to echo off the cavern walls. "Remember when we first left the port of Icly. We were tugging you behind like we were using you for bait, though nothing would dare bite your nasty skin."

"Shut up, you damn thief! I swear I'll cut your pathetic tail off and feed it to you for dinner if you speak one more word!"

Fehr appeared stung as the dwarf stared down upon him and was about to speak, but then held his words as Jermys continued. "And besides, with all the weight and size you've put on, I do not think you'd be too buoyant yourself nowadays. I am just glad you can walk on your own because I was not about to lift your chunk of a body now."

Fehr was steamed. "I knew you could not resist attacking my weight. It did not take you long before you had to..." He paused and his face softened. "I do miss the days with Krirtie and how she would carry me everywhere we went. However, any weight I *might* have added is due to that dwarven food you have been stuffing down me lately. All you guys do is eat and smoke."

"Stuffing! I never saw you turn down a meal, much less not have between-meal snacks on top of it. Yes, I've seen and heard you creeping the hallways at night, and the cooks have watched you pick their locks on the food cabinets. That is why we added those new locks."

Fehr smiled. "Yes, those new ones took almost thirty seconds to get through, truly worth their weight in gold."

"They were when you consider all the food hidden in storage behind them was, shall we say, enchanted with a special sauce."

Jermys was talking over the laughter in the corridor as the rat's smile vanished. "What are you talking about, dwarven scum?"

Jermys's potbelly jumped irregularly. He was so pleased with what he was about to say. He faced the now-white-with-anger rat and replied, "To put it most simply, if anyone is to be green on our voyage, it will not be me."

Fehr appeared somewhere between disbelief and total confusion. He stared hard at the dwarf but knew that he was not bluffing. His laughter was too pure and his expression too pleased with the success of his plan. "I will get you for this, dwarf. If anything should happen to me, I will get you for this, and trust you will not be so pleased with the result."

Strange garbled noises echoed through the hallway as Jermys simply smiled and shook his head. The only words that were issued was a simple statement between gags. "Zule tanka dvarpha."

Jermys's jaw dropped as he absorbed the ancient dwarven language being used so graphically and directed toward him. The green rat slowly made his way back to the dwarf but only stared hard at him, not able to truly speak.

Jermys raised his hand and motioned the rat forward. "Hush now, we are about to enter the king's chambers, and I don't want your lunch spread across his throne. Your sickness has slowed us down enough already."

"You should have thought of that before you poisoned my food. I'll be lucky to stay on my feet before King Kapmann, much less control my overactive stomach." He completed his comment with a high-pitched belch to make a pirate proud. The Antaagian dwarves leading them now glared down in disgust. No dwarf but Jermys greeted rats as friends, but because of who Jermys was, Fehr had to be accepted. Still, Antaag was nearly totally against the newfound relations. Though Fehr was the only one who had ever made any contact with the taller, potbellied dwarves of Antaag, he was enough to completely halt any further exploration of the idea.

Jermys began to enter the large throne room depicting King Kapmann's royal chamber when he stopped and whispered something to the lead dwarf. With a slight chuckle, the dwarf agreed and let Jermys pass. As Fehr pushed his way through, he was greeted with dwarven axes and a slamming door. "Jermys asked that we keep you busy while he talks with the king. I think we can find some light work that someone of your size could handle." Laughter filled the hall as one of the dwarves scooped the rodent from the ground and carried his long-faced body toward the river. Fehr, in his sickened state, could do nothing but close his eyes and concentrate on his stomach, helpless to prevent whatever was about to happen.

"Is the ship ready?" asked Jermys, ignoring all formalities of speaking to a king as his adherence to customs had become somewhat desensitized with his close relationship with King Krystof of Feldschlosschen.

Kapmann looked noticeably disturbed by the blatant disregard of policy but answered the question put forth. "Yes, Jermys, the ship is ready."

Jermys frowned. "I am sorry if my abrupt words offend you, King Kapmann, but I have much on my mind and little time to resolve it. This voyage is sudden and I am second-guessing my judgment regarding it."

Kapmann rose. "You have not told me your destination or plans at all. You have expected me to fulfill your every wish without regard for policy or order." Kapmann was becoming even more noticeably disturbed, and then suddenly his expression relaxed. "I see you still carry the Hatchet of Claude by your side. In this I know your actions must be true and probably very dangerous.

Perhaps the fewer who know of your plans, the safer you will be. Your raft is ready, my friend, and you two can leave when you are prepared. The guards will help you load should you require aid." He paused then added, "Good luck, wherever your path takes you."

Jermys had heard all that had been said, and although something seemed strange about Kapmann, discovering what all was going on in his mind would have to wait until the key thing he heard was clearly resolved. "Raft? Shouldn't there be a large crew of some kind for such a large ship?"

Kapmann shook his head. "I am sorry. I thought word had been passed to you already. Gnausanne needed a shipment of minerals immediately, so the ship I originally planned for you to use left yesterday. However, it is not a problem, as I set aside another boat for you that you will be able to have totally at your disposal for as long as you will need it. Your party will be the only cargo, so it should better fit into your plans as well."

Jermys's heart sunk as the vision of the large sea liner was replaced with a picture of a bathtub with a sheet for a sail. Fehr was going to have his revenge, he was sure of it.

Seeing his displeasure, Kapmann added, "I hope this is all right. It is really the only boat I could spare. I thought you would be pleased."

Jermys forced a smile. "Thank you, King Kapmann. It is just my head and belly both prefer a larger, smooth-riding ship that tosses waves, not a small one that gets tossed by them."

The king laughed and slapped the dwarf on the back. "I sometimes forget you Feldschlosschen dwarves don't take to the water well. Here"—he reached beneath his long white beard and pulled out a small pouch—"some of my special mix of tobac. It will make your ride more pleasant."

Jermys's face lit up as he reached out to grab the small bag. "Perhaps you would like a smudge now, before I leave."

"Aye, Jermys, it's a right, nice time for a smoke."

He pulled out his long, delicately carved wooden pipe that hooked downward nearly twelve inches before turning back up to open into a small cup. The two sat back as a strange green haze began to fill the room being accompanied by an ear-to-ear grin across both their faces.

A New Direction

"I am sorry that I could not speak with you earlier, Krirtie, but there were matters with Elvinott I had to see to immediately regarding the flyer scouts that were returning. What is it that could be so important as you implied earlier?" Stepha began shaking out her wings in the fountain as she inquisitively gazed toward the human girl who stood with a worried and impatient look about her.

Krirtie replied, "I want to ask your help in something I have planned, but I want to emphasize that there is no obligation."

Stepha stepped out of the fountain bath while Krirtie struggled to find her next words. She was intrigued with her serious tone but had no idea where it was going. She placed her hand on her shoulder. "Come on, Krirtie, tell me what troubles you so."

She giggled slightly. "You sound just like my mother."

Stepha too smiled. "Is that what this is about, your mother? Well, I think it is wonderful that you have found..."

Krirtie raised her hand. "No, my mother is a more-than-welcome sight, but she left a short while ago with the elf party heading for Toopek. This is over a completely different matter, and I guess the easiest thing to do is simply spit it out." She paused and moved with Stepha at her side to sit on the edge of the fountain. "I am going to Draag to find Maldor."

Her mouth fell wide open to join her eyes in disbelief. "Krirtie, that is crazy! Going in alone would not help Maldor, it would only get you both captured." She avoided speaking of the possibility of death in elven fashion, but she knew that it was a more likely possibility. "Schram will be back soon, and we will all go to help him. Only then can we hope to save Maldor from the evil clutches of the dragons." She paused, then added in a softer tone, "We all miss him dearly, for he is as much a part of our family as anyone, but we have to act in a way with the best possibility to help him. You know he would not wish us to risk even the slightest chances of harm in his rescue. You know if anything happens to you, he will be destroyed."

"No! I feel Maldor's time grows shorter by the day. You heard what the dragon lord said about him. He may be facing death as we speak."

"Those were just words to scare you," replied the elf as she placed her arm around the trembling woman. "Do not fall into his trap. We must wait for Schram."

Krirtie's face grew long. "I cannot wait for him, and I don't believe he wanted me to. Could you wait if it were Schram who was being held?"

She stared at the elf, hoping to gain some support, but she quickly realized she would not be finding any there. Stepha replied, "If I believed in what he fought for, I would wait. Also, it is ridiculous if you think Schram wanted you to go. He made it abundantly clear to me before he left that he would speak to the canoks and then return, unless his business took him elsewhere first. Then, when he returned, we will assault Draag with whatever it takes to save Maldor."

Krirtie, with tears now falling helplessly across her cheeks, pushed herself up. Her voice cracked under the stress and emotion, but she knew she had to force her words out. Stepha was her only chance. She knew she could not do this alone. "What if he can't return right away? We both know what he has before him. It may take time, and time is the one luxury Maldor is without. Stepha, I came back to ask you to accompany me because your aid would be extremely valuable. However, if you refuse, I will still go."

She put her face into her hands, and when Stepha rose to comfort her, she turned and disappeared into the nearby forest. The city of trees, with all its beauty and excitement, gave no cure for the pain Stepha was feeling. She turned and stared at the wondrous statue of the Princess of the Flyer Elves, her long golden hair falling down the intricate carvings making up her wings and back. As the water from the fountain trickled down the face of the statue, so did it down the one it was modeled after.

With a long sigh, she glanced to where Krirtie had disappeared, and seeing no sign of the girl, she turned and headed toward the castle. She knew the only one who might be able to make some sense of this was her brother, if she could be lucky enough to find him.

"Madeiris, are you here?"

The elf nearly jumped from his seat as he swung and faced the girl whose entrance had gone completely unobserved. "Martak, sis, you about shook my heart free from my body." His shocked expression calmed when he noticed the stress in her eyes, and he added, "Please sit here by the fire. It seems you have much on your mind, and even if I am not as wise as many kings before me, perhaps as a big brother I can find some answers."

Stepha moved over and sat next to her brother in front of the fire in the great hall. To her left rested the large wall plate tablet depicting the treaty between the elves and the humans, drawn up in the wake of Schram's kidnapping by Hoangis over twenty-six years ago. A sadness filled her eyes as she thought about her now-distant husband. Her loneliness and longing for his presence were evident in her actions, but she knew there were matters at hand that had to be discussed. She cleared her mind and concentrated on her reasons for coming before Madeiris with her troubles.

She placed her hand on her brother's as it rested on his knee and said, "Madeiris, I have much that sits poorly within me at this time, but what I wish to discuss with you is something I do not believe even you have considered."

The elven king seemed intrigued with his sister's statement and used her pause in speech to add, "I can see whatever it is troubles you gravely, and I hope I may hold the answers and wisdom you desire."

She smiled and continued her thought. "I must leave with Krirtie tomorrow."

Madeiris's head tilted slightly in surprise, and he placed his free hand to his chin. "Where must you go on such short notice, and why does it involve Krirtie? In the past you two have accompanied others on very dangerous treks; I don't want you now getting into something that might be too much for you both to handle alone."

Stepha appeared offended and agitated, but before she could respond, Madeiris added, "Do not think I don't have total and complete confidence in your abilities. I know you are both incredible warriors, but I also know how your minds work, and I have seen that look in your eyes before. If what I suspect is true, where you plan to go may be more than even your abilities are prepared to handle."

Stepha shook her head. "I fear that what you suspect *is* what I have in mind, but my reasons for such a dangerous journey are unknown to you. We have to go to Draag and attempt to find and save Maldor."

Madeiris stood. "Out of the question! I discussed this possibility at length with Schram prior to his leave, and he made it adamantly clear that by no means was anyone to attempt such a plan. His reasons were well-said and not open for negotiation."

Stepha joined her brother, both of them standing and showing great determination in their faces. "Krirtie carries Maldor's child."

"What? She told you this? How can it be? They have been apart so long."

No, she did not have to tell me. You know as well as I that an elf who is close to one can sense these things. And you also know maneth young are carried for up to two years. I believe Krirtie is starting to feel the burden of the life within her, and she will stop at nothing to attempt to save him. Without my help, she won't have a chance at Draag."

"No, even with your help you both won't have a chance. There has got to be another way." Madeiris began pacing around the room, searching his mind for any answers he could find. "Send for Krirtie. I want to speak to her myself. Possibly I will be able to make you both understand what our options are, and that a futile rescue attempt is not one of them."

Stepha smiled. "I have sent for her already, for I knew you would wish it."

"Fine. Perhaps you also know what I should say to a stubborn-headed sister and her bull-headed human friend." His voice was clearly showing the burdens he now had resting on his shoulders. Leader over a nation at war with forces of evil, architect for rebuilding a society, and big brother to a powerful and confident sister all rolled up into one young elf.

Stepha smiled again. "Consider my other option is to follow my husband." She paused then added, "But Schram would strip the green from your skin should you allow that action. Therefore, now I am giving you another choice."

Madeiris smiled in return to the comment as he pictured Schram's face should Stepha's suggestion be brought to light. "Yes, Schram would not stop with my skin. However, offering me the better of two evils is not an acceptable answer."

His comment was cut short as an elven guard appeared in the doorway, his face showing a strange unknown distress. "Pardon my interruption, King Madeiris, but the princess asked me to locate the human woman. I found her trail. Attempts to cover it had been made, but I could follow it easily enough. She appeared to have stopped briefly, backtracked, and then turned and continued southwesterly. I felt I should check here before forcing her to return, but her pace is such that only a flyer could reach her before she leaves our forest, and I could not even guarantee that."

Madeiris frowned. "Southwesterly? What city would she come to first, assuming her course stayed as such?"

Stepha stepped forward. "She does not know the woods well. She most likely is attempting to reach Feldschlosschen and seek the aid of Jermys. However, if the direction is as he says, she will be well west of the dwarven cities."

"That she will be," added the guard.

The king sat back against the long table, which was placed in the center of the room. He looked toward the two in the room as they peered back awaiting his command or blessing, depending upon who was to be spoken to first. His lips began to turn slightly upward as he focused his eyes on his sister. "Go catch her and lead her to Feldschlosschen. If Jermys accompanies you and Krystof will give his blessing, then you have mine as well." She grinned and was nearly out the door when he called her back. "And Stepha, you had better be damn careful. I do not want to have to tell Schram that now all his closest friends and deepest love have been captured as well. That human will have my head if he finds out about any of this."

She hurried over and gave Madeiris a long, deep hug and small kiss on the cheek. "Don't worry, big brother. I will take care of everyone, including myself."

"You better," he said as she disappeared through the door. To the guard he added, "Prepare a small party to make ready for a journey to Draag. If I know my sister, she will have King Krystof giving his blessing before she even arrives, and if they are going to go, I am going to make damn sure they make it there. Assemble a half dozen, putting yourself in charge, and then make trail to Gnausanne. From there, join them and lend any support they require." The guard nodded and quickly disappeared. "May Shriak fly with you, sister," he said to himself as he fell back to sit in front of the fire and became lost in his own thoughts.

The sounds of steel crashing against one another echoed from ahead as Stepha raced through the air trying to locate where the fighting was taking place and who was behind it. She rose over a clump of trees to look upon a clearing spotted with a half dozen goblins, two of which fought fiercely against Krirtie, who now was on one knee. Beside her rested the body of one freshly killed blackened goblin corpse, and the three others remaining alive sat and watched from the side, yelling taunts and jeers at the girl in between laughs.

Sweat beaded down Krirtie's face, and it was obvious to Stepha as she let her first arrow fly that the girl was growing weak and tired. The arrow struck true, and without the ability to even gargle a sound, one goblin fell to the ground. The shock of seeing his comrade fall right in the face of victory caused the other to lower his guard, and quickly he joined his friend as Krirtie's sword split his throat. Two of the remaining three were quickly greeted with elven arrows, and with only a slight motion and turn, again Krirtie finished the last in the same fashion. With a sigh of relief and exhaustion, she fell to the ground motionless.

Stepha landed and moved directly to Krirtie's side. Lifting her head in her arms, she softly asked, "Are you injured?"

Krirtie opened her eyes and looked toward the elf. "I don't think so, just a little tired. I seem to have lost some of my endurance, but I will be fine."

"That is common among humans during pregnancy. You will have to act more responsibly and keep that fact in mind."

Krirtie looked astonished. "You know...but how?"

Stepha smiled and helped the girl to her feet. "Elves hold many mysteries about them regarding life. I was not sure until I saw you fighting in the glade. You were fighting more in defense than your usual offensive nature. Furthermore, the fact that you would not wait for my decision, fearing I would refuse to help, only added to the thought. I realize the time you have left that you will be able to act grows short. We will continue on to Draag, but we will first head to Feldschlosschen."

Krirtie showed the deepest relief and gratitude possible to fit onto one face, but also there was a note of surprise in her gaze. "Is that not where I am headed? Also, what are goblins doing in the elven forests? I thought the enchantment would keep them from entering."

Stepha replaced her bow and began walking back toward the east, motioning to Krirtie to follow. "First of all, you left Elvinott boundaries nearly an hour ago, and the path you are following will take you west of Gnausanne. We will have to make good time and be free of further interference if we are to reach the dwarven lands before night becomes too thick, so why don't I lead the way for a while?"

Krirtie skipped forward to catch the elf's pace, both girls smiling at the last statement. "Stepha, thank you for everything. Thank you for the goblins at the glade, for talking with me before, and for just being here now. Every day I learn a little more why Schram fell in love with you so long ago, and why that love never faded for him." This brought a smile to the elf's face, and she thought about the human she loved so. Krirtie saw her reaction and felt the love they carried for each other. She added, "Does he know about the child I carry?"

She shook her head. "I was not even sure until recently, and since he said nothing to me or Madeiris, I suspect that he does not, though he may, because he is also elven, at least in part."

"I think he became elven the first five years of his life," added Krirtie. "The physical changes that occurred over the past years with his training involving the Ring of Ku were only a formality to complete the process."

The elf smiled. "The more I learn about Schram, the more I believe that is an accurate evaluation. He is truly a deep and intricate elf and man."

"As are you...elf that is." Krirtie did not bother to repeat the statement, though she knew it had gone unheard. Stepha was consumed with thoughts of the magician who, although he had only left that morning, had already been gone too long. She hoped

Schram was doing well and his journey would be free of problems, though she knew that was unlikely, as hers had met with goblin attacks only a short ways outside the elven forest.

Krirtie lowered her head. Her thoughts turned from Schram and Stepha to the maneth she had learned to love so and whose child she now carried. She prayed that he was still alive but knew very well that he did not have long in the hell he was now trapped within. Every time she thought about him, all she could see was the pain in his eyes as he was tortured by Slayne in the dragon's attempts to get the magical hammer that had become a part of the maneth's body. Though the tortures were only illusions, the pain was real; and Maldor, no matter how strong he was, could not face them indefinitely. She rubbed her stomach and whispered, "We are coming, Maldor. We are on our way."

<hr />

"Well, you have decided to stray from the protective walls of Elvinott."

His knuckles gripped his staff tightly while he moved toward the one who now blocked his path. "Yes, I did, Almok. I have business in another land."

"I know of your journey to my homeland, Schram. In fact, I know everything about you."

Schram felt the searching magical hands of the canok as he tried to pry into his mind. However, this time he was prepared, and no such invasion was possible. "You do not know everything, or you would not be searching for what has put fear in your eyes." He felt the strike in the canok that his words had created. He took another step forward, and in a tone hardly his own, he added, "And furthermore, I don't think any canok would consider where I am headed to be *your* homeland."

"I fear nothing, human! You would be wise to remember that."

"Then leave me now, for a battle this night would only tire me and delay my arrival."

"You speak with confidence. Perhaps when you defeated my brother, you lost his wisdom he taught you over the years and replaced it with arrogance. It could be your undoing."

Schram tightened his lips. "Don't try and a put fear in me. Your conversation has grown bothersome." He arched his staff, pointing it directly toward the figure before him. With a short chant, the darkness of the woods exploded as a beam of light erupted from his staff. Shrieks of laughter split the night air as Schram watched his attack pass through the canok's black body.

After his outburst had subsided and its effect had been felt completely through the human's mind, the canok cleared its raspy voice and added, "Do you know that your beloved elven princess has decided to leave Elvinott as well?" Almok created a vision of the beautiful Princess of the Flyer Elves walking through some trees. "Indeed, she is a wondrous creature. Perhaps I will have to pay her a visit."

Schram looked on in horror while the canok turned, sending a bolt of magical power directly into the human. Schram cringed and sat up, beads of cold sweat present on every part of his body. He swung his head surveying the glade, freezing on the point where he had thought Almok had stood. His heartbeat was racing as he pushed himself to his feet, leaving his resting spot unchanged as he again began to walk. He checked the stars to see how long he had slept to find he had only sat down just over an hour ago.

His nights had been filled with dreams, but never as vivid as that one. Could that be what Stepha had talked about her father experiencing? Was it possible to send messages so real between magic sources in the form of dreams; and if so, how was it controlled? Schram was lost in thought, totally consumed by his dream, which had been real enough to cause him to call on the staff's power in his sleep. It was well into morning when he remembered Stepha. He prayed she had not been fool enough to leave Elvinott, but in his heart he knew she had. He could feel she had. Something was different about Krirtie, and although he could not put his finger on it, he knew it to be strong. He only hoped his pleading with Madeiris would be sufficient to persuade them to wait, but as he thought about Stepha and Krirtie, he only shook his head. Even the trees understood.

Schram closed his eyes and searched his mind, trying to locate or speak to Stepha. He concentrated, focusing solely on every fiber of being which made the elf princess what she was, and right when Schram felt contact was about to be made, all was lost and a piercing screech shook the trees.

Schram raised his staff to greet the bent talons of a scavenging minok. Schram's action was too slow, and the human was struck across the chest as the beast soared toward the clearing. It's talon-like feet bit deep into the human's flesh, sending him back over a fallen log, striking the ground with enough force to free his staff to the side. The minok turned in flight and immediately crashed down on the magician's chest. Schram was caught momentarily as the creature's weight forced all his air to be released, but due to his greater strength and agility, it was only a second later when he swung his arm forward, sending the four-foot brown minok's body into a nearby tree with a thud. The creature sat motionless while Schram sucked in deeply and grabbed his staff. He walked toward the fallen minok, but as he pointed the staff toward it, another screech was heard followed by intense pain in his shoulders as two talons bit through his skin hooking under his backbone. The second creature kicked up dust from the ground, beating its huge wings to lift the human above the trees. Schram knew that this second minok was much larger and probably the mother of the first.

Pain shot down his back and spine while the creature bent its talons into fists, tearing at Schram's muscles and bones. Blood was seeping freely from his wounds, but his hands only clutched his staff tightly, not struggling or fighting the attacker at all. Softly he began to chant, causing the pain in his body to subside, and the subsequent altering of the minok's flight pattern. He opened his eyes, when he felt the air being pushed upward across his face depicting the descent of the creature. He looked up toward the minok that held him, seeing its ten-foot wingspan. It was struggling to keep aloft. Suddenly, knowing it could no longer hold its catch, the creature opened its fists, sending Schram plummeting toward the fast-approaching forest ground. With two quick words, his fall gradually slowed until he gently landed, standing above the younger minok.

He raised his staff and shot two beams into the motionless body at the base of the tree. As he left the glade, he heard its wings begin flapping and then saw its shadow pass when it crossed the morning sun.

"Gone? Where did he go?"

Krystof shook his head and replied, "Well, he and that vile fleabag left the day after the elves made it back to Elvinott. Did he know your visit to be forthcoming?"

There was a slight note of sarcasm carried in his tone that both Stepha and Krirtie noticed but did not know what to make of it. Stepha ignored his question and firmly resaid her own. "Where did he and Fehr go?"

The dwarven king looked annoyed now by the two girls and leaned back in his throne, lifting his long white beard high enough to now fall short of striking the floor. After lighting his pipe, he said, "Well, I suppose you will find out eventually. King Kapmann held a ship for them, and they were to take it down the river. Jermys got the idea and convinced me of the necessity and high probability of success to sail down the Ozaky as far as he could make it and attempt to rescue Maldor. I know of the hammer he possesses, and if legend is correct, in the wrong hands it could be a dangerous weapon. Jermys convinced me that to strike now would be intelligent because they would not be expecting it. Furthermore, their forces would be set to defend an all-out offensive, if anything.

There would be a good chance for a dwarf and rat to sneak in totally unnoticed."

"Why did he not send word to us?" asked Krirtie.

"He felt, and I agreed, that the fewer who knew, the better for everyone." There was a pause, then he added, "They are probably already on the ship and will be in Gnausanne by nightfall."

"Then we will be there in their wake," replied Stepha, her anger at the unexpected turn of events evident in her voice. "Come on, Krirtie, we have a great distance to travel. I hope my wings are up to the challenge."

Suddenly, as the two were walking out of Krystof's chamber, Stepha became dizzy and disoriented, nearly falling to the ground if not for Krirtie's arms pressed around her. "Are you all right?" she whispered.

Stepha shook her head as if she was trying to free some twisted thoughts. With a slight nod, she replied, "I think so. It was the strangest thing. For a moment, just a brief instant, I felt as if Schram were right here in front of me."

Krirtie smiled. "He is always with you, and I imagine he knows we are no longer in Elvinott."

"Are you well?" asked Stepha as she shook out her wings and relaxed her arms that had become seemingly permanently locked around the girl. "We will have to walk from here. My wings are too tired to carry you any further, and I don't like flying at night without having my hands free to grab my bow."

"I am fine," Krirtie replied, "and you should begin to think of your own health first." She paused while she helped Stepha rinse her wings with water from a nearby spring. "How much farther is it to Gnausanne?"

"About another hour by foot. We shall arrive well into the night, but unless Jermys is in some incredible hurry, he will remain in port until dawn. Knowing how he hates water travel and how dangerous Lake Ozak can be in the dark, I feel confident he will be there."

Krirtie looked over the area as best as her human eyes would allow. "Yes, remembering the experience at the South Sea leaving Icly, I can't believe he would ever get on a ship again, much less develop an entire rescue plan around one."

"I am sure it is a rather large ship that will only travel at a less-than-walking pace, not to mention that it would probably take a tidal wave to rock it and Troyf exploding for it to sink."

Both laughed while Stepha saw Krirtie's questionable gaze. With a quick motion, the elf added, "This way, Krirtie. All I can say is I sure am glad I will never need you to lead me anywhere. You seem like you could get turned around in a tunnel with one exit."

Krirtie smiled and shrugged. "It's just that I haven't spent much time learning the names and identifications of all the different trees. Once I get in a forest, they all start to look the same."

The elf saw the embarrassment in her eyes even in the blackness of the night, and with a smile of her own, she said, "Do not worry about such things now, for in time you will have someone with you who can point out every type of life in the forests for you and your child."

The expected result occurred and the concern across Krirtie's face vanished, being replaced with a grin of pleasure as she thought about the situation Stepha had described. For the rest of the journey, neither girl spoke but let their minds wander to think about the ones they loved.

They arrived in Gnausanne about the time Stepha had said, and quickly they made their way to the docks. The night air coming from the water delivered a chill across the small city, which greeted the two girls as a tigon would greet a rat, with a devouring, unrelenting snap of a jaw. Stepha's elven body prepared her for the drastic change in temperature common in the forest, but Krirtie did not fare as well. Both realized the cold was intense; and although the human woman never complained, Stepha quickly abandoned her search for the ship they believed Jermys to be on and found a room at a nearby inn. Though they both would have preferred to locate the dwarf tonight, they knew he would not leave so early as to escape their detection. They agreed that keeping watch was not a necessity this night, as the gnomes seemed to keep their city well under control, finding a peaceful equilibrium between goblin and troll forces and the free populous. They felt a few solid hours of sleep would outweigh any possible threat they could be facing from attack. They would rise before dawn and begin searching where they had left off.

It was now well past dawn, and although they had come upon three ships that had previously departed from Antaag, none of the dwarves on board knew anything about Jermys or his whereabouts. Furthermore, the ships they had come to had all been in dock over a week in Gnausanne. Jermys, at the earliest, could have only left two days ago, and more than likely it was only one day he had been traveling. The captain of the last ship that they had visited said he believed one large Antaagian ship had come in two days ago at the far dock and by all his knowledge still remained, as their cargo unloading was proving to be quite a chore.

At every ship, the two women had been greeted with jeers and calls from various parts of the dock; but the ship of humans, most probably pirates, seemed to take the calls to a new level. The captain had been overly helpful with his guidance, but as they had been talking, several of the crew had moved in behind the girls. All their lips showed crooked smiles through their unshaven faces usually proudly displaying missing teeth or other such malformations, and both girls quickly realized that they were in serious danger.

Krirtie immediately drew her sword to be joined by Stepha who, although rarely chose to fight with such a weapon, preferring the accuracy and civility of her bow, knew in these close quarters her sword would serve much more efficiently.

The crewmen laughed deeply in unison, each egging the others forward. The first daring attacker who approached carried only a small dagger and was issuing various filths and disgusts, to the approval of his fellow shipmates. The jeers quickly ended when Krirtie's sword bit through his throat, severing his head. The decapitated figure fell limp on the deck, his head rolling to the side still showing the same smirk.

There was a momentary lapse, which took an unknown length of time before the rest of the pirates decided that their original plans were now changed and these two women no longer would be toys for their pleasure but rather become bait to better their fishing. Several men began moving forward, their faces now devoid of the recent humor, and it was apparent that only one idea was fixed in their menial minds—to kill.

The girls surveyed the situation, and although Krirtie's expression showed nothing but the desire to kill these rogues, both knew that they would eventually be overpowered. There were nearly thirty or so crewmen within their sights and probably just as many or more below deck. Stepha reached over without saying a word, and with a single motion of replacing her sword, grabbed her companion and stretched her wings into a magnificent flight. The two girls rose slowly into the air. Krirtie used her shield to protect them from the few arrows or daggers that flew their way, but since it was clear while they were on the boat that most of the crew was waking from a rough night at the hands of dwarven ale, their arrows were rarely near their mark. Krirtie removed the goblin dagger Maldor had given her when they had first begun their journey so long ago, and with a quick flip launched it into the captain's shoulder. Seeing him wince in pain as he fought to remove the knife, she said, "Now maybe he won't be so quick to judge women as pets. I always told Maldor I would only use that dagger for a special occasion. I think he would be satisfied with my choice."

Stepha smiled. "Yes, I suppose he probably would." She paused and became more serious. "I hope that captain was serious about the other boat, for if he was only speaking cheaply to draw us in, we are going to be continuing to Draag alone, a thought I really don't find that appealing. Jermys is only one dwarf, but remember he carries the ring's hatchet at his side. Together, that would make three of four weapons being carried with us. I like those odds much better."

Krirtie only nodded while Stepha landed nearly half a mile from the position of the pirate ship's dock. After a brief relaxing of the elf's muscles and wings, along with a calming of the adrenaline flowing through both their bodies, the two warriors began walking toward where the pirate captain had described the dwarven boat. Krirtie peered ahead and then pointed. "They fly the flags of Antaag, and that is a massive ship. It must be the one Jermys is on. It has got his terrified face written all over it.

"Come on, dwarf! You got us into this, you green-faced maggot."

Jermys scowled at the rat. "I was told we would have a large ship capable of traversing any waters." He had to cease talking while his eyes rolled to the back of his head, and once again he leaned over the side of the raft. "Don't think I am enjoying this in the least either. At least you are starting to get over the sickness."

Fehr moved to where Jermys had been working the rudder, and throwing the weight of his small body across it, began to slowly guide the raft as it floated with the currents. With a slight smile, he added, "At least your sickness was naturally caused. Not caused by a foul joke that really showed no humor. However, I now am finding extreme pleasure in your, shall I say, discoloration."

"Shut up, rat! Or you will find yourself swimming home."

Fehr frowned, and with a sharp tone added, "Say, Jermys, will it make it any better for you if I did this?" He shifted his weight to the side and slammed the rudder opposite, causing the small raft to rock downward, splashing the dwarf's still overhanging face and nearly tossing him in the water.

Jermys swung his dripping face upward, causing his beard to whip up and spray water across himself once again. The anger within him boiled a mean force beneath his skin, but in his body's current state, he could only sit frozen, not moving for fear of losing more of the little food, which consists mostly of breads, that he had been able to get down. Fehr only greeted his displeasure with a large grin while he moved to steady the boat on its course.

༺༻

A deep moan echoed from the boat. Fehr groggily got up and walked over to where he had tied the boat with the bow resting on the land. He lifted his front legs over the side and peeked down at the dwarf who was starting to wake up. "So you are finally starting to come around?"

"Where are we?" gargled the dwarf, lifting his head. His memory was not fully in place, but as he lifted his head and the green color he had carried the entire trip quickly flowed back to his face, all memories returned in force.

Fehr replied, "I don't know. Somewhere on the southern shores of Lake Ozak. We are fairly near the outskirts of the Gar Swamp. Did I ever tell you about the time I took my family there for a vac—?"

"Yes, damn it, you told me! Why didn't we stop in Gnausanne? We could have gotten a better boat there."

Fehr smiled. "Well, I asked you if you wanted to go there or take the shorter route toward the southern bank. You replied that you only wanted to be free of these currents as soon as possible, so I took that as an order for the southern bank. We made our way down most of the coastline until you started mumbling annoyingly loud, so then I pulled the boat ashore and started a big fire. However, since you looked so comfortable in the boat, I decided that I would leave you there for the night."

Jermys sat up, frowned, and as his head began to spin once again with the environment around him, he crashed back down against the bottom of the raft. Fehr giggled under his breath and added, "Did I do well?"

He was answered with silence.

Gnausanne: The River

Stepha and Krirtie walked the remaining docks quickly, heading directly toward the Antaagian ship resting its sails at a far pier. Though this was the best lead they had followed all morning and their expectations were at their peak, both tried to remain calm and well-composed since they knew that there were a hundred possible ships Jermys could have taken, and this was only appearing to be a normal cargo ship. Krirtie almost cried when she saw Roepkee, one of the first dwarves she ever met, whom Maldor had nearly killed.

His eyes met the two approaching girls, and a broad smile grew across his face. "Ahoy," he yelled, laughing a bit at his attempt at human pirate talk.

The two hurried and greeted the Feldschlosschen dwarf as he moved down the landing plank of the ship to intercept. Stepha was the first to speak, seemingly asserting herself as leader over the two. "Roepkee, pardoning all formalities, but it is truly wonderful to see you, though a surprise. Might I ask what a Feldschlosschen dwarf is doing on an Antaagian cargo ship in Gnausanne?"

The dwarf grinned. "Offering my support for moving cargo, and in return taken along to bring the load here. Where better to go but Gnausanne, the city of the richest food and specialties in all of Troyf."

"Aye," added Krirtie. "I remember when I came here for the first time. I thought my stomach would burst from all the wonderful delicacies we ate. I swore I would never come back here for fear of wanting to stay for good."

Roepkee nodded. "And I wish to never leave myself, and I have only been here for two days. Luckily, as fate would have it, this ship will remain docked here for longer than planned, and thus I have been granted a few extra days of pleasure." His voice changed from the lost revelry of his good fortune to one of serious concern when he turned to address mainly the elf. "Now can I ask, what great evil has occurred that has brought you here? I can tell from your expression that it is not one of pleasure, as is mine."

"We actually came looking for one of your friends and fellow dwarves. We had hoped he would have been on this ship with you, but if this ship is staying in port for several days, I must assume that Jermys and Fehr were not part of the cargo?"

Roepkee nodded. "Well, it is really Jermys's doing that we are in port the extra days." Both the girls became intrigued and excited when it became apparent that the whereabouts of their companions was known. The dwarf continued. "He was supposed to be on this ship as you suspected, but because Gnausanne needed these supplies earlier than it was originally planned, we left before he was able to join us. Kapmann was supposed to supply him with another boat upon his arrival, and it was assumed that he would switch to this ship and take it on to his destination right away. However, as of this morning, he is one day late, and since the captain is not that excited about relieving his command to Jermys, he has said that we will wait one more day before heading back up the river. I, of course, have not spoken to Jermys, but it is believed he either decided on another route and method of travel or simply did not wish to waste the time stopping in Gnausanne and continued across the lake in whatever boat he had acquired. However, either way does not help you."

With Roepkee's speech, both girls seemed to have the final winds blown out of their sails. Krirtie dropped to the ground with a loud sigh, and although Stepha remained standing, it was obvious as she randomly paced about that this additional setback was not well-taken.

Finally, the elf turned back and asked, "Since you have been here, have you seen any merchants who might be selling either boats or passage down the Draag River?"

Roepkee looked concerned. "From what I have heard, Draag is not a safe place to be during these oppressed times. Shouldn't you consider…"

The elf was in no mood to explain her wishes, nor did she want to waste anymore time unnecessarily, and her interruption expressed both feelings clearly. "If we do not make it to our destination within two days, many lives, including Jermys's, could be in jeopardy. Now, do you know where we might find passage?"

The dwarf remained obviously against the notion but told what he knew, seeing that the elf was determined. "I saw a merchant who had small rafts. Maybe even one or two larger ones. They were set along the water just outside the western boundaries of the city. Perhaps one of hers would be sufficient for your needs, though none looked extremely seaworthy. Also, there is one large human ship that, if rumor serves, will be leaving for Icly this day. They would travel halfway down the Draag River, but again, this was a pirate ship, and I'd just as soon see you walk or swim than be trapped on board with that scum. From what I hear, they are some of the worst lot still pirating the river and South Sea."

Krirtie smiled. "Yes, I believe we already met that bunch. I don't think we would be extremely welcome on their ship anyway."

The dwarf caught both the girl's grins, and realizing that he would probably hear the story that night over ales at a local pub, he let the matter drop. However, he also knew the pirate's version of it would probably speak of how two misfit women wandered onboard their ship, and after the crew had their way with them, they discarded the girls overboard. Looking at their faces, Roepkee was certain that was not the case in this situation. He laughed a chuckle in return, and while lighting his pipe, he motioned for them to follow.

"Come on with me. I will walk you two down to where I saw the merchant the other day. She was female and exceptionally beautiful, with long but exquisite bushy hair. Maybe I can bargain with her to get you a good price."

Krirtie and Stepha smiled at each other, each thinking that to see this four-foot, rough-bearded, and nearly 200-year-old dwarf using his debonair abilities to charm a merchant should be quite humorous, to say the least. Without further comment on the subject, Roepkee snagged one hand from each woman, both who stood well above him, and departed at a happy skip, adding a snuff to his pipe before beginning.

A desperate sight we must make, Stepha thought. However, when they passed the band of pirates who stopped and frowned at them, with Roepkee there, the humans only kept their comments to themselves. They would as soon go about their business than risk fighting off a town that was half dwarven and nearly all dwarven allies.

Krirtie realized that the pirates did recognize them and were grimacing in anger under their filthy skin, but also that they were not about to cause a scene or dispute. Therefore, she chose to seize the opportunity and let the cackling behavior she had learned from her closeness with Fehr come to a full blossom. Taunt after taunt shot like daggers into the bellies of the four pirates, and if not for the gesturing hand of the now-terrified dwarf, it was clear that the pirates would attack, regardless of what the repercussions might be. However, when Stepha and Roepkee finally quieted the girl, the four rogues lost interest and continued to their ship, exchanging comments on how their fierceness had scared the group into an utter pale-white silent horror.

Krirtie replaced her scimitar to its scabbard as a proud look of achievement grew across her face. Stepha joined her with a smile, but the angered dwarf only sighed, letting his disapproval shine distinctly through. However, when his eyes caught the beauty he had seen the previous day, all happenings with the pirate band were forgotten, and quickly he began making himself look clean and tidy, finishing by tucking his rough and tangled beard into his belt. Stepha held her smile while she watched the dwarf's preparations, but Krirtie's expression turned long and flat, and she stared blankly toward the female merchant whose eyes were fixed upon her.

Stepha whispered. "Krirtie, what is it?" When the girl did not answer, the elf joined her gaze on the woman they were approaching.

She was of human build; however, her skin was slightly tainted, almost elven in nature. Her hair was light-brown and bushy, with blonde streaks etched through it. Her dress was that of a common peddler, but it was apparent by her exceptional beauty, as Roepkee had rightly described, that she was no ordinary citizen of Gnausanne. The elf tossed different possibilities over in her mind but decided that as long as they could get a boat from her, she could be a dragon and it would not matter.

By now they had left the city and were standing before the woman who still remained locked in a stare with Krirtie. With a sudden tilt of her head, her broad smile soothed everyone and her voice sang like a gentle breeze across the water. To Roepkee, she asked, "What can I do for you, my friends?"

Stepha began to speak but was cut off by the now-much-deeper voice of the dwarf. "It seems my friends here have become stranded and would like to inquire about purchasing a boat, if you might have one that could stand the fast currents of the River Draag?"

The woman's face lost its smile and began to grow with intrigue. "Draag? Not a good time to travel those waters." She was speaking to the two girls, but she clearly focused on Krirtie. Only when Stepha cut her off did the mysterious woman's gaze turn.

"We have business and friends, which take us down that path. If you can help us, we would be much obliged, and we will pay well."

The woman tilted her head again, seemingly sizing up the elf and human before her. With a slight grin, she said, "I have a raft that should suit you. It is not my largest vessel, but it takes the waves well. However, it will cost you. Two hundred sovereigns."

"Two hun…" began Krirtie before being hushed by Stepha's raised hand.

"We can pay you one hundred now, and the other hundred after our business is completed. I am Stephanatilantilis, Princess of the Flyer Elves of Elvinott, and you have my word."

The woman smiled. "I know who you are, Stephanatilantilis"—she began speaking in elven—"and I know your word is good." She turned to the now-blank faces of the small group and in common tongue added, "In my home, I am Enroht-Wah (pronounced "Jenro-Wa"), but you may just call me Lauren, should you ever need to ask for my whereabouts."

There was a brief silence as all were stunned by the speech and the strange content it entailed. Finally, Stepha said, "I will remember your name, Enroht-Wah, for I will return to see you. My companion is Krirtie of the human city of Toopek, and this is Roepkee of the Feldschlosschen dwarves. We are in your gratitude."

Roepkee interjected, speaking primarily to Stepha. "Pardon the interruption, but we have more than enough sovereigns on our ship. I will cover your fare and then you can return it to the dwarves when you are better able. Besides, you are traveling now in aid to Feldschlosschen, it is only fitting we should aid you if we are able."

Stepha smiled and placed her hand on his shoulder. "Thank you, old friend. We appreciate the help and will be sure to repay any we owe."

The dwarf glanced at the woman merchant and shared her smile as he shrugged. "Do not think about it again, Stepha. Now, if you can spare the time, I would like to invite you all to a quick meal before you leave."

Stepha and Krirtie both agreed, as their desires for food had fallen second to their finding passage. Now they remembered their body's needs and were most readily happy to answer them. All eyes fell questionably toward the woman, but none looked closer than Krirtie, who did not know why this mysterious woman bothered her so. With a smile that rivaled the sun's light, Lauren agreed, and all accompanied the dwarf to a nearby inn. Krirtie remained suspicious as they walked all the way to the first few minutes at the table. However, as the good cheer and humor was passed among the small group, all suspicions were seemingly forgotten. It was as if Lauren had gone into their minds and snatched the doubts away.

They all enjoyed their brief time together, but Stepha and Krirtie had a mission that did not have the luxury of time. It was only a short period later, and they were shoving their small raft onto the glass-like surface of Lake Ozak under the late morning sun. They looked back at the two figures of the dwarf and merchant woman standing practically arm in arm. They hoisted their makeshift sail, and the gentle breeze slowly pushed their boat along smoothly, as if they were floating on air. After several minutes, they both became settled, and Stepha turned to bid one more farewell wave to those on the shore. To her surprise, all was still, and all signs of the merchant or the dwarf were absent. Stepha used her elven sight to explore every hidden shadow along the bank, following it all the way back well into the city. Yet still, there appeared to be no trace of those they had just left.

She tapped Krirtie on the shoulder and, without speaking, motioned back toward the land. Krirtie stared blankly at the beach, not seeing anything out of order at first, and then she too saw the emptiness where the past merchant's area had been located. Now, only white sand was shown reflecting the sun's bright light. A worried and somewhat fearful expression grew over Krirtie's face, and suddenly a damper in her mind seemed to be opened and a barrage of knowledge, which had previously been blocked or out of her reach, was thrust upon her.

She stared back up at Stepha. "I know the woman who sold us the raft."

"Know her?" replied the elf. "What do you mean? Who is she?"

Krirtie again stared back to the shore. "I don't know why I couldn't remember before, but she is the one who sold me the sword I now carry and all my armor. Schram bought it last time we were in Gnausanne."

"I was not with you that morning when you two bought the weapon and armor. Schram never spoke about your weapon as being one of the ring until later. What happened when you acquired it?"

Krirtie fell back, totally ignoring the rudder and becoming absorbed by the workings of her mind while she fought to remember the time Stepha had asked about. Gradually, her head lifted, and she began retelling the story. "We had searched for a peddler with armor that would fit me for a good part of the morning. I had disposed of the goblin armor I had worn previously when Maldor told me about what you had seen in the forest that day so long ago." Her voice faded as she remembered the horror of the past. "The day you saw my father leading the attack on Elvinott."

There was a long pause as both girls seemed to become seduced by the harsh memories they were reliving in their minds. Krirtie lifted her head and, gathering her strength, continued where she had left off. "I no longer wished to wear the goblin armor to avenge my father's death. The strange thing was, and I did not notice it at the time, each time we found a merchant with armor that seemed suitable to me, Schram would rule it out immediately for one reason or another. Until…finally we arrived to a merchant just outside of town. She was beautiful, with bushy brown hair just like Lauren's, only shorter. She did, however, have the same smile, which seemed to sing a magical song as you looked upon it."

"Then you felt it too?" interrupted Stepha. "When we first approached, her smile shot a feeling of peace through my elven skin, relaxing my entire body and mind."

"Yes, just like before. Schram spoke to her like they had been friends all their lives. She only had one set of armor, and when I first looked at it, it seemed way too small. However, when I tried it, it fit snugly and wore lighter than any armor I have ever had. She had six swords. I can still see them just like they still were resting in front of me. I liked a sword that had a blue hilt and magnificent double-edged blade, but Schram would have nothing to do with it. He insisted on this sword"—she rubbed the curved scimitar resting at her side—"and now I suppose I know why. The woman did not want to part with it, and thus the price was high. I think she asked 200 sovereigns for it, and he paid them without question. Now that I think about it, the whole situation seemed weird, but at the time I did not take notice, either due to all the troubles already flowing through my mind or some outside force not allowing me to focus on the situation properly." She turned her head to face the elf and took on a much more serious tone. "I don't know what part Enroht-Wah, or Lauren, is playing in this whole ordeal, but I do think it is much more than coincidence we met her here again."

Stepha looked out over the water. In a soft voice she added, "I agree, and I do not know what to think about it. I only hope we can be lucky enough to cross Jermys and Fehr's path and join them on their trek to Draag. Otherwise, we should come to the realization that we are on our own, and this journey has become that much more difficult and that much less likely for success."

Are we going to leave today, dwarf, or spend another entire day moving a couple hundred feet down the shore, stopping every minute so you can heave…?"

"Shut up," yelled Jermys as once again he sat down on the rocks to rest and settle his stomach. "You are lucky you're out there in the boat and not within my reach, or so help me I would…"

"You'd what?" taunted Fehr. "You'd deposit your breakfast on me?"

His laughs and jeers gained in strength as they crossed the water's surface and struck Jermys, causing his green-with-sickness-face to become red with anger. "Fine! Get that boat over here, rat. We head down the river today, for the weather is in our favor."

"Oh, Jermys, take it easy. I was just fooling with you. If you are not ready to leave, then we won't. There is no reason to risk you feeling worse." Although his words seemed sincere, his tone still carried the rat's sarcastic edge, whether it was meant or not.

"I am in charge and I say when we leave. Bring the boat ashore. We have much time to make up for what we lost during my brief illness."

Fehr frowned, knowing that the dwarf was nowhere near travel-ready, but did as he asked just the same. Slowly the raft made its way to the shore, striking the rocky wall making up the lake bottom several feet short of the actual edge only close enough to set the dwarf on fire. Fehr cringed backward while the dwarf laid into him with jeers of his own depicting the rat's inability to do anything correctly. The thought of wading through two feet of water for a short bodied dwarf was not something that was well received.

However, after Jermys was on board and the boat broke free from its secured landing and began to rock with the waves, his jeers stopped and it was clear if Fehr wanted the upper hand, he would have it. Jermys curled up in a little ball on the floor of the small raft allowing his beard to seep up the loose water along the bottom cooling his body after the beads of sweat had covered nearly every inch of him. Fehr only shook his head and then turned their small raft back toward the center of the lake. To the west, a light rumbling could be heard and the river that the lake emptied into shown clearly on the horizon as a light haze rose over where the rapids began.

The small raft rocked forward bringing the bow to point nearly straight downward, and with a thunderous scream broken only by Jermys's moans, nature grabbed hold of the boat and all means of control and guidance were lost. Fehr's little body was tossed wildly about as the fierce temper of the river slammed their raft sideways, and then with a backward thrust, ripped it around so now they sailed in reverse. Even in his worn and sickening state, the much-stronger Jermys had the presence to snatch the rat and secure him under his body, holding the two of them pinned to the base of the raft. They removed the sail to keep the wind from affecting their voyage more, but it was obvious that the current would provide more than enough momentum. The two tightly clutched each other and the boat while they were belted with sprays of water and debris. A loud cracking was heard when the raft struck a rock causing the wood bottom of the boat to splinter and break. Water quickly began flowing throughout the small raft, making it difficult to even be certain where the raft and the river separated. However, with the rapid pace and force of the water, there was little chance the vessel would completely sink.

Jermys carefully moved toward the fracture and tried to cover it with every loose object and debris he could find. However, each time he had a piece of wood in place, the boat would be issued another jolt, and both he and his patch would be tossed aside. He reached his head up and took a quick gaze at the waters which lay ahead. The adrenaline of the situation had given him a brief freedom from the seasickness he had felt earlier, and he wanted now to try to gain control of their raft before it was torn apart completely. But when he looked at nothing but violent hands of white splashing water reaching out to grab them, his fears and dizziness returned in force, sending the pale-faced dwarf down to again fall beside Fehr, the two remaining motionless on the bottom of the beaten raft.

An uncountable amount of time passed before the hardest jolt yet was experienced, causing the raft to nearly explode. Wood went in every direction, but the two terrified individuals remained lodged in a main piece of hull. There were no longer any sides, and it more appeared that the dwarf and rat were traveling down the rapids on no more than a single board. Fehr kept his face covered, trying to concentrate on digging his claws into the wood to ensure his firm position.

The farther they traveled, the angrier the river seemed to get. The two were tossed every direction with the ferocity of a tigon playing with its catch. The green that had accompanied Jermys's face the past days was now totally absent, to be replaced by the pale white of pure horror. His arms were outstretched, wrapping his fingers around both sides of the board they floated on, with Fehr locked beneath his chest. The dwarf's body was rigid, not letting any of the violent attacks win over in their test of wills. It was Fehr's near-silent voice which broke the dwarf from his fierce concentration.

"The rapids have subsided a bit. Perhaps we can make it to a bank?"

Jermys raised his head but refused to unlock his grip from the board. The water around them was still moving rapidly, but its surface was smooth. They were being carried along at a fast pace and rumblings could be heard both in their wake and from those waters in their path ahead. Jermys lifted his hands, and quickly blood began to return to his whitened fingers. Immediately he started paddling, kicking, and doing anything he could to move what was left of their boat to the only shore he could see. The river itself was over a half mile across at this point, and the shore line they could see was at least half that distance away. Their pace with the currents gradually began picking up speed, and the thunder ahead of them grew louder and louder.

Suddenly Fehr quit paddling and moved to stand before his companion. "Our only chance is to swim. We will make better effort against the current even being able to touch bottom in places. If not, we will be sucked down for anther ride to hell, and this 'boat' can't take that."

Jermys frowned. "Out of the question. We are getting closer to the shore every second."

However, it was too late, as the rat had already leaped into the water and was quickly leaving the raft behind, as his steady strokes were indeed more effective against the swift current. Jermys swung his head to the doom, which willingly awaited his arrival, and then back to the rat who was wildly fighting to continue to the side. The dwarf was completely lost in decision-making abilities as he was only weighing the extent of the fears involved with each of his choices. With a loud scream and flailing arms, he launched his body into the water.

Quickly, all his senses vanished as he was freed from the one thing which had given him a slight feeling of safety a moment ago. His body broke the plane of the water and his hollers and flapping arms greeted any within earshot. It immediately became clear to Fehr that Jermys had gained nothing by leaving the board. He was still being carried down the river by the current at the same pace as before, only he now had the additional concern of staying afloat. He stopped wildly swinging his arms when he felt the sharp pain of something biting at his shoulder.

"SHARK!" screamed Jermys in a fear-stricken panic.

The bite released only long enough for the dwarf to hear., "Shut up, you stupid dwarf, and work with me on this."

Jermys swung one hand back to try to free his attacker but froze when he heard Fehr's voice and felt his wet fur against his hand. The rat growled at the dwarf, but his displeasure was only temporary as he tried to concentrate on swimming against the current while pulling more than three times his weight.

Jermys fought and struggled, thinking he was trying to swim and aid the rat's efforts, but in actuality he was only making things that much more difficult. The rat fought and fought, sometimes gaining, sometime losing the battle against the fierce water. The rumblings from ahead were still growing louder with each passing second, and the current was getting noticeably quicker. The rat bit hard into Jermys's arm as he struggled to reach anything they could use to gain an advantage.

Thirty minutes passed of constant fighting, anguish, and pain until suddenly Jermys nearly leaped out of the water. "SHARK!"

The dwarf began flailing his arms wildly, again knocking Fehr free from his grip and actually sending the rat ten to fifteen feet through the air. Jermys continued flopping and flailing, trying to ensure that this underwater attacker did not get another chance to use his body as a midday meal. Fehr's giggles in the background finally broke the dwarf from his stupor.

"Put your feet down, dwarf. Your shark is the river bottom. If I can touch, I know you can too." Fehr's voice was a good attempt at sarcasm once again; however, his exhaustion and panting made his tone get lost in his deep breaths, and Jermys only heard the words as helpful, instead of the rat's usual snideness.

Stretching his feet down, Jermys gripped the river bottom and stood strong against the current. He cleared his eyes and turned to the shore in time to see the rat fall flat on the dry beach, nearly unconscious.

The heat from the fire soothed the dwarf's face, and slowly he began to stir. The pains from the day's activities grew throughout his body, making their staunch presence known. He opened his eyes trying to focus, and he realized that the sun was nearly set, and the shadows of the surrounding forests further swallowed any available light. Gingerly he raised his head to immediately let it return to the ground when the fire began spinning and swirling with a violent passion about him. He issued several grunts, which alerted Fehr that his companion was trying to rejoin the world of the living.

In the background, the thunderous roar of the rolling rapids filled the air, and Fehr moved to sit beside his friend. In a deep and completely out-of-character caring voice, the rat said, "Jermys, are you all right? I have been worried that you would not return."

The dwarf tried to look at his small companion whose little eyes stared blankly back toward him. He coughed slightly, sending a bit more river water from his mouth. Softly, he said, "Thank you, Fehr. You saved me. I shall not forget."

With that he fell back into sleep, and the rat moved closer, placing his head across the dwarf's belly and closing his eyes as well.

"What do you think we should do?" asked Krirtie, looking down the mouth of what appeared to be vicious and unforgiving rapids.

"It is getting near sundown, and I don't think I would want to be caught in those once it gets dark. We will camp along the north shore and, at first light, do our best to navigate them." Stepha pointed toward the rapids, and it was obvious in her tone and expression that she was not looking forward to their next day's activities. However, knowing Jermys and the extent of his stubbornness, she was sure the dwarf would not hesitate to enter these rapids regardless of his boat and the condition it was in. She believed that if they ever wanted to join with the two ahead of them, they had to continue along their last known course, and that meant the river.

As Krirtie guided their raft toward the nearby shore, both girls got a good look at what lay ahead for them. The first hundred yards or so looked fairly smooth, as far as rapids went, but judging from the noise and the high amount of white foam and spray shooting into the air beyond that point, it was apparent that the first hundred yards was only a test to prepare them for the real rapids. The girls made a small camp in the marshy beach marking the outskirts of the Gar Swamp, and after Stepha checked the area for anything that should not be there, she returned and shared in a meal Krirtie had prepared. The two ate heartily, since it had been late morning since their last meal, and it was now falling well into night. The sounds of the forest were alive with life, which soothed the elf's mind but made Krirtie uncomfortable and nervous.

Stepha saw her discomfort and moved to sit beside her. Softly she said, "That was the mating call of a male cervu. He will bugle like that to mark females that he claims to his herd. It is both a warning to other males and a song to lure other perspective mates."

Krirtie looked toward the elf with a slightly lost and embarrassed expression. "Is it that obvious that I am lost in the forest? In fact it often scares me."

The elf smiled. "Among any but an elf, you would appear like any other? I know the signs when someone is faced with that, which they do not understand. You are not lost in the forest. It is just not known to you. As far as humans go, only Schram was able to find peace among the trees. I believe he is more at home here than in the cities he claims as home."

Krirtie nodded. "Yes, that much is certain. Even when we were growing up, at our closest times he was still distant. There was always something blocking our friendship, a part of him he would never let me near. Often I would go out at night and see him and Kirven, I mean his canok friend, alone talking at the Toopekian forest boundary. Schram would often stare blankly into the trees as if he knew he was missing something—something he could only find out there." Her head jerked slightly in her revelry. "Now I know it was you he was looking to."

Stepha rose and walked toward the fire. "Night after night I would sit and look toward the stars, wishing I could be on one of them looking down at Toopek. My entire life, the only elf I ever loved was Schram, and he was human."

There was a long silence before Krirtie rose and joined the elf's side in front of the fire. "Perhaps some time, when Maldor has taught me more about the trees and animals, all four of us will walk together and share a moment of peace in the forest."

Stepha smiled and placed her hand on Krirtie's stomach. "Don't you mean the five of us?"

Captured: The Boat

A roar sounded through the trees, causing Fehr to freeze in the same position he had slept in the night before. Hesitantly, he opened one eye and alerted all his other senses to be aware of any movement in the nearby area. An odd silence crept over the usually active morning air, giving the rat the feeling something was not right. Suddenly, there was another roar, which shook the rat's body at its closeness in proximity. He rolled over and began shouting curses in dwarven as he kicked the snoring dwarf still sleeping next to him. Jermys mumbled a bit but only turned to his side, not coming to complete consciousness but still showing he would be feeling better this day. Thankfully for Fehr, his new position also silenced his echoing snores, so once again there would be some peace for the area.

The rat stretched his cramped muscles and gazed his eyes across their crude excuse for a camp. Quickly, he noticed their fire was all but diminished, and he darted into the nearby woods to gather a few more branches to burn for the morning. Before leaving the area, he took one more brief glance back toward the dwarf to be certain that he was still well and then darted into the trees. Finding the necessary logs proved easy; and knowing that the dwarf would remain asleep for some time yet, he decided to go exploring. It had been a long time since he had been able to go off on his own, and besides, he knew he could not get in any trouble out here, in the middle of nowhere. He would be hard-pressed to even find another form of animal life.

The thick tree cover was providing the utmost excitement for the rat as he leaped over fallen trees and ducked beneath wild brush and shrubs. He climbed and crawled, moving with the silence common among his kind, but not consciously trying to be quiet. As he traveled, any sound which did occur seemed only to be its rightful place in nature. Whether a tree branch snapped or leaves rustled against each other, all seemed to be simply the forest greeting the morning light.

Suddenly, Fehr leaped past an outcropping of trees and landed on a well-marked and seemingly well-traveled path. He stared at the cleared surface, and slowly a completely puzzled and confused look grew across his face. This lost expression froze the rat in his tracks.

"What in the—." His words were cut off in mid-sentence as an arrow thudded in the ground nearly severing his tail.

"Oh, you missed, you clumsy fool!" echoed a rusty voice butchering the dwarven tongue. Fehr knew without looking that this meant dark dwarves, and to dark dwarves, he meant breakfast. "Here, I will show you how to kill tree scum like this."

Fehr did not hesitate a moment longer. He leaped back into the brush from which he had come. He began retracing his steps as fast as he could go while a few more arrows struck his path behind him. However, due to the thick cover and rough traveling, he was certain he could safely put some distance between himself and the bumbling dwarves who had just missed a completely unprotected shot at a meal.

"Wake up, Feldschlosschen scum!" hollered a voice from above.

Jermys opened his eyes to greet a dagger tip pressed to his throat. He gulped deeply then tried to speak. His words were chalky, and he knew that although most of his sickness seemed to have passed, he was still far from well. "I am Jermys Ironshield. I wish to speak to your leader, for I carry with me the Hatchet of Claude."

He slid his hand to his belt but found only an empty buckle. His face dropped when the dwarves around him started to laugh and shout jeers. The one who had spoken before kicked him in the gut again and removed a small ax, placing it to Jermys's face. In a gnarled voice, much like scraping sandpaper, he said, "Do you mean this hatchet, dwarf?" Again laughter filled the small clearing.

Jermys raised his head and peered around as much as he could, knowing that too much movement may cause the dagger at his throat to become active and begin pressing much closer to his skin than he would be comfortable with. What he saw was a party of about ten DDs around a fire, many eating or talking among themselves, but the ones to be concerned with were the three standing beside him. He looked back up to stare at their leader, who now possessed the hatchet.

He coughed to clear his throat and then in a stern voice, he said, "I trust you will return that to me in time."

The dark dwarf frowned. "I am Eb-Brown, and you would do well to remain silent. It would serve no purpose to return this ax to a dead dwarf."

Jermys stood strong as the jeers and calls once again erupted. "Eb-Brown? Does that mean you are cousin to one Lyl-Brown?"

All noise ceased at the mention of the once-second-in-command over the dark dwarf reign; the one which Bretten, Jermys's twin brother, had brutally killed over a year ago outside Eltak, the old mountain elf city. Eb-Brown grew totally stoic and serious, placing his own knife at Jermys's throat. "You know something about my brother? Speak now, or die!"

His words were harsh, and there was no doubt in Jermys's mind that he was sincere in his threat. Jermys fought to keep the fear from entering his speech, but he knew not what to say. If he said the truth, he would most likely be killed. If he lied, he may not be able to convince them of its merit. His face grew slightly pale before he uttered the words, "Your brother is dead."

He knew he could not speak the entire truth. He knew that if he told the dark dwarf that Bretten killed his brother, vengeance would be his only reward. He ended his statement without comment, waiting for the result, the outcome of which he could not even imagine.

Eb-Brown turned cold, his face dropping without actually showing any physical movement. His eyes turned fire-red as if hot coals were about to explode within him. Jermys knew he was about to be struck dead, but he was helpless to prevent it. Brown's muscle flexed tightly, and he pressed his dagger deep into Jermys's skin, causing blood to begin to ooze from around the blade. "How do you know this, Jermys Ironshield? I give you moments to live save you speak the truth."

He was now being pressed between the sandy soil of the ground and Eb-Brown's sharp dagger. With each passing moment, more blood began to ooze between the blade and flesh and trickle down his neck into his long beard. Jermys stared back deep into the dark dwarf's eyes, and for a moment, he saw only the pain he felt—a pain Jermys knew as well as anyone. For that brief instant, Eb-Brown looked no different from any mining dwarf except for his much darker color. Jermys shook his head, for he knew what he had to do.

His stare carried the same pain when he began to issue forth a response. "Formerly I traveled with a group of companions in search of my brother. It was many, many days ago we found him. His body was cold and still, for he had been passed for many moons. Next to him lay your brother, his life also ended. We found them outside the southernmost entrance to the dwarven mines of Antaag. By the looks of the surroundings, the two appeared to be fighting against a common enemy, although no signs of this enemy remained. The ground was scorched with something equaled only to dragon fire, but it was magical bursts of energy, which opened both our brother's chests. An elf traveled with me. With his help, both Lyl-Brown and my brother, Bretten Ironshield, were granted grace in passing."

The dark dwarf's eyes became transparent, and he slowly removed his dagger. However, when Jermys began to sit up, two hands grabbed his shoulders and held him down. Eb-Brown climbed back to his feet and paced the ground in front of the dwarf before turning back to face him. Raising his dagger to use it as a pointer, he said, "We will take you to our leader. I will leave it in his hands whether to believe you or not, but let it be known that at this point, I do not. If you make any attempts at escape, I will not hesitate to kill you myself."

With a quick motion, the dark dwarf behind him lifted Jermys to his feet. The world began to spin furiously, and Jermys nearly fell straight back to the ground before the dwarf grabbed his arm. "He said not to try anything, scum! Fake a fall again, and I will be the one pushing a blade through your back."

Jermys frowned and concentrated on keeping his eyes forward and walking steadily. He found himself in the middle of the pack as they were leaving the campsite. The DDs paid no mind to the fire, leaving it burning at a full blaze while they disappeared from sight.

Slowly, Fehr crept out from the bushes he had been hiding in and approached the fire. He looked about and then turned to stare over the rapids, which still thundered past. With a long sigh, he gathered anything the dark dwarves had rummaged through and discarded but sighed even deeper when he found nothing that could be considered worth keeping for his collection. Kicking a bit of sand on the fire to lower its stiff flame, the rat disappeared behind the path the group of dwarves had taken.

He remained a good distance back, but following their trail did not prove difficult as they were not trying to hide it. He was out of earshot so the sounds of the forest coming back to rest after a large group had passed, and the now-distant rumbling of the river rapids were all he could hear. It was a much more soothing feeling than he had been experiencing lately, almost giving Fehr the sense that he was back roaming the forests surrounding Toopek and Lawren. The birds were singing and a gentle breeze rustled the leaves, making the dark forest they were in become increasingly friendly.

Fehr bounded along the trail completely carefree. He knew that the only danger he could face in these woods was the large group of dark dwarves traveling ahead of him, and he knew exactly where they were at all times. He thought that this group was probably a scouting party, and now they were heading back to the main camp. Suddenly, Fehr's mind locked. If they were heading back to the main camp, then it was certain there would be more dark dwarves there and thus become less likely that he would be able to attempt a successful rescue. Perhaps his best opportunity would be to act now.

Fehr began to move up the trail more quickly, trying to overtake those ahead and better inspect the situation. However, voices and movement from behind him halted his progress, and the rat leaped into the bushes for cover.

⊙⁕⊙

The girls woke early that morning as the first light of the day greeted their tired faces like that of an unwanted visitor. The two stumbled about, and although they had switched turns at watch, by the time dawn rolled near, Krirtie allowed the stillness of the night to overtake her, and she joined her companion in sleep. Now, however, was a time for serious action. The journey which lay ahead was dangerous and full of many obstacles, the first of which was in the form of a violent storm calling itself the River Draag. Krirtie immediately began preparing a bit of food to hold their bodies for the majority of the day, since there was no telling if they would be able to find a break in their navigations. It was agreed, however, that if a smooth current did interject itself somewhere between rapids, then they would use it as their resting spot. Both only hoped that there were more than one, and that however many there were, they were not short.

The elf moved from the campsite and followed the lakeshore to where it emptied into the river. The beach she was walking along was spongy due to the swamp mud making up its base, and when Krirtie had finished preparing her gear for their trek, her footfalls made gurgling noises as she ran to catch up to her friend. The two circled the edge of the river and began walking its length.

Krirtie stopped and pointed. "Stepha, I cannot be sure, but if you look closely at the water here and then toward the water at the other side, it appears as if this side is much rougher just by comparing the amount of white caps, much rougher at the mouth anyway."

Stepha stared at the river and quickly evaluated the human's observation. With a nod, she replied, "I believe you are correct. It would probably be to our benefit to sail to the other side before beginning our descent."

"Shouldn't we simply begin where it looks the calmest, not necessarily all the way to the other bank, if the situation does not demand it?" added Krirtie.

Stepha nodded again. "That would be true, except because we have such a small raft and neither of us knows much about navigating such a river, I would prefer to stay near one of the banks. At least then if we did capsize, we may still have half a chance to reach safety by swimming. However, looking at these jagged rocks near this shore, and considering the size of our small raft, I think saying half a chance may be stretching our odds."

Krirtie nodded acceptance. "You are right, Stepha. Would it be possible for us to fly? I know it takes much out of you, but it would solve the rapids issue."

Stepha shook her head. "Flight is an option, but only our last option. My wings are tired and it is difficult with the combined weight." She looked back, more serious. "But mostly, I am fearful that we would be easy targets in the sky. These are not friendly forests."

Krirtie shook her head that she understood, and then tilted her head slightly and added, "By the way, you never did finish telling me how you got your brother's blessing to go on this trek. I would have thought he would have insisted you stay in Elvinott, and I know you would not act against his word."

Stepha took Krirtie's arm and began to walk back to the raft. "Well, actually, I have not *yet* gone against his word. I promised I would not continue to Draag without Jermys accompanying us and Krystof's blessing. I didn't give Krystof time to say anything against our plans because I was so infuriated at the situation we were thrust into. I will be accompanying Jermys and Fehr if we could ever catch them. I hope we greet them before we reach Draag because, besides the obvious reason, I would not want to be dishonest to my brother and king.

Stepha threw their last bit of stored food into the raft, which marked the end of their loitering. They could delay the inevitable no longer, which was evident in the total lack of conversation that had ensued. Both girls knew that once they started their small craft toward the moving currents, there would be no turning back. This last chance to back out was issued silently between both their stares, and both answered the same.

Stepha shoved the raft into the water and leaped over the side, never letting water touch her body. And like being pulled toward a magnet, the majestic river sucked them downward. Krirtie worked the rudder and angled the sail while Stepha dug the oars into the water to give the boat the extra surge to push away from the dangerous jagged shore.

Once they had moved about 500 yards out, she turned the rudder, and the small raft began to parallel the river's mouth. Just looking down the massive expanse as they passed gave the girls the feeling that the river was satisfied to simply wait for them, as if it was even daring them to come.

Stepha pushed the raft along using all her strength combined with Krirtie's guidance to keep the river from choosing the time they entered. They studied what they saw before them, with Stepha searching for anything that might give them an advantage. She began thinking about her family and then Schram, wishing any of them were here with her now. Krirtie held the boat turned against the current while she joined the elf in the spectacle rumbling at their doorstep.

The boat fought along its course, slowly finding its way to the southern shore of the river. Stepha dug the oars deep, pushing the small craft backward while swinging its bow around to face the splashing water. Neither girl spoke, but it was obvious both were as uncertain about their next actions as they had ever been in their entire lives. Krirtie had even begun to tremble, doing well to hide her fears from Stepha but not from herself. She was terrified for what they were about to undertake. The horror she was feeling, however, was matched only by that which was experienced by the elf. Stepha's face was pale. Much of her natural green-brown color was lost only to be replaced by an empty hue lacking any definable shade.

Both girls heard the rumble and felt their raft being slowly pulled toward it but were helpless to act. They had been staring at the rapids for the entire morning, but only now, when they were graphically confronted with the idea of traversing them, did the reality of the situation hit.

Stepha broke from her momentary trance to turn and face Krirtie. She wished to speak, but the fear within her made words come difficult. Krirtie noticed her discomfort and, by displaying the same feelings, answered what the elf wished to ask. Only giving a nod, Stepha marked the beginning of the next leg of their journey, the Draag River.

Krirtie lowered the sail while Stepha moved the oars to a closer notch so her use of them would be more quickly answered by the boat. Once the sail was down, Krirtie returned to the back and took her seat by the arm of the rudder. Neither girl had any idea what to expect or how much control they were actually going to have, but both were prepared to give it everything they had, and both knew it was too late to decide otherwise now.

The raft began to increase in speed as it caught the swifter currents, but to Stepha, it did not appear that it was moving as fast as the laws of physics said it should be. It had picked up momentum, but quickly it had seemed to reach an apex; and although the water was moving continually faster, the boat remained at the same pace. However, the elf glanced ahead and tossed her feelings aside, realizing that their current speed was more than sufficient to send them tumbling topside.

A spray of water exploded upward as the bow of the raft took the first wall. They plunged, driving the tip of the boat into the swirling waves before whipping it back to be temporarily level to the surface again. All of Stepha's muscles locked, becoming firmly fastened to the handles of the oars, driving both paddles deep against the current.

Krirtie kept her eyes focused ahead, working the rudder by feel. When the raft was shoved one way, she threw all her weight back trying to counter it in return. She could feel the bruises beginning to form around her shoulders as she leaned with all her might against nature's forces, finding either the rudder arm or her own armor being shoved back just as hard. However, even as bad as it seemed, there was something that was not right, and that something was giving them the advantage they desperately needed.

A large wave crashed sideways into the boat, causing the entire vessel to rock well to its left and then quickly, seemingly unnaturally, roll back flat. Stepha was thrown off her seat; and when she immediately shifted her weight to hold against the new obscured position, she was thrown back to the right as the raft reassumed its old direction. The elf looked up in horror but was not able to spare the time to examine what had happened as now the violent storm surrounded them on all sides.

Stepha rocked back, forcing the oars down to bite into the water, and Krirtie slammed the rudder arm starboard trying to force the boat far enough to pass by the huge, jagged rock face protruding through the white foam in their path. The boat slowly fought against the raging current. Beads of sweat rolled down both their faces but only remained moments until a splash of water washed them away, only to be quickly replaced, starting the cycle over again.

Then, as they looked ahead, at nearly the same time they both saw what was in their path. Their faces remained pale, completely devoid of color, as they realized the raft was not going to turn fast enough to miss the large, jagged boulder breaking the water's surface directly in their line. Krirtie fought as hard as she could, but with every foot they gained, one large rapid would shove them violently back into the original direction. Scratches echoed with the first contact, then a loud crack followed closely by a smash, as the raft was turned broadside against its unforgiving edge. The small craft lunged sideways, becoming perpendicular to the now-incredible pace of the water. Stepha dug her oars in once again, but this time nature won out and the handle of one oar snapped and sliced back toward Krirtie, nearly sending the woman into the water. The elf fell back, but simultaneously the boat struck a second rock, which worked in their favor to straighten their course and throw Stepha back to her seat. She removed her remaining oar and used it as a paddle, switching sides and thrusting it vertically into the water to aid Krirtie in control.

The raft surged forward, but now their ability to guide it was even more hampered. Their speed, however, still puzzled the elf. They remained at the same constant rate. Furthermore, she wondered what had brought the raft back to be flat on the water when everything in nature said they should have capsized. She had not been looking at Krirtie, but nothing the human could have done would have brought the boat back as it had. Stepha's revelry was ended abruptly when a jolt of unimaginable force brought their small boat to a momentary halt in the fast rapids. The elf lay facedown in a pool of water along the baseboards of the hull. Her arms were firmly pressed back, protecting her head from the huge rock protruding through the bottom. Cold river water began flowing over Stepha's hands, and at the rate it was seeping in, the elf knew their boat would stay afloat only minutes longer.

She pushed herself to her knees, hollering to Krirtie that they needed to make a swim for it. When she did not respond, Stepha swung around to see a pool of red water filling the back half of the raft with Krirtie's head submerged in it.

Stepha leaped up and then collapsed again. Her eyes rolled back into her head, and she became disoriented and lost. She shifted her weight completely off her legs, enabling her to regain some conscious control of her thought process. It was at that moment she realized both her legs were broken. The pain previously unnoticed now was unleashed through her body. She looked down to where she had fallen to see the propped-up oar she had landed across. Blood now became visible in her half of the raft as well, and the shock nearly made her fall unconscious again. She struggled to keep her mind clear, knowing that to give in now would be both their undoing. She adjusted her position, and once again pain shot like flesh being torn from the bone. She leaned over the seat while further cracking and breaking wood splintered from the damaged hull. She could tell that the boat was being pushed free from its temporary resting spot.

She reached over and pulled Krirtie toward her, seeing a large gash across the woman's forehead. Yet the blood flowing from it had already ceased. Her eyes remained closed, but her breathing was strong so the elf knew she was well, at least for the moment. Suddenly the boat rocked, and once again it became the play toy for a vicious, unrelenting force of nature. The lunge threw Stepha back against the side, but this time the expected pain from her injuries was absent. However, the shock of this reality was nothing compared to what she felt when she looked to see how the water had changed and witnessed the completely sealed and undamaged surface of the raft.

Then, mumblings of Krirtie's voice broke the air, and Stepha turned to greet the stunned, clean face of the girl whose only sign of injury was a slight scar, which seemed to be fading as she watched. Krirtie immediately came to her senses and was back working the rudder, hollering questions at the bewildered elf pertaining to what had happened. Stepha, having no answers, only stared first back at Krirtie then to the boat. Not only had the hole the rock had ripped through the hull magically vanished, but also the oar which had snapped earlier now rested in its notch, ready to be used in guidance.

Stepha grabbed the handles of both oars and better situated herself to attempt to maneuver the raft toward the shore. Tears began to flow, causing Krirtie to grow instantly concerned for Stepha, not just their situation.

"Stepha, what is it?"

The elf wiped her eyes, the stress clearly showing on her face. She whispered, "My legs are no longer broken."

"What, Stepha?" hollered Krirtie back. "What is broken?"

Stepha turned and dropped her arms down, causing both oars to fall free, splashing off the water's surface. Turning to face the concentrating stare of Krirtie, she hollered, "Let it go! This boat could no longer crash than you could fly. If we get in trouble, I believe my wings have enough strength left in them to lift us out of here."

She spoke firmly, but her voice still carried a clear note of exhaustion. Krirtie looked questionably toward the elf but refused to release the rudder. The raft continued down the river, both oars dangling uselessly to the sides and Stepha simply holding on with both hands, using her feet and legs to secure her position should they greet another rock as before.

Suddenly Krirtie screamed, causing the elf to rip her head back toward the woman as a large jolt from the rear struck their little raft. Stepha saw a large chunk of the wooden rudder being tossed in their wake while Krirtie sat huddled to the side, the broken handle still in her hand. "Now we are lost for sure!" she cried, throwing the rudder handle to the floor of the boat. "We have no way to steer."

The elf motioned with her eyes. "We were never steering before. This raft has a strong will to survive. It is not our doing that we are afloat right now. Some other force guides us."

Krirtie followed Stepha's gaze to see a sight which nearly knocked her from the boat. The previously shattered rudder now appeared brand new as it turned back and forth below the water.

Krirtie's eyes turned back in disbelief. She stared toward the elf and then back toward the rudder. She noticed the sharp, newly carved handle. It appeared as if it had been cut from its birth tree only moments earlier. The water from the river gave the look of sap seeping from its veins. Krirtie flashed her eyes back to where the original broken rudder handle had been tossed. She reached down a grabbed the handle to inspect it more closely. As she lifted the wooden post into the air, it slowly began to fade and become transparent. Within a moment, it had disappeared altogether.

Krirtie's jaw dropped completely. She wanted to speak but all she could utter was, "But how?"

"*How* is not important," replied Stepha. "What is important is to hold on for our lives. As sure as what is now only a faint scar on your head but moments ago spilled all the blood at your feet, it simply appears that we cannot be hurt while we remain inside. I also believe this raft can't be damaged."

Krirtie glanced down and was shocked by the sight of the large amounts of red color mixed with the water at her feet, but even while she looked, it seemed to be lessening in depth, now even showing dryness in several places. Her hand went to her forehead, and although she felt she had been seriously wounded recently, to her touch and sensations in her mind there was no sign of it. She stared blankly at the elf in front of her. "When this is all over, I wish to have a word with Enroht-Wah, or Lauren, or whatever her name really was."

Following that, the girls remained silent, concentrating solely on holding on for their lives while the raft they were in faced bombardment after bombardment of a ruthless and angered river. Several times both girls thought they were about to capsize only to find themselves flopping back down correctly. Twice they struck large rocks, once simply giving the boat a mighty jolt but the second ripped a gaping hole through the bow. Water seeped into the craft, and both Stepha and Krirtie were helpless to stop the roaring water. However, as they could feel the boat begin to waver under the torrid waves, it again began to right the wrong. The torn planks along the base of the raft suddenly began to regenerate. The water slowly vanished, and in only moments, it appeared undamaged.

Stepha looked on in disbelief but thankful just the same. There was no way of knowing how far they had traveled since entering the rapids, but she hoped there would be a break soon. Essentially, having the added pressure of navigating the river lifted. It still was incredible work just to stay inside the raft. It was constantly knocked from every direction, and even holding on and securing a position was a chore. There was a brief channel of smooth current, which gave the elf a chance to survey what lay ahead of them. She pointed to Krirtie when the human woman saw the fork and nudged the rudder to try to guide the boat to stay on their planned course. That small nudge was all it took, and suddenly the raft dove right, taking the rougher water without question.

Krirtie hollered forward, trying to carry her voice over the fierce rumbling of the water. "I only touched it a bit. I can't believe it was enough to throw us this far. Should I try to take us back?"

The elf heard her words but could not risk turning her head to reply. Instead, she nodded and yelled. "No, I think it was only waiting for us to make a decision on our course."

She did not know if she had been heard or not, but at this point not much other than staying inside mattered. Even if Krirtie did try and take control of the rudder, Stepha doubted that it would have any effect. The exiting tributary of the River Ozaky meant they had already traveled over five miles. The boat may be able to make it the entire length of Draag in one shot, but Stepha was certain they would not. They were being desperately shaken about; and although none of their serious injuries seemed to be that serious after the boat's magic took effect, they still were being dealt a tremendous battering. Both girls constantly let out cries when their bodies struck the side or were thrown to the bottom, only to get back up, narrowly avoiding a wave crashing broadside upon the raft's bow.

Suddenly, all motion seemed to stop while a loud creaking and scraping sound spit through the thunder of the water. Both girls rocked forward, with Stepha even cracking her head along the side of the boat. They lifted their eyes to greet nothing but crystal blue sky. The river in front of them had vanished, and both knew exactly what this meant. Their boat was lodged on a rock at the top of a large water fall the depth of which could not be seen. Stepha's eyes drew a deep terror as she absorbed their situation. She lifted her hand to try to signal Krirtie to lean as far back as she could. They had to keep their weight to the rear, or they would fall free of their sensitive hold.

Krirtie understood the signal but she could do little to aid the effort. Water was continually pounding against her back as well as the back of the boat. Slowly, they began to rock back, only to get hit by a strong burst of water, which shifted the raft's resting spot freeing it from its hold to the bottom. With one soft slide, the raft rocked forward, and Krirtie and Stepha could only follow the bow downward.

The total length of the falls was only about ten to fifteen feet, but both girls knew without it being said that a normal raft would have exploded at the force of landing in the liquid storm. However, their boat landed tip downward, and while the rough water kicked and beat the boat at contact, with the aid of their respective forces, it immediately worked back level.

Krirtie crashed into the seat ahead of her, and Stepha was thrown overboard landing several feet ahead of the raft but directly in its path. She burst back up through the water's surface to see the boat being pushed directly toward her body, which was also being carried rapidly downstream with the current. She sucked in a deep breath and dove downward, kicking her feet up in the process and feeling the bottom of the hull strike them as it passed. Krirtie was quickly on her feet, yelling, but had no idea what had happened. The rapids had found a momentary lag following the large falls, and now the boat merely moved with the current smoothly, no longer being tossed by the fierce waves.

Krirtie was still yelling when Stepha answered her call from the far left. "I am over here. See if you can turn the boat and guide it to this shore. It looks as if these waters might be navigatable."

The girl sent an affirmative wave and quickly moved back to grab the rudder arm. At first touch, the raft made a perfect ninety-degree turn and began moving with increasing speed across the current, acting as if it too were ready for a rest. The raft and the elf reached the southern shore at nearly the same time, and after Krirtie had pulled it a safe distance from the edge, both girls collapsed on the ground.

"That was the most unbelievable journey of my life," said Krirtie, gasping for air between broken words.

"Indeed," replied the elf. "I hope the remainder of the river proves less difficult." She shifted her eyes toward the boat. "I do not wish to have to discover any other secrets hidden within this mysterious vessel."

"Nor do I," added the human woman, who had now fallen completely flat along the ground.

Stepha nodded, and then her eyes narrowed. She tilted her head slightly and then she leaped to her feet and drew her bow, placing an arrow in the same motion. Krirtie lifted her head in surprise and whispered at a level that should not be considered a whisper, "What is it?"

As Krirtie moved her hand to the hilt of her sword, the elf continued to focus on her surroundings. In a slightly distressed voice, Stepha said, "There is something wrong. It is well past noon, but I hear no animals or birds. Even at this hour there should be some activity about." She lifted her face to the air. "There, do you smell it? A fire. The scent comes from farther downstream."

"I can't tell," shrugged Krirtie. "Is it from a camp, or do you mean a large fire in the trees?"

The elf smiled. "No, it's not quite that big. Probably a camp."

"Then maybe we have found what we…"

"Do not get your hopes up, Krirtie," interrupted Stepha as she shook her head, giving the impression that she had just identified something about the mysterious scent. "We should investigate, but there is a much higher percentage of dark brothers in these woods. Only a dwarf would start a fire such as this. It burns with a sour odor that is near deadly to many small creatures. I doubt even a human would set fire to a knot-lack tree." She paused as she replaced her bow and then noticed Krirtie's expression and felt a slight guilt grow within her. "I am sorry. I did not mean to…"

Krirtie laughed. "Don't worry about it. Most humans probably would not know, but I don't aim to be one of those for too much longer." She motioned and added, "You lead the way, and while you are at it, why don't you show me what those trees look like?"

Stepha led them toward the source of the fire's scent, stopping momentarily now and again to investigate various sounds she had heard and then continuing ahead. As they drew closer, even Krirtie could sense the harsh odor from the burning wood, and she too began to feel uncomfortable at the unnatural lack of noise in the forest. After nearly half a mile on foot, Stepha rose a hand, and both she and Krirtie peered into a small clearing, which opened onto the face of the river.

"Do you see anyone?" asked the human as she pushed a branch from in front of her face.

"No, but someone had to start that fire, although it does appear to have been burning for some time as it has nearly burned its life away."

"What do you think we should do?" she asked, already stepping through the brush.

Stepha answered, "I'll cover you."

Krirtie hesitantly moved forward, following closely behind the point of her sword. She walked past the glowing fire and scouted through the entire glade, ending near the water's edge. Picking up a piece of torn cloth, she yelled toward the elf.

The elf released her breath and lowered her bow, giving her worn arms a brief break before bounding through the brush. When she arrived at the water, her expression turned to displeasure and she whispered, "Keep your voice down. Whoever's camp this is could be returning, especially if they are within earshot of your hollers."

Krirtie ignored the comment other than showing a distinct frown before continuing in a normal tone. "This material is from the lining of Jermys's armor, and all these prints are dwarven. If what I think is true, nobody will be returning any time soon. Jermys and Fehr have been taken prisoner by the DDs and are either already dead or have been taken somewhere to meet that fate.

The elf displayed great disapproval for the presumption of death but made no comment on the subject. Instead, she inspected the area more closely, and upon finding a trail leading away, she motioned Krirtie over. "Whoever left followed this trail. See here, they tried to cover their tracks near the clearing, and even did a poor job of that. However, if you look a few feet ahead, you can see them plain as day. A blind minok could pick up and follow this band."

"Stepha, look here." Krirtie pointed to the ground near the side of the trail. "That looks like a rat's print, but it can't be Fehr's, it's too big."

The elf looked. "Well, it definitely is a rat's print. No other creature in all of Troyf that I know of has a paw with only four claws. Whether it's Fehr's or not, you would know better than I."

"Can you tell how old they are?"

"A matter of hours, maybe as many as ten, but more than likely about five, if you take into account how the fire has burned down. I suspect they were camped here at night, then sometime this morning they were greeted with company. Fehr might have found a friend or something, and that is who trails them now."

Krirtie thought a moment then replied, "I doubt it. No rat would survive long out here. They do better when they have humans nearby to torment. There must be something else at work here." She paused then added, "Should we follow?"

Stepha was smiling after the first 'human' comment, but now her face grew stoic, and a deep, serious stare seduced her. "First, we will give the birds a break and put that fire completely out. Then, we will follow."

They were making pretty good time along the trail, cutting through the thicket of trees. They seemed somewhat rejuvenated by the knowledge that they now had a definite lead on finding Jermys, although they both carried a certain unsteadiness as to his current situation. However, coupled with the fact that they no longer had to reenter the river, their pace was swift and their faith was high.

Following the dwarves' trail was simply a matter of moving as fast as they could, and every once in a while glancing down to make certain the prints were still there. Both girls had drawn their weapons, and although Krirtie acted better in sword fighting confrontations, Stepha led the way as she was better able to interpret the forest and recognize trouble before it occurred.

The elf had to duck to the side when her sudden stop caught Krirtie by surprise and her momentum carried her sword tip just beyond Stepha's neck. Quickly recovering, Krirtie began to ask what the elf had seen but stopped when she saw Stepha's expression and raised hand.

The Reunion

Fehr crouched in the brush, remaining completely still while the commotion behind him gradually grew louder. His idea that he would be safe while trailing the dark dwarf's party had quickly vanished, and now he sat waiting to see who was following him. A look of anguish crossed his face when he glanced toward the ground to see his footprints clearly showing where he stopped and turned into the brush.

I can't believe I was so stupid to leave a trail that even Krirtie would be bright enough to follow, the rat thought to himself. He knew anyone would be able to find him regardless of whether they were looking or not. After the recent morning's activities and the fact that everyone in this area saw the large rat as breakfast, Fehr knew his options were limited. He cursed under his breath, as he could now see the outline of two figures breaking through the brush down the trail moving at a fairly intense pace.

He toyed with the idea of fleeing but figured he would do better to wait. It could be that whoever it was could only be trailing the dwarven party or, even more likely, simply be following this path back to their camp. If he ran now, he could only be asking to be followed himself, as they would have no idea what actually made the noise. Furthermore, he would have the same chances of a successful escape whether he fled now, or if he waited to be discovered.

Fehr sat motionless while the voices of those who approached were now fairly loud, but he still could not see them clearly due to the depth and thickness of the brush in which he was hiding. As they approached, he could tell the two were arguing, and by the tones of their voices, he also knew of what race they were. The two black bodies reached where the rat was hiding and continued at a pace just shy of a run, without even taking a second notice toward Fehr's tracks, only concerned with blaming the other on why they had been left behind.

Judging from their voices and the fact that both carried bows but were short on several arrows, Fehr assumed these were the two he had met earlier that had been searching for some breakfast. He gathered that their leader, the one called Eb-Brown, either had forgotten about them or wished them dead. Whichever mattered not to Fehr, for all they were to him was a better trail to follow. Not only were they totally unconcerned with their prints, but their chatter could be heard clearly through the thick brush. He only hoped they would catch the main party soon, because if Fehr was to attempt a rescue, he knew it had to be before they reached the main camp, and he knew that had to be soon. However, he still had no idea what he was going to do.

He followed at a heartbeat's distance behind the two, and for the first time in his life, he saw firsthand evidence that the dark dwarves and the mining dwarves were more similar than any would ever had admitted. If the two had been able to keep a steady pace through the trees, Fehr was certain they could have caught the group ahead. However, their constant bickering and fighting frequently delayed them, often causing them to stop and duke it out, once even bringing them to draw weapons. One had drawn a sword and the other a bow. Fehr imagined that if they had both squared off with battle axes, it would have looked identical to Bretten and Jermys the first time he ever saw them in the tunnel leading under the river between Antaag and Feldschlosschen. However, he thought the dark dwarves' disputes could end up being battles to the death, whereas Jermys and Bretten could not have hurt each other regardless of what the argument was about. He took a moment and thought about Bretten and the ordeal at Anbari's Dominion and the staff. He began to wonder if everything was really worth it, and then, hearing another of the disputes end with some harmless shoving, continued behind the dark brothers.

As fate would have it, after nearly a full day of following the two, just when the darkness of late evening began to engulf the forest, they squared off in a fight, which left one dead and the other bearing an arrow through the chest, lying in a bed created from his own blood. Fehr approached the small clearing that had served as their last battleground; and realizing the first dwarf he came to was already a rotting corpse, he moved toward the other. Blood seeped from this one's lips as his hands fought desperately to remove the blood-greased shaft from deep within his beaten body. He issued a deadening groan when Fehr leaped onto his belly just below where the arrow had struck.

The rat showed no remorse for the pain and death he was seeing, nor did he attempt to make the dwarf's suffering any less. If anything, he went out of his way to make certain the pain was as intense as it could be. He found a spot on the dark dwarf's chest above the arrow and pressed his hind claws deep into the DD's chin, tearing at the flesh and hair making up his beard while leaning back against the shaft of the arrow. The dwarf winced in pain, but due to the loss of blood he had already endured, he was helpless to do anything.

Fehr used his laugh to taunt the near-dead figure before saying in perfect dwarven, "I followed you the entire day to find your camp and free my friend, and all you two imbeciles could do is argue the whole time. Well, I suggest that if you wish me to remove this arrow, you will point me in the direction of the camp I speak of, you disgusting river slug." He was using his deepest and most strong voice and drawing on his library of dwarven languages and curses; and although most of what he said was not really true and he knew finding the trail the dark dwarf party had left would be as easy as stealing food from Jermys's locked chest in Feldschlosschen, he was having a good time tormenting this dark dwarf upon his death.

The dwarf spit blood as he replied. "You'll get no such help from me, rodent scum. Go back to your pathetic rock you live under and see if you can torment a snail with your taunts."

Fehr did not reply and, shifting his weight back, pushed the arrow at a new angle, tearing it through the dwarf's insides. He cried in pain, and sheets of blood seeped from the wound and his mouth. Fehr released his weight and his only comment began, "I don't think that was the answer that I was…"

He broke off when the dwarf heaved his body in one last spastic contraction and then fell limp. Fehr stared at him in surprise and then dove to the side, his senses telling him that something was wrong. Just as he leaped from his body, another arrow struck the dwarf exactly where Fehr had been sitting. Looking across the body, he saw the second arrow shaft which had killed the dwarf but had probably been meant for him. Fehr's attention turned to witness three dark dwarves breaking through the far brush, one preparing to release a third arrow at the rat. Fehr hesitated not a moment longer, and as the shot planted itself in the ground behind him, he issued a slight whimper and disappeared into the trees.

He ran hard through the thickest of paths he could find for several hundred yards before turning around and checking for pursuit. Seeing none, he began to try to calm himself and curled up into a small ball to cover the pain of his severed tail. The arrow had pinned his tail to the ground, and even though a bandicoot's tail will separate from its body and almost immediately grow back, that does not stop the intense pain. Fehr cursed a bit under his breath, feeling sorry for the hardships he had faced but gradually brightening when he realized what a fine story this would make. After an unknown length of time, which allowed the pain to subside, the rat leaped to his feet and began backtracking through the underbrush. It was now deep black in the forest, the tree cover even blocking the light reflecting from both moons. However, since a bandicoot did most of its work during the night, the darkness was not a hindrance for Fehr. Within minutes he was back to the edge of the small glade.

He looked across, gathering any light he could from the now-exposed moons but still not seeing with any clarity. He could make out the outlines of the two dead figures, and scanning the rest of the area, he saw no movement or appearance of remaining guards. Knowing dark dwarves, he knew they probably left the corpses to rot and would only steer clear of the area for several days until the bodies were swallowed by the forest. Very rarely did the lighthearted rat feel any fear, and this instance was no exception. With a slight sigh, he bounded forward, landing well inside the boundary of the clearing only feet from the first dwarf. Learning his lesson from earlier, he decided not to remain in the open area for too long; and after rummaging through the dead figure's belongings, only finding a small dagger, which he stuffed in his pouch, the rat departed, taking a quick look for the arrow that had severed his tail but knowing that it and his missing appendage were now trophies on some dwarven wall. He cursed again, and after inspecting the outer ring of the glade, he disappeared down the most recently traveled trail.

It was only about a half hour's walk until he came onto an outbreak of trees overlooking a huge opening spotted with small glows from several campfires. All in all the area looked to be roughly 400 square meters, but he was only judging this by the skeleton created by the positioning of the fires. It was too dark to determine specifics. However, he was aware that the path he currently stood on was probably a main access point to the camp and would be heavily used by leaving and returning scouting parties; possibly even more so with the capture of Jermys sure to send a stir through the entire camp. Knowing this, Fehr had a choice. He could either sneak into the camp tonight and see what he could find out, or wait until morning and survey the conditions from a safe distance, waiting to see what the dark dwarves had planned. His natural-born instinct was telling him not to worry and simply plow forward, locate the dwarf, free him, and escape. However, his common sense told him it would be better to wait. If the dark dwarves had wanted Jermys dead, he would be as such already. Something was amiss here, and Fehr had already had one confrontation that left him without a tail.

With one more glance downward across the camp, he sighed and started to leave to find a comfortable and safe haven to rest for the night. As he left, however, an unseen hand reached down and snagged his tuft of hair between his ears, placing a dagger to his throat. The only thing heard was the rat's deafening dwarven curses.

Stepha knelt down and began running her fingers over the ground, motioning with her other hand at Krirtie signaling her to remain quiet. She heeded the warning and quickly knelt beside the elf who leaned near her as she moved. "Someone has joined the trail here after the rat passed. It looks to be two dwarves moving at a quick pace." Her voice was only a whisper but it still carried great concern in its tone.

Krirtie squinted at the new prints. "I would never have noticed them. Is there any way to tell about how soon after they passed?"

The elf smiled. "Not with any accuracy. However, I would say they will probably overtake the rat by nightfall at the latest if their pace was to remain at this rate. By the length between their steps they seem to be trying to catch up to someone, or something." She paused, then added, "We will only catch them if they stop." She said no more, but both women understood the danger that may lie ahead for their companions.

Krirtie broke the silence in the strongest, upbeat voice she could muster. "Then we should be on our way."

"Yes," replied Stepha, "but also take note that I do not believe we should be in any hurry. If they walked throughout the day beginning in the early morning, as it appears they did, then we will not have a chance of catching them by sundown. If their final destination is not a full day's walk, then we, starting as far behind as we did, still will probably only reach it after dark. Either way, we will be able to learn nothing until morning. I think we would be better served to save our strength for when we need it. If it is Jermys and Fehr ahead, then any escape will be followed by a sprint back toward our raft. I think the better rested our arms and legs are, the better off we will be."

"I can't argue with that," said Krirtie as she stood and continued, now at a much more leisurely pace, although it was still much greater than a casual walk. "Who do you think those two dwarves following them are?"

Stepha shrugged. "I was just thinking the same thing. All I can say is that I have no idea."

"That isn't very reassuring."

The elf smiled slightly at her tone. "I was wondering if they could have been planted to watch for any pursuit, but I cannot imagine any dark dwarf leader being that adept to prepare that carefully…unless there is another force at work here."

Krirtie's eyes grew dark and she seemed almost scared to say the word. "Dragons?"

Stepha did not answer at first as she lifted her eyes to the sky. Finally she replied, "I do not feel as confident with my previous thoughts as I did when I first spoke them. Perhaps we should keep as quick a pace as possible."

That was all the enticement Krirtie needed to belt ahead at a gallop. Stepha was impressed with the woman because despite being barbarian-like with the way she wielded her sword, she had a more elven-like quality about her when she ran, not to mention being with child. She made very little noise as she ducked below the branches and leaped fallen logs or rocks; and although Stepha could do the same, even a slight bit quieter, there was no reason to fear alerting anyone nearby with their movement. The elf would have preferred to remain in the lead, but Krirtie had a certain passion about her now that would work in their favor should any confrontations commence. Stepha kept her eye on the trail but she was confident the woman ahead of her would not have a problem tracking this bunch. It almost seemed like they wanted to be followed. This idea began to haunt Stepha's mind, falling into one of the old human proverbs Schram used to spit at her: *If something seems too easy, it usually is.* The elf pushed the feelings out of her head but kept all her senses pierced at their surroundings. She wanted to be ready for even the slightest sound or movement that was out of order. They could not afford to be captured as well, even if it meant leaving their friends on their own.

They had moved at a steady pace throughout the day and although Stepha had wanted to make camp several times, Krirtie insisted on pushing ahead. It was now well into the night, and as they approached a small clearing, it was Stepha's elven sight that caused her to grab Krirtie's shoulder and pull her to the ground.

"What is it?"

The elf pointed. "Two dead dwarves. Probably the two we were tracking. Let's remain here a moment. I am not sure everything is as it should be."

The two sat motionless for nearly half an hour, waiting for anything in the night to make a sound. There was a long, ominous silence. It even seemed unnaturally quiet to the elf. They waited for what seemed like the entire night before Stepha slowly motioned to her companion. "Come, let's go." Taking very small and careful steps, they moved into the glade.

They inspected the two corpses carefully, taking notice that the dwarves had died in combat against each other. However, the extra arrows in one of them and the fact that his face was torn and covered in dried, dwarven blood worried Stepha. She could not determine exactly what had happened, but as an elf, she had certain concerns for those passed, which must always be fulfilled given proper time. Reaching into her armor, she removed a small pouch and sprinkled some dust from within it over the motionless bodies. A cold chill streaked down the girl's spine and vanished as quickly as it had been felt.

Krirtie leaned toward the elf. "Don't those passed usually vanish with the chill?"

The elf looked solemn. "Some are taken by the princess and vanish, as you have seen before, while others remain to slowly become part of the forest they lived their lives within. Both are admirable closings for a true life. However, some may be sentenced to be received only by the powers of darkness. This is the case for these souls. It is truly a sad thing to witness, a sad thing for friend or enemy. No creature should ever face such an ending." She paused then added sadly, "We should be going."

Krirtie followed the elf's lead, and after a brief inspection of their choices of trails, Stepha motioned and the two left following a path west. As they were leaving the glade, Krirtie took one more glance back across the opening and even in the dead of night, she could see dark shadows engulfing the bodies where they lay. She squeezed her eyes and turned away, hurrying to fall in behind the elf. Stepha did not look back, yet a tear still slid down the side of her face.

They walked for some time without speaking and remained consumed with their own thoughts. The silence they were experiencing as they walked became quite unnerving for the human. She found herself wanting to hum or whistle but knowing that to do so could mean their death or capture. She broke the monotonous silence by hesitantly asking, "What does the dust you and Schram carry do?"

As if expecting the question, Stepha replied, "It prepares and protects." She paused. "For those who have been forbidden passage, it allows it. It is pure life in death."

The words seemed alien to the human. It was apparent that this was something deep and very elven. The two continued again in silence, but now with a mood of intense emotion about them. They had no guess as to what they would greet next, but without speaking, they both knew they hoped that it did not come too soon.

They followed the trail for a short distance, making no sound with their feet or in speech. Krirtie had begun to relax and calm herself. She had tried to push the emotions she was feeling aside and concentrate on their progress forward. It did not take long for all the previous feelings to return when Stepha raised her hand

and pointed. It was difficult for her to see but when she stared hard enough, the outline could be made out under the moon's light.

Krirtie reached silently down to pull a small dagger from inside her armor, and after handing her sword to Stepha, she leaped forward and grabbed the creature, placing the blade flush against its neck.

Vicious taunts and hollers echoed through the trees, but the language was foreign to the girl. However, the voice was not. She swung the rat around to face her and in a questioning and whispered voice said, "Fehr?"

The rat's grimacing smirk turned into an inverted rainbow, and he began to shout his best friend's name, "KRI—"

The girl pressed her hand over Fehr's mouth to muffle his calls while Stepha quickly moved forward. "Ssshhh! Do you want to get us all captured?"

"Same old Stepha," he chattered happily. "Boy, am I glad to see you two. I have got some story to tell you. First, Jermys has been—"

"Captured," interrupted Stepha. "We know some of your story, and we are anxious to hear the rest, in due time. However, we must first find some cover for the night." She looked across the dwarven camp. "By the look and the spread of those fires, we will have our hands full tomorrow. This looks to be closer to a city than a camp, but why so secretive and well-hidden?"

Krirtie loosened her grip on the rat and was about to answer but then thought better of it. In a tone devoid of pleasure, she said, "Well, whatever story you do tell, please have it start by explaining how the diet I instructed you to follow allowed you to triple in size."

Fehr blushed under his fur but was not allowed to speak, as the elf had darted into the trees and both he and Krirtie had to hurry behind. After a short while, they fell into a tiny break in the trees and here the elf motioned that they would make camp. When Krirtie and Fehr arrived, they were already involved in an argument, and although they were keeping their voices low, Stepha was annoyed just the same.

"You can't tell me dwarven food made you this fat."

"Yes, it did. All they do is eat, drink ale, and smoke. They made me feel bad when I refused to join—"

"Yes," interrupted the elf. "I am sure you just hated having to eat and drink all the time. It goes against your total character."

Her sarcasm struck the rat, and Krirtie fought to hold back a smile, knowing that to further irritate him could only be asking for trouble. Grinning, she added, "Don't tell me you've taken up smoking as well?"

Fehr groaned a bit, leaning back and placing his front paws across his now-rolled-out belly. "Yes, and could I use a puff right now. Some of their tobac is simply amazing. Unfortunately, that damn dwarf has our only pouch."

Krirtie frowned. "I can't let you out of my sights for a minute. After this is all over, you will start eating with me, and while we're at it, no more smoking."

"Who do you think you are?" spat the rat, but he knew it was a battle he would not win this night.

She ignored the question and continued her orders. "And from now on, you will travel by your own resources. I will no longer be responsible for carrying you. Not that I could even do so for long now anyway."

They were glaring at each other when Stepha finished setting up her sleeping area. She stepped over. "Will you two stop this bickering?" Turning to Fehr, she added, "Now I want to know everything that has happened, but keep it short." She smiled deeply then added, "And speaking of short, make sure you include the part about your tail."

Krirtie chuckled, caught off guard by the unexpected shot toward the rat's newfound injury. Fehr's lips tightened into a white pucker, appearing to be a bomb about ready to explode. However, he quickly realized that he was just asked to be the center of attention and to tell a story, his two most favorite things. With his anger soothed, he dove into his tale.

He hurried through all the events leading to the dwarf's capture and his diligent tracking through the forests. However, it was still over an hour before he finished, and Krirtie had already nodded off. Stepha, on the other hand took everything in, and was left with more questions than she had to begin with.

Whatever had caused the dark dwarves to take a prisoner—something they never did unless it absolutely served their gain—probably was very important for both their causes. Whether Jermys's life was in immediate danger could not be determined, but she believed she must assume that it was, or he would not be held against his will. However, if they would truly be able to help the dwarf or not was another more difficult question. She knew they were in unfriendly forests and the longer they remained here, the greater chance they had of being captured. She made a mental note to herself that regardless of the other's objectives, tomorrow they would evaluate the situation as a whole. If she felt that to attempt to help Jermys would be too great of a risk, then they would head back to their raft and continue without him. The thought was not at all pleasing to her, but she knew it was the correct one; and although she knew Krirtie would at first protest, eventually she would see that as well. However, Fehr would be a problem. She glanced over at the sleeping rat nestled closely against his lost friend's curled arms. With a soft sigh, the elf shifted some branches to better cover her two companions in the night and then disappeared into the shadows of nearby trees to keep watch.

Jermys's groggy eyes peered around the sides of the tent, which was being used as his cell. In it he sat alone. The only other objects in the room were a small wooden table, on which sat a single candle to give light, with a serving of food and a large mug of ale to the side. The dwarf was in no mood for eating but he also was not one to act unintelligently, especially with the pounding he was currently experiencing in his head.

In what amounted to one swallow and gulp, the plate was clean and the mug empty. With a deep, bellowing belch, he leaned back and pulled out his pouch of tobac and pipe. The green haze depicting his special dwarven blend filled the small room, and gradually the tobac began to work its magic. His body relaxed, allowing every muscle to soften and fall limp against the ground. He noticed no pain in his head as his eyes gently fell closed.

There was no telling how long he had slept when a loud argument ensued outside his door. The dwarf looked up in time to see two dark brothers nose to nose in cursing yells, which ended in two violent swings and then one dwarf being removed by two others that approached. Jermys froze as the remaining figure's shadow moved toward the door. The slit slowly lifted and the dark dwarf pushed through to stand before the still-motionless dwarf.

"Awe, I am pleased to see that your stubbornness did not keep you from eating. The trip was long and I guessed you would be hungry."

Jermys was surprised and somewhat suspicious of the sincerity he heard in Eb-Brown's voice. "I may be stubborn, but so is an empty stomach."

"Yes," replied Brown. "I took the odds that you would eat. I heard your belly shouting the last hour of our trip. I will be pleased to inform them of the outcome."

Jermys raised his eyebrow, and his mood instantly lightened. "You were wagering on my appetite?"

The dark brother laughed. "Yes, but there were no odds on the drink. Everyone knew a Feldschlosschen dwarf could never pass on a mug of ale."

He shrugged. "Aye, the food alone might have been questionable, but with the ale by its side, I had no hesitations."

Now they both chuckled in an uncomfortable tone, and for Jermys, it was the first time he had ever exchanged pleasantries with a dark dwarf, if in fact that is what they were doing. He assumed it was the same situation in reverse. However, he was also aware that this visit was not brought on by the need to determine the outcome of their wagers, but a much deeper problem was at its source. As their smiles slowly faded and an ominous silence seduced the tent, Jermys knew he was about to find out exactly what the true problem was.

Brown paced the small room for a short time, creating a longer period of intense silence. It was a room full of nervousness and emotion. Jermys followed the dark dwarf's motion with his eyes, but looked away when Brown turned to speak. "I have told my leader what you said to me regarding my brother. He says you have no reason to lie about such a thing and therefore should be believed until we learn different." Jermys nodded understanding before the dwarf continued. "However, as for the Hatchet of Claude, my leader has many questions."

Jermys knew he was in no position to bargain, but as far as he was concerned, his life meant nothing if he was to lose the hatchet. "Twice you have referred to him as your leader. Does he not have a name? You may have plans for the hatchet, but let it be known that I will not leave here without it, regardless of the cost."

Brown appeared angered and stung, but he seemed to fight through his natural reactions, keeping a polite atmosphere. "You will learn all you wish to know in good time, but also know that you would do well to improve your attitude. My leader has agreed to meet with you personally, something only three dwarves in this camp have ever done. You will be blindfolded and led for some distance with many different dwarves leading you. Any attempt to escape, and you will be killed immediately. Any knowledge you gain once you meet my leader must be kept with you forever. Any inclination that you will reveal that may jeopardize what we are achieving here will also result in your immediate death. Do you understand and agree?"

Jermys was totally taken by surprise, and although he was not ready to trust those he had hated for so long, he believed that this may be the only way to locate the hatchet. Furthermore, even though Brown had not said anything relating to it, he believed that to disagree now would probably also result in his death seconds after his reply was issued.

Weighing these ideas, Jermys replied, "I agree, Brown, but remember my last words. I will not leave without the hatchet by my side." He paused and lifted himself from where he had been sitting. "Now, when do we leave?"

Shaking his head, the dark dwarf turned his expression into a slight smirk. He walked near Jermys and gave a motion that he was going to blindfold him. However, in one quick movement he removed his ax and, with the blunt end, clubbed the dwarf over the head. Jermys gave a grunt and then fell to the ground, unconscious. In a chuckling voice to himself, Brown said, "We leave right away."

"So you finally decided to wake up."

Jermys groggily grabbed his head and tried to sit up and focus on his surroundings. "What happened?" he asked toward the voice that had spoken. Then remembering he had been slugged, he turned with tightened lips toward the dark dwarf guilty of inflicting his pain. "Where are we, Brown?"

The dark dwarf grinned, causing his black cheeks to wrinkle all the way up to his bald head. "Sorry for having to hit you, but it was necessary. As for where we are, that is something you should hope you never discover."

Jermys only nodded, but his agitation was still apparent. He replied, "Can you at least tell me what hour it is?"

"A handful before first light," the dwarf replied. "Are you able to walk?"

"I suppose."

"Good. Put this on and grab hold of the rope, and remember, to let go of the rope will mean your instant death."

He handed a piece of cloth to Jermys, and reluctantly, the dwarf tied it around his face, covering his eyes. Brown handed him the rope, and feeling it pull tight, Jermys began walking behind. He knew he was being led through the forest, and frequently there were stops where he believed those leading him switched positions. Several times he heard soft chuckles to the sides and assumed that he was being paraded in front of some of the other dwarven guards. For all he knew, they simply had made additional wagers that he could actually be made to do all these things. However, for whatever reason, he felt Brown was being honest. He knew that the dark dwarf would never had gone through all these elaborate measures if he was not on the level. Something out of the ordinary was at work here. If not, Jermys knew he would already be dead.

They walked for some time. It was unclear to the dwarf what direction they were or had been heading, but he could tell that it was now well past dawn as light had begun breaking through the loose material of his blindfold. Two hands grabbed his shoulders and their journey seemed to be brought to an abrupt end. Jermys reached up to begin to uncover his eyes, and his hands were slapped away without comment. He heard the faint sounds of two dwarves talking in soft voices some distance ahead of him, but he could not understand or identify the words. The hands holding the dwarf in place were removed, and in their wake was the rustle of several leaving behind him. There was a brief silence before a second movement was detected approaching. Jermys felt a hand reach around his neck and the point of a dagger bite lightly into his scalp. With a snap, the blindfold was cut, and the dwarf squinted as the onrush of light attacked his eyes. Quickly he adjusted and opened up to see the bald face of Eb-Brown staring back at him. He looked briefly around and was quite taken by the scenery. Large trees shot hundreds of feet into the air on all sides except one, which opened into the brightest, most green field Jermys had ever seen. Two bongos were grazing at the far side of the glade, but his eyes were focused on a small black tent erected in a near corner.

Eb-Brown followed his gaze and said, "That is where my leader waits, but there is more I must tell you before you go. What you will learn here will make your immediate inclination to strike out against him. However, hear him out. In the end, if you deem him a traitor and you so desire, I think his honor will allow you to kill him. But, do not underestimate what he is trying to do. If I had been informed of your plans in time, I would have steered clear of your party, never capturing you in the first place. As it worked out, I am only glad I did not kill you during our confrontation. That would only work against what we fight for."

Brown stared for a moment deeply into Jermys's eyes. Then after issuing a motion forward, added, "Remember all that I have said."

The dwarf was now completely confused about the entire situation, but his confusion only grew when he started to walk toward the tent. Eb-Brown hollered one more comment. "We have been searching for your companion, the rat, and he has been spotted several times near our camp. However, he repeatedly eludes us. If we find him, we will bring him along."

Now Jermys was totally at a loss. Why would dark dwarves ever consider doing anything with a bandicoot other than eat it? Furthermore, how did they know of Fehr's existence? The entire time Jermys had assumed that the rat had followed him and now probably was randomly exploring through the camp looking for him. However, now he was several hours' walk away, and the only help he thought he could count on was from those he had called enemies his entire life.

He approached the tent and, with a quick inspection, he could see that it had only been erected within the last hour or so. The flap making the doorway was closed, and as Jermys lifted it, he could see that there was no light within it. Tension the likes of which he had never felt in his life engulfed his body. Part of him said turn and run, find Fehr, and continue on their mission, until a voice from inside, which seemed to be somewhat disguised but still familiar, asked him to enter. When he did so, all light from outside vanished. His eyes could see nothing in the blackness. He could hear the breathing of another to the left, but with the loss of light, he could not even make out his outline.

There was a strike of flint, and suddenly a large flame ignited on a candle, and the room was filled with light. The tent was empty except for a table and two chairs. One of the chairs was empty while in the other sat a figure Jermys could not believe he was looking at. In a soft voice, he said, "King Kapmann."

"I do not see anything," said Stepha as she looked over the camp. "Do either of you?"

"I don't," replied Fehr, but that does not mean anything. We need to get a closer look."

Stepha turned. "Out of the question. Unless we can locate him for sure, we will not even consider any advancement. It is too dangerous and our mission too important."

"Fehr, look," issued Krirtie, ignoring the elf's comments and pointing to a spot at the base of one of the tents.

"Yeah, I see it. Disgusting sight it is as well." He paused and then glanced up to catch the girl's considering grin. "Surely you don't expect me to. No! Absolutely out of the question! No possible way!"

"What?" asked Stepha. "Another bandicoot?"

Fehr swung with hatred painted clearly on his face. "I should kill you now, elf, for even suggesting such a thing. A cotton sig is the lowest form of life there is, not even close to the superior minds of the bandicoots."

She was surprised by the outburst but when Krirtie giggled a little, the elf quickly relaxed. She sent a questioning glance toward the girl who shifted her gaze back toward the camp and then answered Stepha's unspoken question. "You know bandicoots. Most of them have a very choppy language at best. However, cotton sigs have never even developed that. By all appearances and actions, they are bandicoots"—Fehr grumbled and turned away—"but to my knowledge, they cannot communicate even among themselves."

"Is this true, Fehr?" asked the elf.

"No. Their fur is rougher. They are not as large or as fast and by far not as intelligent. Also, if a bandicoot wants to know anything, a cotton sig's menial mind is no match. I could get anything I wanted to know from that scoundrel." Suddenly his eyes fell as he knew he had been tricked.

Krirtie smiled proudly but Stepha drew a frown. "I do not like this a bit."

"It is our only choice, and not a bad one," said Krirtie. "Fehr could get through that camp with his eyes closed."

"Yes, but to lower myself to seek aid from a sig—I just don't know."

Stepha peered down to the camp. "It is your choice, of course, Fehr, but you need to know the risks involved. If you should be captured, we cannot come after you. Furthermore, if you do not return by midday, then we will head back to the river and our raft without you. Finally, if you do not wish to go, then we will all leave now. That is how it must be."

The rat frowned. "I will go, and I understand the situation. However, if I discover that it is possible to help Jermys, then we, or at least I, will do so, regardless of the costs. That is what you should know."

With that, he nodded to Krirtie and then bounded through the trees. The girl looked over to Stepha. "Would you really leave them both here?"

Stepha said nothing.

They sat in silence for the next few minutes, both peering through the trees surrounding the dark dwarf camp looking for any sign of movement. Krirtie pointed to a clump of trees about fifty feet from where the cotton sig still was gnawing at the meshing of a tent. Stepha followed her hand and then sighed. "Amazing, how could he get there so quickly and how could you locate him?"

"You can learn about how the little guys act if you are around them enough. They are really not that much different from other forest creatures, although Fehr is definitely unique. Most can communicate on some scale, but the different languages he knows is really extraordinary. I think there is some mystery about Fehr we don't yet know, and possibly never will."

Stepha smiled. "I have thought that same thing many times." She paused, and then as she thought about their situation, a worried look grew across her face. "Tell me, Krirtie, are cotton sigs as widely hunted by dark dwarves as bandicoots?"

"I really wouldn't know, but I assume so. I know very little about any race outside humans, but since I understand that they like bandicoots because of the taste, I imagine that sigs can't be that different. Why do you ask?"

Stepha pointed. "Look down at the sig. Do you see anything out of the ordinary?"

"Well, nothing too extreme. He is trying to get into that tent for something, but that would be normal for the rodent."

"Why then, when guards pass, do none of them kill the rat? I am sure they must see or at least hear him gnawing."

Krirtie thought a moment then her face began to grow much more solemn. "You don't suppose it is some sort of trap, do you?"

She shrugged. "We do know that they are aware of Fehr's presence. After all, they did take shots at him back in the field. Also, we cannot see well enough from here to determine if that cotton sig is free or if it could be tied up to something in the tent. If the latter is the case, Fehr may be in over his head.

"I never even thought," exclaimed the girl as she turned back to the camp. "Cotton sigs would no longer make a home here than a bandicoot would. We have to warn Fehr."

"It is too late," said the elf, pointing. "Look!"

Fehr slowly crept forward, keeping to the shadows as best he could. He saw the rodent chewing away now less than ten feet in front of him. He stopped a moment when he noticed the odd chain tied around its neck. The thought had never occurred to him before but now he knew. This sig had been captured and was being saved to be eaten later. Now Fehr was especially glad he had come. He knew he could save the rat from certain death and definitely get any information he needed from him in return.

He inched his way out and made an almost silent chirp to draw the cotton sig's attention. Fehr was nearly twice this animal's size, and when the sig looked over, surprise and fear showed in his eyes. Fehr mumbled a few words but when there was no response, it became clear that this rodent was even a lower intelligence than Fehr was accustomed to. He decided he would free him first and then attempt to dig for information.

He sat next to the rat and examined the lock holding the chain about his neck. With a quick sigh, he dug into his pouch and removed a small bent pin. "Don't worry, it should only be a moment," he said, though he was not sure if the sig could even understand. He started to toy with the lock, and the second before it opened, two black arms tore through the side of the tent and snagged the rat, quickly drawing him inside.

Stepha and Krirtie both bowed their heads as they watched, knowing that they were helpless to act. Without a word, Stepha rose and threw her pack over her shoulder.

Krirtie turned to her. "We can't just leave them. Fehr will be killed."

Again the elf could do nothing but lower her eyes. Both knew Fehr was probably already dead, and if not, would be soon. Any attempted rescue would only get them captured as well. She leaned down, offering her hand to help the girl to her feet. Krirtie refused it, jumping up on her own and moving in the direction of the path leading toward the camp. Stepha grabbed her shoulder and in a stern voice said, "I will not let you go."

She swung to face her. "I will not hesitate to take arms against you now, Stepha. I can move through the trees as well as Fehr, and that tent backs against the forest. In less than a minute I can be in, get Fehr, and be gone."

"And can you outrun the hundreds of dwarves who will follow?" Her voice softened. "I need you, Krirtie. Without your help, there is no way I can hope to save Maldor. Don't let one loss make us lose another. Fehr knew the risks when he went down there. I should not have let him go, but if Jermys lives, he must save Fehr now. Our path must lead elsewhere."

Krirtie broke free from the elf's hold, but she did not continue toward the path. Tears began to fill her eyes and she whispered, "Good luck, you no-good rat. I'll miss you."

⚬⚭⚬

Dwarven curses filled the tent while large black fingers tried to cover the rat's mouth. "Would you be quiet, you no-good rat. I'll kill you now if you don't shut your jabbering trap!"

Fehr bit at anything he could reach, making contact with either a finger or arm; he could not be sure. The dwarf screeched in pain and slapped the rat across the face. "Hit me again, you fat-bellied gar sucker, and I'll bite another piece of your anatomy off."

A deep, bellowing laugh echoed from the dwarf. "A rat that speaks dwarven and carries a temper as well. I never thought I would see the day."

Fehr was caught off guard by the response but was liking the dark dwarf's good humor and quickly forgot any differences he might be feeling. "Well, seeing as I am nothing more than breakfast around here, do you mind if I smoke?"

Again the dwarf laughed. "As you wish," he replied, loosening his grip as he felt the rat begin to calm.

Fehr smiled. "Then, might I borrow a pipe and tobac? Preferably some that burns with a faint green color."

The dark brother shook his head and smiled. "Only a rat would ask for permission to smoke from those who planned on eating him and then not even have any of his own tobac. Then, not only does he ask for tobac, but he asks for the best there is." The dwarf rose, setting the rat down in the process. "Now, Fehr, I trust you will not run off when I go to bring you back your smoke?"

He nodded in reply, completely taken by the fact that the dark dwarf had called him by name and that he was still alive, not to mention about to get a smoke. Whatever was happening, his curiosity would not allow him to leave, though he suspected a dwarf guard remained outside the door anyway.

Moments later, the dwarf returned, carrying a small pipe, a pouch, and leading another dwarf. They both stared at the rat briefly and then the second handed the first a couple of coins. After placing them somewhere inside his armor, he said, "Sorry to keep you waiting Fehr, but we had a bet on whether you would try anything when we entered. As you can see, I won."

He handed the pipe and tobac to a bewildered rat and used the flame from the candle to help him light it. "I am Tal-Gentry and this is Dol-Teo. Believe it or not, we will not hurt you."

Fehr looked suspicious but was becoming more relaxed with each puff. However, as he sized up those before him, one thing seemed to grab his attention. Hanging from the belt of the one called Dol-Teo was a long, curled white-gray tail. Fehr's eyes became fire, and in one leap he was attached to the face of the dwarf digging his claws in for all he was worth. The dwarf winced in pain, and as Tal-Gentry grabbed the rat, pulling him free, Dol-Teo reached to his belt and removed his dagger, preparing to drive it into Fehr's body.

Gentry shoved the dwarf back, putting himself between the two but not being able to stop Fehr's constant taunts and yells. In one motion, he belted the rat across the face, drawing a flow of blood from his nose and successfully shutting his mouth. Then, he turned his scalding voice on Teo. "Stop it now, Teo. We have our orders, and I doubt even you would act against the leader."

Teo's face was oozing blood from Fehr's attack, and his level of anger showed clearly between the deep crevices planted across his stoic stare. However, moments after Gentry's words, his expression softened, and he took his seat without further comment. Gentry looked back at Fehr, and although he could not be certain of predicting the rat's behaviors, by his look he was fairly confident that there would be calm for a short while.

He turned his attention back to Teo who had not moved. In a motion as calm as a gentle spring breeze across a lonely lake, Gentry removed the coins Teo had previously given him and returned them to the dwarf, who accepted without motion. Turning back to Fehr, he said, "I bet him you would not react badly when you saw your tail. By the appearance, I believe I was wrong."

Gentry turned and sat adjacent to the two. Fehr immediately retrieved his pipe and then set it down once more, now completely agitated. "All right, dwarven scum. Tell me why Scrappy Face here first uses me as target practice and now you claim you will not harm me?"

Dol-Teo glared back but made no motion for his dagger. Gentry smiled. "You truly have a way with words, little one. I think it would be in your best interest to hold your tongue for a day. If all goes as planned, you will be with Jermys by nightfall and can continue your journey to Draag tomorrow. However, the only one who can take you there is my counterpart here, and right now, to use your words, you are nothing more than breakfast."

Kapmann Captured

The king grinned slightly. "That's right, Jermys, and let me assure you that I am as surprised to see you as you are to see me."

Jermys frowned and ignored the comment. "Then it is true. You have been a traitor to our people from the start. You tried to stop my companions and I over a year ago, and now you have prevented my advancement as well."

Kapmann was not pleased with the response, and his expression showed it. "We have much to discuss, young Ironshield. I would be pleased if you hold your accusations until the end. However, if the only way for you to hear me out is to give back what you lost, then let it be done." Kapmann still displayed displeasure as he reached down below the table and removed a small item he had locked in his chest. Moving his hands to the table, he placed the Hatchet of Claude across it. "Now will you take your weapon and sit with me a spell?"

The dwarf's face brightened for a moment, then he quickly hid his pleasure with the suspicion he still had harboring within him. He reached over and picked up the hatchet, and immediately it began to glow and then faded. Jermys felt a surge of power flow through his body, to be replaced by a soothing calm. He moved over and took the seat across from the Antaagian king. Lighting his pipe to join Kapmann in a smoke, he said, "I believe you should tell me the entire story."

Kapmann leaned back, letting his beard fall to the floor. After a deep breath from his pipe, he began. "First, let me tell you that from day one, you and your companions have caused me nothing but stress. Nearly two years ago, a dark dwarf leader by the name of Den-Hrube approached me secretively and spoke to me about some changes he saw occurring that he did not like. Of course I thought it was some kind of trick, knowing Den-Hrube and his reputation for acting only in his own best interests. However, when he began to speak of dragons coming to them seeking their aid in exchange for leadership in the 'new world,' I began to see the truth in his words."

The king paused a moment to give Jermys time to absorb what he was saying. His eyes showed confusion. Kapmann waited a moment longer before he continued. "You see, Den-Hrube may have been many things I do not respect, but one thing he was not was unintelligent. He knew that if the dragons did move to take over all of Troyf, dark dwarves would not be near the top of the list to rule under them. He felt a temporary alliance with Antaag would be necessary to help fight against the dragons. However, we both knew that if this alliance was made common knowledge, then he—and I, most probably—would be overthrown in a matter of days. He had nearly 600 or 700 dark brothers who had gained his trust and defected, so to speak, under his leadership. I sent minerals as often as I could, and we kept contact through the secret tunnels of the southern mines." Jermys looked up, about to add something before Kapmann cut him off. "Yes, the ones you and your companions destroyed. However, worse than that was just your simple appearance in Antaag. It was to be the largest shipment of minerals yet. Den-Hrube himself had come to oversee its deliverance. When you showed up, though, all of the scales were moved up for fear that we would be discovered. We sent his ship out a day early before we had the river secured, and as you know, all was lost."

"Why then did you arrest me that night and throw me in that cell?"

Kapmann frowned at the interruption but then continued when he thought about the question, remembering what he had not mentioned. "When I told Den-Hrube about your group's visit, he immediately centered on the fact that I had mentioned dwarven twins. At this time, our camp here in the woods did not exist, so his command was a secretive existence among all the dark dwarves in the Canyon of Icly. You can think of it as a band of rebels not building against their own nation but not willing to follow their leadership either."

Jermys shook his head in understanding but still awaited the king's answer. Kapmann continued in a slightly softer voice. "Well, this situation actually made it better in that they could keep abreast of all the new plans that the ever-growing dragon loyal dwarves had made. Den-Hrube had heard rumors that some Feldschlosschen twin was going to join forces with the dragons and really turn the scales to their favor. When I thought about the two of you, I wrongly assumed it was you who would betray your homeland. In my opinion, you were the most strong-willed, and because of that, I thought you would be more attracted by the dragons' lure. By capturing you, I could solve two problems. First, I might be able to find out for sure where your loyalty fell, and second, if your friends did try and rescue you, it would keep them away from the docks until Den-Hrube could escape."

Jermys eyes fell. "If we had only known!"

"Yes, I know that now. But at the time, I could not be sure. If I brought you into our secret circle and you were to betray us, all that we had worked for would be destroyed."

"What happened following Den-Hrube's ambush on the river?"

The king sucked in another deep breath of smoke and then gave a long, depressing sigh. "Many months went by, and I had not heard a word from any of the dark dwarves. I had instructed our search parties not to attack them unless they had already been attacked. Additionally, if any of the dark brothers wished to speak with me, then they were to be allowed."

"These orders did not cause dissension among your nation?"

Kapmann shrugged. "At this time, I think many already suspected that some sort of alliance had been formed. Furthermore, I feel all believed that if we were to curve the dragons' onslaught across Troyf, all dwarves must bind together. Even with these facts in mind, there are only a few that have openly been brought into this plan. By keeping the number low, if this ever did collapse around me, there would be only a few dead by my side."

Jermys nodded understanding and agreement. "Did any dark dwarves come?"

No, and I feared that the rebel forces had disbanded with the loss of their leader and joined with the dragon forces. Then, more on a thought of desperation rather than true belief, I decided to check the southern mines on my own. That is when I came across Lyl-Brown. He had been wandering them for days, not able to find the entrance because Krystof had changed the magic to block against any unexpected visitors. Lyl-Brown is the dwarf who organized the evacuation from Icly and set up the secret camp here in what he called the Forgotten Forests.

Immediately I began running minerals down the river, and despite a few attacks, nearly all got through. These procedures have gone along steadily since that time, with only a few hitches. Upon Lyl-Brown's disappearance, I moved in and took over the leadership, unknown to all but five of the dark brothers. Most believe that their leader is still Lyl-Brown, though none have seen him in over a year. His brother, Eb-Brown, whom you know intimately, convinced me that this would be the most intelligent way to handle it. They needed an experienced leader, and they feared if word got out of Lyl-Brown's death, then the group might fall apart. That is why when you openly spoke about his death, you created such a stir. Eb, however, passed it off as your foolish whimpers trying to save yourself. Only when he said that he had spoken with Lyl yesterday did he soothe the damage. It was indeed a close call, but we have gotten past it."

"How then did you make it here so quickly? I was only captured less than a day ago."

He shook his head. "If I had ever believed you would end up anywhere near the Forgotten Forests, I would have sent word down ahead of you. Eb and his search parties would have steered well clear, letting you have the run of the forest. As it was, I left a day later telling those in Antaag that I was going to Gnausanne, as I usually did. However, instead, I was traveling here to prepare a small company to act as a sort of cavalry if you needed the support. I was not ready to expose this group of dark dwarves as allies, but if it turned out they could help, we would not hesitate to do so."

Jermys shrugged and restuffed his pipe. "All this is so hard to believe. So much could have been different, but I understand that to trust too many would seal your fate as well. You have done well to hide it."

Kapmann nodded. "Yes, but now that you know, has anything changed?"

Jermys thought a minute, then replied. "How many dwarves do you have here at the camp?"

"There are 500, maybe 600. Our numbers are not growing. If anything, we lose more than we gain. By this, I mean if someone is going to leave our camp to return to Icly, we will do everything in our power to kill them before they get there. Our secret must remain just that—a secret."

Again there was a pause, and both dwarves filled the small tent with their exhale. Jermys leaned forward. "Then we will keep things just as they are. I shall not tell anyone unless the situation deems it necessary and I am sure they can be trusted."

The king replied, "But won't you require some help from the forces here? I assure you they would be loyal to any cause that fights against the dragons, as long as it did not involve fighting their kin." He paused and thought a minute before adding, "Though, if they had to, I believe they would."

"At this time your numbers are not large enough to make a major difference should a massive offensive be planned. However, if we can keep them a secret, they could become extremely important as a strong cavalry. They may just be able to tip the scales if used at the right time. I feel this band could prove very beneficial to our cause, and they should never have to face those they separated from. To do so would split your troops and destroy all you have fought to create and hold."

The king nodded. "I believe your words to be sound and am pleased to hear of your loyalty to us here. I trust what you say, and we will help you if it is ever within our power. However, I also wish you to know that my first loyalty is with Antaag, and I will never allow any evil to infiltrate its boundaries."

He smiled. "I respect all that you have done here and understand your motives. I too agree that Antaag must not pay the price for your actions. If it did, defend you I would not. No matter what happens here or as a result of any dragon army progression, you must never forget your home."

Kapmann shook his head before Jermys continued, his tone and appearance changing as he spoke. "I will be asking for your assistance sooner than you may have wanted."

Kapmann looked surprised. "What is it you would ask?"

"I traveled with Fehr, and due to my capture, we have become separated. I freely admit that wanting that annoying pest back may be considered impossible to understand by most, but he has become a counterpart that each gives strength to the other. If your troops locate him, please point him in my direction. Also, could you give me a direction?"

Kapmann smiled again. "I already have Eb-Brown organizing parties looking for him. There have been several sightings, but he always alludes us." Jermys joined in the smile as the king continued, "And passage for you to Draag has already been prepared. The dwarves here have dug a secret tunnel under the most fierce section of the Draag River. Because the rapids are so trying there, the goblin forces are at a minimum on the other side. You should be able to approach unobserved, but after you pass the river, you will be on your own. I have several dwarves which have been planted in some of the forces around Draag, but they are few and far between. Also, they will not risk exposing themselves to help you. Therefore, even if you could make contact, their help would be small. You will stay here through the day, and then Eb-Brown and two others will lead you to the river. I must return to Gnausanne so I don't bring further suspicion upon myself. Already I fear some of the Antaagian dwarves have begun to doubt my loyalty. In these times of evil, the last thing I need is to have civil war in my own nation. As of today, I am turning over full command to Brown and a dwarf called Dol-Teo, who you will meet when you head toward the river. We all agree that due to your comments during your capture, many are going to begin to talk, and soon the fact that none have seen their leader in over a year will start to make them suspicious. However, Brown has much support and he is certain that with Teo's help, he will be able to keep the band together. I only hope he is right. If word leaks out, it would be a devastating blow to all who have fought to make this possible. After all, we are not many in number; and being so close to Draag, it would be like swatting a fly to wipe our band from existence."

"We will keep it a secret, King Kapmann. That much I promise." Jermys rose to his feet and let out a long breath before adding in a strong, deep tone. "You have returned the Hatchet of Claude, and with it I will free my friend and then move to crush the dragons and the wrath they bring. Above all else I could say, though, I wish to express my deepest appreciation to you and the dark brothers. Your actions will never be forgotten."

The king bowed slightly. "And a thank you goes to you as well, and good luck. You will be faced with much more than can be described or even imagined here, and I pray that even one blessed with such a weapon will be strong enough to face it. May Claudos guard your travels."

The two embraced, and then the king bid him farewell, making a somewhat hasty exit. Eb-Brown returned, throwing down a pack and some blankets. "You would do well to get some sleep. We have a long journey ahead of us, and the forests are not considered friendly, especially for a mining dwarf. We must be alert." He paused, and then sensing Jermys's question, added, "And there is still no word on Fehr, but I also have not spoken with any since I left you. We will not know anything until this evening when the others arrive. Now, get some rest if you can."

Brown left, and being as how Jermys had not slept in over a day's time, he drifted off to a restless sleep. The many worries of the period bit at his mind, but mostly his thoughts centered on the rat who had become his best friend. Questions regarding his whereabouts filled his mind and dreams.

Two arguing voices woke the dwarf, and judging from the lack of light that penetrated the black fabric of the tent, he guessed it was near sunset. He gathered his belongings, placing his pipe and tobac, which he had left on the table, into his pouch; and after briefly rubbing his hand over the helve of his hatchet, he moved and pushed through the door of the tent. When he looked across the field, the sight which greeted him made his jaw drop, and he drew his weapon while starting a full run for those ahead of him.

"I'll take no more of your lip, rat!"

"Awe, shut up, you fat lump of maggot dump! You are not fit to…"

"Fehr! One more word and I will kill you myself!" Jermys was shouting at the top of his lungs as he approached.

Immediately, the dark dwarf holding the rat dropped him and drew his sword, turning to face the surprise visitor. Seeing it was Jermys, he lowered his weapon and issued an angry stare, which was meant to silence the dwarf.

Jermys caught the look and knew right away he had acted poorly. He drew an apologetic frown when he arrived, but it quickly changed to a hidden smile when Fehr leaped into the dwarf's arms and began licking his face. The embarrassed Jermys pushed the rat down and gave him a stern look of his own. "If you ever do anything like that again, I will cut off your tail." He laughed. "Well, it looks like someone has beat me to it."

Jermys turned to face the dark brother who stood beside him, and seeing the rat's tail still dangling from his belt, held his smile and said, "I am Jermys Ironshield, and you must be one powerful dwarf to cut off my friend's tail and then be able to put up with his annoying chatter about it."

The dwarf shook his head. "If he keeps the chatter up, more than his tail will come off. I am Dol-Teo, and I am pleased to make your acquaintance, though your friend leaves much to be desired."

Fehr grumbled, and when neither acknowledged his displeasure, he stormed off to where a small campfire burned and two more dwarves sat eating. Jermys watched the small critter waddle off but hid his joy at seeing his friend behind the stoic masks all dwarves carried. He removed his pipe and offered some to Dol-Teo as the two turned and made idle conversation on their way toward the fire.

The conversation was cheap and served only to fill Jermys and Fehr in on the plans and what they could expect in the way of resistance. The trip itself was to take the entire night but they would be on a well-traveled path, and the walk should not be difficult. All enjoyed the moments of peace before the journey and the plentiful amounts of food each was served, but most of all, the two reunited companions were pleased with the other's presence.

Despite the brief good cheer, Fehr leaned over and whispered to Jermys, "Stepha and Krirtie were with me in the forest. They are most likely on their way to Draag on their own on the river. They have some magic boat or something."

Jermys jaw dropped. "They're here? Why didn't you say something?"

Fehr frowned. "I was spending time with people who normally eat me. Trust was not high on my list." Fehr then continued to tell all he knew about the two and his time with them in the forest.

Jermys turned to Eb-Brown. "Can we get word to the camp to aid the elf and human?

"Out of the question. Your presence alone is enough to drive a stake through this band. Now help an elf and human, both women no less? Out of the question."

"Then we are leaving," said Jermys. "Thank you again for your time."

Hesitantly, Eb-Brown raised his hand. "Wait, dwarf, don't be too tough around here. You are still in mixed company, and your friend here does look tasty, with all the meat on those bones. I would hate to kill you and be forced to banquet on him." He paused, then motioned to one of the dwarves. "Go take this message back and send six dwarves to the area described by the rat. Make sure they know not to attack. The elf is with the forest. If they approach without weapons raised, they will not attack first." He turned back to Jermys and Fehr with a stern gaze. "Sit down." He paused with a deep breath. "This is of little use. Based on the rat's words, there will be no way to catch the elf and human before they reach the river."

When they finally left the glade, it looked to be nothing more than an empty field. Eb-Brown, Dol-Teo, Fehr, and Jermys began their long walk through the night toward the heart of the dragon's stronghold, Draag. Jermys had been given dark dwarven armor and then used mud to hide his lighter skin. Fehr was instructed to dive into the trees should they encounter any others in the forest. To an unexpecting observer, they looked like a stray band of dark dwarves heading to Draag to find a new command to serve under. That was to be their story, and Brown or Teo would be the ones to do the talking. They traveled without exchanging words, all hoping that their silence might aid their chances of success, but none knowing what their chances really were.

※

Stepha stretched her arms and then glanced over to where Krirtie had a fire going and breakfast ready. The roar of the River Draag could be heard thundering down their path, and their raft, which had again taken them down the rapids without any problems, rested well upon the shore. The elf rose and walked over to the fire, bidding a morning greeting to the human who returned it with a large serving of food.

Stepha's expression clearly demonstrated her deep hunger and pleasure as she received the morning meal. As they ate, both looked around the area they had arrived at late the night before. The river had been exceptionally fierce, and if not for a brief period of calm, they probably would still be fighting its violent hold with all their collective forces being drained in the process. They had guided their raft to the northwest shore, but with all the thick tree cover, they had no idea where they were. For all they knew, they had sailed beyond the caverns of Draag long ago.

They seemed to be able to read each other's thoughts when their eyes met, and they both laughed. Stepha spoke first. "I have no idea where we are. What do you think?"

Krirtie grinned. "You are asking me? You obviously don't remember that I got us lost between Elvinott and Feldschlosschen one day after being there. Your question alone demonstrates how truly desperate you have become."

"I am by no means desperate, but I am definitely in unfamiliar territory. By the length of time we were on the river, I would say we traveled most of its length, which would put the Draag Caverns to our west, possibly a bit north as well."

Krirtie tried to look that direction but the tree cover was still too thick. "I really have no idea. All I know is that I do not want to get back on that river if we do not have to. If you think we can walk from here, I say let's head northwest."

The elf finished her food and rose to clean her plate before adding, "I was going to suggest the same thing. However, we should hide the raft in case we need to make some kind of emergency escape down the river. I would sooner sail this river out to sea than be cut off by it and have to either fight, swim, or be an easy target in the air."

Krirtie nodded, and when she finished eating as well, the two set to camouflaging their raft and then departed on foot, the elf marking their trail so they would be able to find their way back if needed. They followed the river a short distance and then set a course by Stepha's lead to the northwest. They moved with utmost caution, and unless they were seen, they would not run into any confrontation, as neither of them made even a twig crack beneath their steps.

Stepha rose her hand to stop their march and peered up the trail questionably. Krirtie slid in next to her but did not speak for fear of giving away their presence. The elf motioned ahead holding up three fingers to alert the girl of their numbers. Krirtie nodded, and then the two separated.

Stepha turned off the trail, as she was more apt to move through the wooded area without disturbance even without a having a path present. Krirtie drew her sword and continued down the trail but at a slow-enough pace to let the elf circle around.

One goblin struck the ground with an arrow squarely through its chest as Krirtie emerged into the clearing, swinging fiercely at another. In only moments, all three goblins were dead, and the two women warriors were replacing their weapons.

Suddenly, the ground beneath them seemed to open up, and both girls were falling downward with a sea of debris and a goblin corpse being carried with them. Stepha reached over and took a firm grip on the human, opening her wings in the same motion. They both glanced down to see the goblin body strike the hard and jagged rock-bottom floor below the trapdoor, but they had already begun to climb. Within seconds, they were back through the opening and safely standing on firm ground.

Stepha turned to motion Krirtie back to the tree cover but screeched as an arrow bit through her wing, tearing through the delicate cell line. Krirtie wheeled around to greet two dozen goblins and a handful of dark dwarves entering the glade from the far side. Already another dwarf was notching an arrow, and if not for the girl's accurate and quick sword work splitting it in flight, Stepha would have been killed. The two looked at each other and quickly realized that to fight would be to die a warrior's death. Without a word exchanged, they turned and fled at the fastest pace they could muster.

Stepha's wing was torn and dangled helplessly down as she ducked beneath branches and shrubs. The pain was intense but she knew that to stop and bandage it would mean to give up the little lead they had gained. They could move through the forest at a much faster pace than the heavier and less coordinated goblins, but that was the end of their advantage. They did not know where they were or what direction they were heading. Furthermore, although they may be able to outrun this band, they both knew these woods were thick with dragon armies. This was only one small group. There were many more scattered throughout the trees, and it would only be a matter of time before they greeted another party. They were both aware of their situation, but all they could do now was run like they had never run before. If they could gain enough of a lead, they would start to hide their trail. Until then, they could only hope they didn't meet any more unwelcome guests.

The two burst through some trees, and Krirtie slammed on the breaks so hard her feet slid out in front of her and she fell hard on her back. Stepha launched an arrow, and its flight passed directly above the fallen woman to strike the dark dwarf through his heart. Krirtie was back to her feet in moments, and an ensuing hand-to-hand combat took place. Both girls fought with terror-driven anger, giving them strength they had never drawn on before. Stepha used her sword like it was her weapon of choice, dropping a half dozen dwarves before any could even mount a defense. Krirtie was cutting a path through the rest as tears of adrenaline and hate covered her face.

They had begun to dent the camp of two-dozen dwarves when the pursuit from earlier provided the needed support to shut the lid on the two girls. Stepha's sword was knocked free, and before she could retrieve her bow, she found a goblin dagger placed to her throat. Krirtie was backed against the tree line, and once the elf was secured, the brunt of the attack was turned on her. Within moments, she too was disarmed and on the ground.

The goblins threw both women on their backs in the center of the clearing, and the one who seemed to be the leader moved to approach. Both girls were sitting with their heads raised, allowing their long golden and black hair to fall freely behind. The goblin knelt behind them and ran his rough, curved, and nasty fingers through each of their hairlines causing both women to shake them off in disgust. The goblin issued a deep, bellowing laugh, which incited the other goblins around to do the same. He leaned toward Stepha, and in a seductive and forward gesture outstretched his long black tongue and moved it around the tip of her pointed ear. Her face grew dark and tears began to flow, bringing even more laughter and cheers from those around. Krirtie moved her hand over and gripped the elf's, hoping to allow them to share each other's strength.

With this, the goblin removed his attention from the elf and turned it toward Krirtie. He ran his hand upward along the back of her armor and then reached around her neck, moving the backs of his bent fingers across the sides of her cheek. He continued stroking her face to the cheers of support from the surrounding goblins, and she could only tighten her lips in disgust trying to pull away but his grip was too firm.

Without a further gesture, he applied force to the side of her head, turning her face to stare directly into his. Krirtie closed her eyes at the gnarled and disfigured goblin appearance. His face was beaten, like it had been ripped apart by an animal. Large black nostrils sat below deep cuts surrounding his eyes, and his lips looked more like bark than skin. The goblin saw her disgust and became angry at the response. He reached his hand around the back of her neck and pulled her head forward, placing his lips across hers. Gripping her neck and throat tightly, he forced his tongue in her mouth.

Suddenly, the goblin fell back with a scream of pain and an issuance of blood from his mouth. He swung his backhand across the human woman's head, sending her back against the elf. Krirtie fell, nearly unconscious, but spit a piece of the goblin tongue back his direction before she faded completely. As jeers and laughter rose from those around, the goblin leader drew a small dagger and raised it before the two girls. Stepha had helped Krirtie recover, and although she was still groggy from the hit, she knew what was about to happen.

Both girls huddled together as the goblin leader rose and stepped closer. The dwarves in the area were not paying much attention, but the surrounding goblins formed a circle around the three to ensure all could see clearly. The goblin leader pulled Krirtie away from Stepha with another goblin placing a knife to the elf's throat to keep her from moving. The goblin shoved the human woman's legs apart and knelt between them, placing both hands on her waist. Tears filled her eyes while the goblin began moving his hands over her armor. He reached up and separated the breastplate from the back, causing it to fall forward. Again cheers and growls echoed from the clearing.

Stepha swung her hand forward, knocking the knife from her throat, and moved to strike the goblin leader only to be violently thrown and pinned to the ground by several other goblins.

Krirtie's face showed nothing but fear and rage when the goblin leader began running his hands over her body. Blood showed through the meshwork of her clothing as his claw-like fingers tore through her garments, biting into much of her flesh in the process. Krirtie quivered, as the pain in her chest was minimal to that which she felt in her heart. He reached his hand around the top of her leg armor and, in one violent motion, ripped it off, causing much of the metal to scrape and cut her skin.

More cheers rang through the trees, with the dwarves still seeming completely uninterested. Most were sitting, discussing the weapons they had taken from the women, not following the commotion brought on by the goblins. Krirtie's eyes were filled with tears and all her thoughts were centering on the child she carried. She issued a silent prayer for the protection of her baby regardless of what happened to her.

The goblin nodded his head to the cheers, inciting even more applause to fill the glade. Stepha screamed, and one of the goblins holding her belted her across the face, knocking her momentarily unconscious. When she began to come to, she heard a dwarf's voice arguing with the goblin leader. She arched her head up to see Krirtie in the same position. Stepha had no idea how long she had been out, but when she looked into Krirtie's eyes, she knew the woman was all right. Krirtie nodded an awkward smile, although her face was still covered in tears. It was clear she did not know what was going on, but more importantly, it was clear that the attack had been halted by the dwarves for some reason. The elf turned her attention to the goblin leader and the dwarf who seemed very agitated at what he was witnessing.

The dark dwarf raised Krirtie's sword to the goblin and was motioning toward both girls. The arguments could not be understood by the girls, but both Stepha and Krirtie assumed something about the sword had alerted the dwarf, and he was extremely aggressive against the goblin. The dwarf was speaking in some unknown goblin tongue so even Stepha was at a loss to understand. Although the dwarf seemed to think that they should not be injured because of the sword Krirtie carried, the goblin was not in agreement. As the discussion continued, the goblin leader was becoming very agitated, and the argument heated. The other goblins, who were greatly outnumbered by the dwarves, began to move around their leader. The ones who had previously held Stepha freed her completely, and they too surrounded the dark brother and goblin leader. Stepha quickly moved beside Krirtie and both tried to slide over out of the way.

The goblin leader drew his sword and thrashed out against the dwarf, only to find five arrows piercing his chest before his sword made half a swing. The other goblins tried to flee when they saw their leader fall but quickly were greeted with sword tips, drawn on by archers. Those that still fled or fought were immediately killed. Those who dropped guard were ordered to fall into ranks with the dwarves.

Both Stepha and Krirtie looked on in disbelief and horror. They had no idea what was going on, and as the dark dwarf turned his attention to them, they feared they were about to be killed. He approached the girls with a look on his face that gave no answers or support. For some reason, he had saved Krirtie and Stepha from the sexual wrath of the goblin force. However, were they saved to simply be killed now? With the tip of Krirtie's sword pointing toward their throats, both felt the end was near.

"Do you understand dwarven tongue?" asked the dark brother to Stepha.

"Yes, I do," she replied in a cracked and broken voice.

The dwarf showed no change of expression but only made a quick motion to his company then turned back to Stepha. In a flat, commanding tone, he said, "Your weapons look to be some we have been searching for. Replace her armor"—he pointed to Krirtie—"and dress any wounds you may have suffered. We are taking you to our leader and will be leaving as soon as you make ready. However, do not delay. Whether we deliver you dead or alive makes little difference to me."

Stepha relayed the message to Krirtie, and soon the two women were on their feet and ready for travel. Most of Krirtie's wounds were superficial, but Stepha's torn wing was serious enough to possibly mean she would never fly again. She made a silent prayer to Shriak as the dwarven leader approached.

"To speak is to die, you make the choice."

The elf looked at Krirtie and placed her finger across her lips and then across her throat. The girl nodded that she understood, and with a gentle shove in the back, the walking began. The dark dwarf leader was in front, followed by two guards, the girls, and then three guards bringing up the rear. The majority of the company remained back to continue their scouting and guard of the surrounding forests.

The dried tears on both their faces shown clearly and spoke of great despair. However, both also knew where they were headed and the leader they were about to be placed before. They both prayed their death would come quickly. Krirtie placed her hands across her stomach and repeated her prayer from earlier as another tear draped across her face.

Hawthorne

Schram broke through a final line of trees to look across a seemingly endless embankment of blowing, grassy fields. Since his run-in with the minoks over a week ago, he had only dealt with two obstacles, both of which consisted of small bands of goblins. However, neither group thought twice about stopping a stray troll, and the confrontations—if you could call them that—were nothing more than passing greetings. Ever since the masquerade that allowed Schram's party to sneak past the troll armies around Elvinott, he had repeatedly used his magic abilities to re-obtain the black body form of the troll; and strangely enough, the more times he did it, the easier it was for him, and the less he relied on the powers of the staff.

As he looked across the large glade, however, he knew it was no longer a necessary disguise. With a quick incantation, his shape became somewhat liquid and flexible until he looked exactly how he should—an elven-human warrior. He sighed slightly and then pulled his staff close, beginning to walk to the only objects, which broke the level plain before him. Two large boulders sat near the center of the field, one the crisp white of new fallen snow and the other darker than the blackest night. They appeared strange against the flat horizon, but none who passed could ever find any value in them. So there they remained, completely undisturbed for eternity.

A strong feeling for the presence of magic grew within Schram as he walked across the field toward the rocks. His mind felt a soothing, which in turn delivered a peaceful sensation throughout his body. When he arrived at the boulders, he hesitated only a moment, running his fingers along the base of the white one before taking his place on his knees between them. He drew a deep breath and then began reciting a poem locked deep within his mind. It was in a total of four languages, but when spoken correctly, the sound formed into a beautiful song. As he spoke, the entire area began to melt as if spurred by the wind that now burst across the grasses. The space between the ground and the horizon became out of focus and uncertain, creating a period where time did not seem to exist. Within that period arose a city. Magnificent buildings or structures shot heavenward, but they were nothing that had ever been built. Moreover, they had been created or reformed from that which was already there. Where originally had rested an open prairie now stood a city. Schram had just entered the homeland of the canoks.

Schram was the only human to have ever laid eyes on the city, and though it held no secret beauty as did Elvinott, he considered it partly his home. The buildings, as they are most easily described, were no more than cavernous mountains whose interiors were home to any who would enter. The city, protected by magic, existed as a vision caught in a rift of time, separate and distinct from Troyf. The only way to enter the city was through the rift. The only way through the rift was to have the key. Schram had the key and stood in time with the city, one black and five white canoks staring back at him.

The human rose and moved from between the rocks. He looked across the familiar faces before him but stopped on the black. "Greetings, Werner. I had hoped that I would find you here."

"Greetings to you, Schram. I was not sure if you would head here or to Icly. I am pleased that I guessed correctly, though I have known so for several days as our scouts located you after you left Elvinott."

Schram turned to the others. "And may I bid my best to all of you as well. It has been a long time, and I bring new hope."

The others nodded appropriately, but it was Werner who continued to speak. "Indeed, there have been great shifts in the forces of evil since we parted last in Icly. With these shifts, I assumed it meant you had been successful. Judging by the staff now by your side and the trollish form you carried as you traveled, I see I was right."

He was about to respond when a soft, human voice interrupted from his side. "Yes, the ability to shape-change truly has dragon origins. Your success is well-displayed."

Schram was startled by the voice, but not just by its presence as much as its familiarity. Furthermore, when he turned to greet who owned the voice, the radiance emanating from her beauty nearly dropped Schram to his knees. She walked as a human, but there was no possible way she could be totally of human origin. Her skin was silky white beneath her long, soft light-brown hair. As she walked nearer, her movement made her appear to be floating rather than stepping. Her legs were long and showed the same delicate tones as her face. She wore no armor, having only two small cream-colored cloths covering her chest and waist. Schram stared at her in disbelief, knowing that he was looking at the only creature on Troyf that had a beauty to rival that of Stepha's.

Werner saw the human's surprise and captured gaze and softly said, "Schram of Toopek, may I present to you Hawthorne. She has come here to help us carry out our plans to return the canok's to the proud race of our ancestors."

Schram made no motion that he had heard or understood the canok, and his stare remained locked on the captivating figure approaching. As she drew near, all the canoks saw that she too looked back at the warrior with the same frozen stare. When she arrived to the group, she ignored the others and placed the back of her fingers on Schram's cheek, running it along his face and over to his ear.

She smiled and in a soft tone, added, "I have learned much about you, Schram Starland. Your story is one which will be told for many years to come. I am very pleased that I will be a part of it, as I have always dreamed I would."

Schram was completely taken with her statement but could muster no words to question their meaning while she touched him. His head swirled while feelings surged and unleashed throughout his body. Great power flowed from this woman, which left the human stumbling over his own thoughts. She suddenly seemed to feel the others' eyes and removed her hand while turning to better face them all. Schram immediately felt his mind clear and stared blankly into open space, trying to understand what was happening. The woman's presence was almost hypnotizing, and the essence of something so familiar still seduced Schram's thoughts. The canoks all displayed questioning expressions but none spoke verbally in regard to them. Instead, Werner made a simple motion with his eyes, and all turned and began to follow. The mysterious woman slipped directly beside Schram.

Werner led the group through one of the cave entrances, which opened into a small enclosed chamber. A small fire burned in a pit in the wall, but as there was no smoke billowing into a chimney, Schram knew it was of magic means. There were no chairs or any other objects in the room save for a long cushion placed across a portion of the floor. The white canoks moved over and immediately took seats along one of the walls while Hawthorne knelt by the fire. Schram began to move nearer the woman, but a nudge from Werner made him halt.

"We have issues we must discuss."

This statement caused a stir among the other canoks, and Schram nodded understanding. The two exited the cave and Werner slowly led them toward a small pile of loose debris and rocks. Schram had always been forbidden to go near this area, though it looked harmless and unimportant, and Kirven had never told him why. As they drew nearer, a growing darkness was felt emanating from its source. Although the sun always shined on their wrinkle in time, this area of the canok's homeland was in permanent darkness. Werner suddenly stopped, and the black's eyes became fixed on the target ahead.

"I can go no further. I know your are not sure of your next actions, but put faith in the staff. It, with the hand of evil behind it, caused this horror. It is only that which you have now harnessed that can undo what has been done."

Schram's uncertainty showed on his face, but he knew he must not let it control his actions. He gripped the staff tightly, and with a quick glance down to the canok, he hesitantly proceeded forward. He felt an odd sensation in his foot, and when he glanced down, he saw it beginning to twist and turn into a gnarled formation. He quickly stepped back in surprise and then realized it was another time barrier protecting, or possibly hiding, whatever was inside. He reached his hand outward. It was as if he was pushing through the surface of a lake as it moved past the barrier separating the two periods. He slowly pushed his whole body forward, holding the staff close to his body as it passed.

A whirlwind of colors flashed before his eyes, and Schram felt his body get ripped into this chasm. He felt as if he was moving faster than humanly possible through a maze of winding and violent turns. His body became contorted and deformed and he could feel his senses beginning to fail. The speed he was traveling was unknown and uncontrollable. He felt himself falling into unconsciousness. Suddenly, the staff began to hum throughout his body and his mind focused on the environment. As the sound began to grow, his travel suddenly came crashing to a halt.

Pain erupted through his head while a barrage of magical hands reached for the staff. Schram fought to keep hold, but the magic driving against him was growing too strong. Too many fists reached, tugged, and stabbed, trying to take control over the staff. Suddenly, branches formed from within the staff and entwined into Schram's arms. The staff had grown into an extension of Schram's own being in an attempt to rid the attackers of their prize. With this, the magical hands turned their fight against the warrior himself. Their fists carried more strength than a hundred maneths. Schram erected no magical defenses, but something was causing the punches to land with force but hinder him little. His eyes were still useless against the environmentless space, but he still could sense a passageway in front of him. He clutched the staff to his body and began to drive forward.

The colors began to streak by him as if his walk was really a pace beyond that capable of any creature on Troyf. He traveled for what seemed like hours, but as adept as his senses were, he actually had no feeling for time. He sensed he was in a place where time did not exist, or at least was not measurable. However, he was certain that time was playing a role on what was happening.

He continued walking, confused at the total inconsistencies with everything he knew to be fact. When he held his legs still and only leaned his head forward, the same rush of colors would nearly blind his eyes as they passed with their lightning speed; and when he would look down at his feet, they appeared as tiny specks nearly a mile behind him as if his body had stretched to unimaginable limits. Then, when he would step forward, it appeared that his body was recoiling like a spring to bring back to its original and proper position. Sounds buzzed by his ears, but even his own words were completely unrecognizable.

Suddenly, he clasped his hands around his head, nearly dropping his staff as a screech of immense intensity shattered his eardrums, dropping the human to his knees. Some power within him calmed his mind while he fought to regain his self. He lifted his head into the air to see a window appear through the explosion of colors and a long, outstretched head peered through. Two large eyes sat atop an oblong disc, with large jagged teeth protruding outward from some type of beak or hard-fleshed mouth. The creature opened wide and emitted a second scream, which this time was high pitched and crystal clear, no longer muffled by the differences in time. Schram still gripped his ears, but there was no protecting from the sound which penetrated his mind, tearing at his nerves like a minok tears at flesh. Schram doubled over, and the creature dove back into its window, causing it to dissolve as it disappeared.

Schram lowered his hands and slowly lifted his head. Again ahead of him was a wall of color, only now it was slightly different. It no longer appeared in the rhythmic motions it had before, possibly due to the intrusion of the creature or some other unknown reason. Whichever did not matter, because Schram now knew what he must do.

The creature had tried to put fear into his mind, crippling him to the point of retreat. However, all it had done was to give him the answer to his quest. Schram had passed into one time shift, and without the staff's protection, he would not have survived. That is why the canoks could not pass. They were strong with magic but this barrier had been erected to directly defend against their attempts. The only way to penetrate this force was with that which created it. If Werner was correct, the staff, under evil guidance, created these traps and barriers. But although Schram experienced their power and force, as long as he possessed staff, they could not be used against him.

Schram rose. With his new understanding he began to speak, attempting with the staff's power to open a window of his own to follow the creature to whatever it was so desperate to protect. However, he stopped after only a few words when he discovered he was deaf.

The monotonous silence bordered on life-threatening to one who had come to rely on his ears as much as any other organ. An overpowering fear and emptiness engulfed him as once again he fell to his knees, only this time he was not certain that he would ever rise. The creature's attack had been precise and well-thought—to destroy that which would be left unprotected but still completely debilitate. Schram had never considered his hearing as a possible choice of attack or he would have protected against it. However, he had underestimated what he faced and now it was too late.

His face grew hard and his mind determined. He did not know how he was to create an incantation such as the one he had planned without speaking, but since he knew every spell originated as just a thought, his belief was that he could. He lifted his body up from where he had collapsed and pointed the staff to where he believed the creature had been, though with every slight moment the environment changed greatly around him. He began reciting his words, but whether any sound emitted was unknown. Suddenly the staff emitted a beam of light, which erupted in the air ahead of him, leaving a tiny black spot where it had appeared to strike the wall of colors. Schram peered at the spot, wondering if what he had tried had actually worked. He took one step forward and the spot more than tripled in size. There was a slight relief planted inside of him when he realized that he had been successful, but it was compounded by the knowledge that he now had the doorway to face what he had come here to face, still having no idea exactly what that might be.

He took two more steps forward, and now that tiny black spot appeared as a large darkened doorway to a place Schram could not fathom. He had worked a spell to follow whatever had previously been there. If he was indeed successful, when he passed through the doorway, he would be at his destination. He circled his staff in front of him, creating a ring of energy around his body, and then he stepped through.

Once again all time shifted and the environment went completely dark. Then suddenly, a bright light filled his eyes. His energy shield acted like a filter to shade his face, and without it, he knew he would now also be blind as well as deaf. He could still hear no sounds, but if the violent swells in the creature's neck and throat were any indication, the walls were shaking with its howls.

He had entered into a small room carved out of solid rock with only two objects in it. Placed on a stone pedestal against the far wall was a black orb with a tiny red light glowing within it, and next to it stood a large brown and heavily scaled body of the same creature as before. It was a creature the likes of which Schram had never seen before. It stood on two legs with taloned feet, but it also had two other limbs, which hung as arms from its body. It had a fat belly, which probably pushed its total weight into the thousands of pounds. Its neck was equal to its tail in length, both incredibly long and well-stocked with heavy armored projections. Schram knew one of its main attacks would be with the violent use of its tail like a sword. One touch with one of its spikes could create a hemorrhage so deep and true that death would be instantaneous.

For a brief moment, the creature calmed and seemed to better inspect the man before him. However, a moment was all Schram was granted before the first attack struck. Magical shells of fire, heat, and wind bombarded Schram, accompanied with the same blinding light as before. The creature moved quickly and followed its magical barrage with a forceful physical attack. Schram held his staff high and let his mind control it faster than his conscious thought would be able to do. The two struck each other with a stubbornness that would rival that of the meanest dwarves. Schram was hit with a blast of energy, which somehow passed unhindered through his defensive barrier. The jolt knocked him back to the ground, sending a piercing pain through his chest. The shield around him still remained, but if the creature had discovered a way though it, Schram knew his time would be limited. He rolled to the side as a second bolt struck the ground behind him. He wheeled to his feet and came up returning the attack with the staff. The creature opened its arms and let the bolt penetrate its chest. Its large eyes turned a beet red while it slowly absorbed the power unleashed upon it. Schram fell back in disbelief. For a moment, he could not even fathom what he was facing until a distant memory curled to the surface of his mind.

His eyes narrowed and he thought deeply to himself. *A bantis? It couldn't be.* Elven for "magic-grabber," a bantis was a mythical creature that was supposedly originally created to be pets of the gods. They eventually turned on their masters and created the first Death of the Ages, a time when all gods ceased to exist as mortals. Never had one ever been seen, and always they were believed to be only a fictitious legend created by some elven storytellers.

Schram now knew different. Who better to guard against that which only magic could free than a creature that would capture any magic used. Slayne had been thorough in his work, more thorough than Schram could have ever dreamed.

The bantis arched back with its newfound strength and put forth another display of incredible power. Once again Schram was beaten down, having to force all of his magical abilities into mounting a defense that might help him survive long enough to escape, whether his mission was successful or not. Moreover, he still was not sure what he was there to do, yet he assumed it must be related to the black, faintly glowing orb that the bantis would not let him near. In fact, this last attack did not seem to be meant to injure, but rather it seemed to be designed to push back and better position the human away from the orb. Now Schram could not even see the orb, much less reach it. Schram held his elven shield, the gift from Stepha before he left Elvinott, up to block those bolts able to pass through his protective barrier. He was at a loss to explain how the creature's magic was penetrating his defenses, but with all his prayers, the elven shield seemed to be efficient where his magic was not.

The creature, no longer satisfied with simply wearing him down, momentarily halted its attack while it fought to develop a way to finish its prey once and for all. Schram saw the porthole he had just passed through to enter the room only a few feet away. During this pause, he knew he must capitalize on the opportunity. He leaped to his feet and made a sudden lunge to the door but then abruptly stopped and turned on the creature. Seconds later an explosion occurred where the door had been, and Schram knew that had he been inside, he would be trapped or dead, or eventually both. Without hesitation, he charged at the creature slapping his shield with as much force as he could muster into the bantis' head. It rocked backward, being caught by surprise, and quickly lost its balance. Schram leaped onto its back, placing the arm holding his shield around its neck, and gripped with all his might. The creature flailed wildly, and just as it appeared it might falter, Schram felt a sharp pain shooting through his back. However, even when his grip fell loose, the creature did not break free. They fell down in a heap, neither making any effort of attack or withdrawal from the other.

Schram reached his hand to his back and could feel a jagged projection from the creature's tail lodged deep within him. Blood was flowing at an alarming rate down the back of his leg, and he was certain that if he could not remove the tail, he would soon pass out from the loss of blood, but to remove it would cause immediate massive loss of blood. The pain was too much for the human magician to bear and he accepted that death was the only option. He thought about Stepha and Kirven, his mom and even his father. He also thought of Hoangis. A tear began to form in his eye as much from the stress he was experiencing, the feelings of failure, and the friends he had lost and those he would not see again. He closed his eyes tight.

In one motion, he gathered up all his remaining strength and pushed at the huge creature, but the tail was wet and slick and would not budge. He studied it as best he could and realized that most of the blood was not his own but was the thick brown blood from the bantis. Schram followed the tail up and saw where another spike had pierced the creature's own throat.

Though the bantis was still alive, it probably would not be for long. Using his staff for leverage, he pried upward at the tail, giving the additional torque needed to break the spines free. The armor projections released from both of them, causing each to give a soft screech of pain as the tail struck the floor. Schram rolled away from the bantis just to be certain the creature would not have one last feat of strength, but when he looked back at its glassy, rolled-back eyes, he became aware that this creature's attacks were over. He felt weak from the loss of blood and collapsed back down on all fours. He slowly reached his hand back to feel the depth of his wound. Blood now flowed freely from his back, but the pain had subsided.

He grabbed some cloth from the lining of his armor and tied it tight across his wound. His only hope was to stop the blood flow long enough to recognize a spell he could draw on to save him.

He gripped his staff between both hands and closed his eyes while his mind began shuffling through various enchantments. Gradually, the remaining pain in his back subsided, and his blood stopped falling onto the ground. In time, no scar would even remain.

Schram leaned back with a long sigh and drew a deep breath of relief. He glanced toward the motionless creature, which looked back at him with mixed terror and mercy as it fought to stay alive. Then, his eyes moved toward the orb. It was a shadow of an object, and Schram could sense the evil magic that created the darkness around it. Still, there was a faint, red light which softly showed through the opaque exterior, which seemed to draw Schram toward it. He gathered his strength and pushed himself forward, a slight fear filling him as he slowly approached the object. As he drew to an area within his reach, great powers struck him back, nearly sending him into the bantis' idle body. He closed his eyes and lifted his staff to face the dark object.

The air around them became ignited when the first bolt struck the orb. A brilliant display of colors and light filled the small room as the faint light from within seemed to burst through the shadowy exterior. Swirls of light encircled every inch of the area as the beams danced about, giving an extensive peace the like of which Schram had never felt before. Several streams of the red-and-blue illuminations began to wrap the human in their brilliance, slowly and gently lifting him into the air. He was amazed at the power and the strength he could feel flowing from their contact. He became aware of nothing else in the room other than his own comfort.

A second group of lights and sensations began to encase the bantis, causing its eyes to return to their natural shade, but its ferocity and hatred was no longer present. It turned its head toward the origin of the lights with an ease as if it had never been injured.

Nodding its head twice and then bowing slightly, it moved to stand beside the now-immense brightness of the light.

Already Schram had his eyes locked closed and was unaware of the bantis' movement due to the bright light and intense power filling the room. However, when the explosion hit, although he could not hear or see it, he still was confident in its existence. The flash penetrated his closed eyes with a painful brightness. The air shook the human as if he was standing on ground that had just ripped open and was trying desperately to swallow him. He was near unconsciousness with his only physical thought being focused on holding onto his staff. Suddenly he felt his body being thrown through the air, and all the fingers of brilliant light which had engulfed him were suddenly stripped away to be replaced with a solemn darkness the level of which he had never before believed could exist.

His body continued through various displacements until he began to realize the sensation of ground beneath his feet. The clutches of magic upon him slowly dissipated, and while the light once again could be sensed through his eyelids, he was released. Schram's body did not react to the freedom well. His muscles gave way to the need to hold his body, and he doubled over onto his knees.

Slowly, he lifted his head and opened his eyes to gaze into the wondering eyes of Werner. He followed the canok's black nose down to his black fur and in a distressing voice said, "I failed."

Then, shock struck him again as he realized he still could not hear. His eyes remained on the canok and he could see that he was speaking, and concern showed on his face. However, there was something else different about him and the entire area, but Schram could not focus well enough to digest it. Now he had to inform his friend all that had happened, including his loss of hearing. He concentrated a bit and tried to put forth a telepathic message. *Werner, my friend. I am sorry I failed you and your nation. I will again try to bring back the canoks' pride and unity, but you must also know that I have been struck with a loss of hearing. The battle I fought was intense, and save for luck, my hearing would not have been all I would have lost.*

Werner smiled softly. *Schram Starland of Toopekian humans, the elves of Elvinott, and the canoks of a home out of time, you did not fail anyone. Look to the sky, my friend, and see what wonder you have returned.*

Schram was startled by the clarity of the canok's telepathy but more so by the words he spoke. The human turned his head to the sky to see what he had not noticed was different about the area. The only sun he had ever gazed upon in the canok homeland was the same in appearance as the one which shined over Toopek. However, now their sun was a magical red color, glowing much more softly, and illuminating the entire area with its reddish brilliance. Schram's amazed gaze was interrupted with another passage from the canok beside him.

You see, you have given us back what was stolen so long ago. Our colors will return in time as each accepts the nation back as a whole. Already blacks and whites from all around Troyf have felt the change, and many have since begun their return. I feel deeply saddened at your losses, but if my suspicion is correct, there is one here who may be able to help you. I wish now to say something you will hear again and again for the rest of your days. Thank you, my friend. What you have given this nation can never be returned.

Again Schram was taken by surprise by the statement and by the embrace from Werner which followed. It was an awkward encounter, as a four-legged creature is not properly designed to fit into a human's arms, but Schram could feel that it was important to Werner. Furthermore, if what he said was true, there would be many more such embraces to come.

Their arms fell limp, and without another word, the two turned and started back toward the cave. Several times whites and blacks alike approached him, bidding thanks and appreciation, which gave the weary human a newfound strength. His mind was essentially bombarded with messages from those around, and only after a message from Werner in return did he find a break. The entire situation was one of the proudest of Schram's life, but nothing could match what he felt when Werner led him to a small cave near the one they originally had gone to. In it he saw a large white female canok who had just given birth to a litter of five pups. The young canoks were being cleaned by their mother when they entered, but it was still obvious beneath their wet fur to see the brilliant color they carried. Each small pup was the color of the light in the black orb, which now rested above their nation. Their eyes, nose, coats and tongue were all a bright, peaceful red.

Schram could not muster a comment, but the white female looked up to him; and although she did not speak, her love and happiness was well communicated. Werner added, *All newborns from this day forward will only feel the peace you have given them. From now on, we will know nothing but one nation beneath our red sun.*

With a slight bow from the mother, Schram and Werner continued on to where they had left the others to what Schram felt was days ago. When they entered the cave, Schram saw the same scene he had left before. The beautiful Hawthorne sat to one side while the small group of white canoks remained huddled together across from her. Werner went over and began speaking to the woman softly in an unrecognizable language while Schram remained staring at the others. They all seemed at peace, and several began to show faint signs of pink and red hues appearing in their fur.

One rose and approached to greet Schram in the same embrace as before. His voice sounded like music in Schram's mind. *We have been instructed not to speak at length, but I wished to extend one notion Werner may not have expressed. The one who first brought you to us, that same one whom you have always felt was your greatest friend, would be very proud of you this day.*

Schram's mind locked on his old friend Kirven, and although canoks did not hold to the beliefs of elves in speaking the names of those who had passed, they still respected all other being's beliefs. Schram nodded in return and closed his eyes as he thought about his old friend. *Yes, he would be proud,* he thought to himself. He reached out and stroked the white canok in return.

A hand on his shoulder broke him from his trance, and he swung up in surprise. The soft eyes of Hawthorne greeted him and quickly calmed his racing mind. She reached her delicate hand to the sides of his face and telepathically said, *I understand you cannot hear. I wish you to relax your mind to me. You have only lost your human hearing, but you have a much deeper sense within you, which only needs to be brought out.*

Schram felt a presence within him, which had a captivating sensation about it. While it was part of him, he knew he was as safe as he would ever be. Somehow he had felt it before but was like from a dream. Suddenly, faint whistles and scratches could be heard until her touch and mind released, and he was again alone.

He watched her mouth move, and although the sound struck his senses fiercely at first, he unconsciously adjusted to where it was correct. "Your hearing range will now surpass anything you have experienced before. Do not be shocked or afraid of it. It is a part of you. I have just pulled from deep within your mind."

He nodded, but it was only due to feeling the need to give some response. He was totally consumed with what he was now experiencing, and although he had heard her words clearly, most of their meaning had been lost in his mind. He experimented with what he was now sensing until Werner added, "Please join us now, my friend. We have much to discuss, beginning with our trip to Cindif."

Slayne's Plan

Schram dug into the meal that had been put before him. It was much more food than he needed, but he knew the conversation could grow long and he was famished. He held his staff close to his side, and frequently he even cradled it across his lap, drawing more strength from it at all times. He kept his eyes on those around him but found he focused on the woman more than any other others. To his surprise and often discomfort, she usually returned his gaze with one of her own.

After the meal, which had been filled with only polite conversation, Werner rose and began speaking. "My friends, we have all felt and witnessed the evil growing across the land for the past 200 years. Each in their own way has fought to defeat that evil. However, it is still among us and becoming more powerful with each passing day. We have now been granted our lives back through the incredible strength of our friend, and with our lives comes our powers to again play a major part in finally bringing to an end the raging terror of one mad dragon."

There was a brief pause while everyone adjusted from the shallow conversations of dinner to the deep and intense words the canok now spoke. Schram was quite taken by Werner's abruptness into the discussion, but he was more surprised with Hawthorne's apparent sadness when he mentioned the dragons. The human rose. "I hear your words now and understand the need for action. However, I am at a loss for what choices we now have. The great Anbari, the master of this staff I now hold, spoke of Slayne's new plan. Now you speak of a trip to Cindif, a place I have never heard of even in ancient elven folklore. I have the feeling that you too know what Slayne and his dragon forces are now planning, and if this is the case, what is it we should do to act against it?"

Werner seemed a slight bit surprised by the interjection and its content, but smiled in response nonetheless. "I was not aware that you did not know of Cindif. This lack of knowledge will also explain why you have not anticipated Slayne's next move to acquire the Rift Amulet."

The human stared on blankly. Hawthorne stood and added, almost in defense of Schram, "Really, Werner, there is no way the boy would have known. He is only just shy of twenty-seven years. Nobody has spoken of the amulet in ten times as many years. Most who even know of it believe it to be nothing more than legend. The times of rift travel have long since died."

"I supposed you are right. Even I did not believe in its existence until you convinced me."

"That may be true," replied her soft, musical voice. "But you were also seeking to find answers to your other suspicions. To those, let me only say that in time you, as well as Schram"—she turned to the human who was totally lost in the conversation's meaning—"will come to understand all."

Werner nodded. "Yes, I suppose we shall." Smiling and joining the beautiful woman in her gaze upon Schram, he added, "I am sorry that I spoke ahead of myself."

"You never have to be sorry to me, my friend, but please do explain further. I need to learn about this amulet and what powers it holds for Slayne."

The canok sat back, stretching to get comfortable, giving the impression that a long speech was forthcoming. His eyes were carrying a soft red tint, but for the most part, his body remained engulfed in shadow. However, it did seem that a giant weight had been removed from his back the moment the sun was returned to the land. Werner was one of the only blacks he had ever spoken to, and most definitely the only one which was a friend. Schram did not know for sure what happened to the minds of those canoks who turned to the dark reign, but he had always assumed some great evil twisted their thoughts to strive for those things that canoks normally would hold unimportant. Schram believed that Werner must have faced a constant battle to be able to hold to his old ideals in the midst of this powerful evil. He was truly a strong canok and one to be trusted.

However, now he looked troubled once again and almost seemed to be struggling for the right words. Hawthorne saw his inability to know exactly where to start, and she broke in, saying, "In actuality, the entire situation revolves around the capture of your friend, the maneth who holds the Anbarian hammer."

"You mean Maldor?" asked Schram, now growing worried as his thoughts trailed to his friend.

Werner now leaned forward. "Yes, the maneth is the key. We have had what essentially were spies planted throughout critical areas in Troyf since the day the evil first struck. We knew that the canoks would not be able to fight as any great force, but we would be able to follow all that was occurring in the hope that someday we might return to strike against those who struck us. With each of Slayne's acts, it seemed fairly clear what he was planning. However, when we received word that he had gone to such lengths to recover the hammer, we became worried. There was no reason the weapon would be of any use to him other than stealing something that could potentially be used against him. However, of all the weapons of the ring, the hammer is the weakest, and his own power could defend against it with ease. There is no logic to it." Werner's voice trailed off slightly as he contemplated the words he had said.

Schram stood and with an inquisitive tone, added, "Yes, I many times have questioned the risks he has gone to for it as well. His motives were not clear to me but very deliberate. He wants the hammer. Why is another question."

The canok nodded. "So you see, we became extremely worried that we had misjudged Slayne and began to believe his plan may be more complicated than we originally had anticipated. We could not construct any theory on why he wanted the hammer's power, not until Hawthorne visited us that is." He motioned to the beautiful woman who was locked in a stare with Schram, measuring his response. "She reminded us about one thing our minds had long since forgotten—the Rift Amulet. We had only been concerned with the idea that Slayne wanted the hammer to use its power, never thinking it to be a possible bargaining tool. However, as the legend holds, those who guard the amulet will only allow its use in return for the only thing that was ever stolen from their keep—the Anbarian hammer. How the hammer came into their belongings or how it was stolen has long since been lost in memories longer than mine, but if all else which remains with the tale is true, then it can be the only answer for Slayne's actions. He seeks to gain the Rift Amulet."

Schram's eyes fell slightly as gaps in his knowledge was something he was not accustomed to dealing with any longer. Somehow, in his training, he had learned more than he ever thought a mind could hold; where it came from and where it was stored was unknown to him, but it was always there. However, he had no knowledge of the Rift Amulet or the legend Werner spun. Further, how could Hawthorne know so much? Who was she? His pause was too long, and as he raised his eyes to address the comments, he saw Werner's crooked glance and could feel Hawthorne's stare still locked upon him. In a softer voice, very distant from that which was his norm, he asked, "What power does this amulet hold? In all my training, I have not experienced it in any fashion."

Werner frowned slightly, expecting Schram to be able to shed additional knowledge to the group. Hawthorne used it as a cue to interject. "All space has counter space. By this same meaning, all universes have counter universes. In these, anything that is naturally occurring—meaning the trees, the creatures, the land— each has its parallel somewhere else. Comparatively, those things created by the different creatures of each world—the buildings, tools, armor—find their existence only in that world for which they were created. Therefore, no magic weapon has an opposite somewhere else that can be used against it because all weapons are created, with one exception."

Schram gripped the ordinary-looking tree branch he held by his side. "The staff, there is another staff like this one on another world, and the Rift Amulet can be used to find it."

"That is what we believe," added Hawthorne softly.

Schram's face now showed deep concern. "Does the other staff have greater power?"

Werner motioned toward Hawthorne, and she returned a smile as the canok stepped forward to reenter the discussion. "All questions regarding the possible strengths of those on other worlds are unknown. We are not sure if a second staff truly exists or if all creatures even have counters somewhere else. All we have are legends and theories and a large group of minds searching constantly for answers. However, with the latest information we received, we cannot wait for those answers. We must seek to reach those who guard the amulet without delay."

Schram's concern had not faded when he hesitantly asked, "Who guards the amulet?"

Werner nodded. "We must go to Cindif."

Schram knew there was more because although the canok had not answered the question, only renaming a place Schram had never heard of, he also felt something within his new friend—something he had not felt for a long time. He turned and softly added, "Werner, what is this new information that you feel so strongly about? Why does it mean we must move with such expedience?"

His voice was caring and held much pain. "We believe that Slayne has acquired the hammer. We received word that he has left Draag on a course directly northward."

The human rose with a look of terror now plain on his face. "What word do you have of Maldor?"

Werner did not answer but only bowed his head. Hawthorne rose and moved beside the human, placing her soft hand on his shoulder. Her touch was as soothing as before and her voice could have calmed a storm. "The friend you knew in the maneth has most likely passed. He will be well-accepted by his princess."

Schram felt his knees begin to weaken, then a surging strength flowed through him from the woman's touch. He moved back to retake his seat, allowing Hawthorne to move to rest beside him. He did not speak for several minutes but he was aware that the group was waiting for a response. His voice was tainted with his emotions pushing him down, but he pushed through knowing there were no other options. "When do we leave for"—he paused then added—"I do not know of Cindif."

Hawthorne replied, "It is the land across the North Sea. It does not have the size to compare with Troyf, but life flourishes there like none you have ever seen. It is truly a beautiful place with many mysteries and hidden powers. The Rift Amulet is but one of them."

He looked completely bewildered. "Across the North Sea? I never even considered. How will we cross? I have an excellent ship and a somewhat trustworthy but definitely fearless captain who would be more than willing to attempt the journey, but he and the ship are in the Toopekian harbor, if they are not out stealing from some innocent merchant somewhere."

The canok smiled. "Our method of travel has already been arranged."

"Then do we leave immediately?"

Hawthorne looked briefly at Werner then turned to face Schram. With a care much like that of a mother, she said, "We will leave when you are ready. However, we do know that your human half requires more sleep, and after this night, sleep may become a luxury you will not find. Search your inner self to determine what you need. Only you have the answer."

Schram was surprised by the "human-half" reference but quickly looked past it. He looked toward the group and replied, "I am ready as we speak. Sleep is something I have learned to do without, and with the aid of the staff and all the powers around me, it is now easier for me to do so."

"Then we will be off at once," replied Werner, who seemed pleased with the response. He turned and telepathically said something to the other canoks, which sent them hurriedly out the door.

Hawthorne and Schram began to move toward the door when Schram stopped. "I do have one small problem which remains."

"What is it?" asked the woman.

"I have a group of friends at Elvinott who are waiting for my return to begin a journey to attempt to rescue our friend, the maneth. They must be informed about what has happened and where I am now preparing to go. Further, I fear they have already began a journey to Draag in my absence, as I have felt certain things about them. Are there any canoks who can carry the message to them?"

Both Werner and Hawthorne appeared surprised, but it was the canok who replied. "Our teams are already following two groups, a dwarf and rat and an elf and human woman. Both trails disappeared in the Forgotten Forests where even canoks rarely go. There was a rumor that the two females were seen days after their disappearance on the River Draag again, but their trail could not be confirmed. Most canoks have been clearing all the dragon-army-held forests for several weeks due to your approach here. I assumed you knew of your friends' attempts, or I would have spoken to you sooner."

Schram did fall to his knees this time before Hawthorne could reach him, the pain in his eyes evident to all those around. Schram had felt this already, but now it became real. Hawthorne knelt beside him, but the human did not even recognize her presence. All his thoughts were on his friends, especially the elf he loved like no other. He turned toward the canok. His pain had be replaced with an emotion more closely related to anger. "I cannot go with you now. If it is true that my maneth friend has been overcome by the evil he has been facing, then my companions currently trying to save him are walking into a trap. I had a dream during my approach here that this had occurred, and if everything in that vision is true, then those forces at Draag know of my friend's approach. I must see to the needs of those who rely on me."

A concern struck both their faces. Hawthorne's soft voice carried a deepened tone. "You cannot jeopardize all they fight for because of love. You have given them the weapons they need to survive. Furthermore, their presence at Draag will benefit our cause if we can recover the amulet. Slayne will have no choice but to return, and although they are not strong enough to fight him alone, they can defend against and possibly defeat the dragon lords. Without the dragon lords, the magic controlling the unity of the goblin, troll, and dark dwarf forces will be broken. Slayne will see his power collapsing around him. Then together, we can overtake him. The best help you could be to them now is to prevent Slayne from recovering the amulet. If he does find the other staff, they will all be killed upon his return. We must act now."

Schram seemed to be fighting through the logic of her words, but the tense level of the situation made rationality out of his reach. He shook his head. "No, I leave at once for Draag."

Werner moved to speak as Schram walked out the doorway, but Hawthorne's hand silenced him. "I believe another can make the boy see what he knows to be true."

Schram was moving at a quick pace, almost as if he wanted to escape this place before he changed his mind. Suddenly he stopped when heard a voice he had not heard for some time. *Schram, my son, be strong for me now.*

Schram looked around, but the voice had not been physical. "Mother?"

If you believe that to be the case, then let it be said, though I was never a mother to you. However, I love you like no mother could. I offer you now my advice as I helped you when I could in the past. Trust in the strength of your friends as they trust in you. If you go to them now, help them you could but risk all life in the process. You must be free to follow your own will, but please search your mind to make the choices you know to be correct.

Schram remained motionless for several moments before replying telepathically, *The first time I met Slayne, you told me the necessary words for my friends and I to escape to the Dry Sea of Nakton. I remember your voice, but, who are you?*

There was no reply and Schram knew he was now once again alone. He turned and slowly walked back to the cave where Hawthorne and Werner still stood at the entrance. "Come on, we have a long journey ahead of us, and we must not delay our leave any longer."

Schram walked off without any further explanation or word. Werner and Hawthorne fell in behind him with the canok telepathically speaking to the woman. *I do not understand all that is occurring, but I suspect, as you have said, that in time all will be told.*

Hawthorne showed no expression but replied, *I hope it will, my friend. I hope it will.*

⊙⊙⊙

Stepha fell to her knees, exhausted from the days' occurrences. The dark dwarf leader approached the two girls but spoke only to the elf. "I have just received word that my leader has long since departed on a mission and will not return for some time."

A worried look grew over her face while she relayed the message to Krirtie, who also had dropped to use the break in the most restful way she could. The dwarf waited for her to finish and then continued, his voice still hard and totally devoid of emotion. "This brings me to the problem of what to do with you. Upon further examination, I am sure your weapons are the ones we seek, so killing you is out of the question, at least not until you are put before my leader." Stepha let out a sigh and quickly recapped again for Krirtie, who also breathed slightly deeper; however, both knew a "but" was probably coming next. "I sent word to the lords and expect they should arrive shortly. We will remain here until then." He paused, and then added in a voice which bordered on sympathetic, "Make yourselves as comfortable as you can, but you will be bound to ensure that you do not get any heroic ideas."

Stepha nodded once again and filled the human woman in on the update. The two girls were tied to each other and to nearby trees, but each binding was not overly tight. Stepha believed these dark dwarves to be high in the dragon army ranks and quite civilized because of it. Furthermore, she knew any escape attempt would be a useless gesture at this stage due to the unknown forests they were in and the high amounts of guards throughout it. She even saw towers in the breaks armed with dwarves ruling out flight as a possible answer even if her damaged wing could handle it. She twisted her hands within the ropes and believed the bindings served more as a symbol to behave rather than to tie down.

The girls sat quietly. Though they were now free to speak, they really had nothing to say. Each went over in her mind what she could have done differently, and both only could come to the realization that their plan had been foolish and not well-thought all the way from the beginning. They had gravely underestimated the now-much-stronger dragon armies than when they had been to Draag previously. Since that time, the armies had become much more organized largely due to the fact that the dragons and dragon lords had effectively taken command. Moreover, besides just the goblins, now both trolls and dark dwarves acted unified with the dragon cause. Stepha wondered if all hope was quickly fading for the old life on Troyf. She let her head fall, and Krirtie heard her saddened plea but could do nothing but sit and experience the same burdens.

Time moved slowly as they waited in the forest somewhere near Draag. It was pushing on sunset when two figures approached, causing a stir through the glade. Both girls had been falling in and out of sleep, but now they were awake and anxious about what was occurring. The two newcomers remained a good distance away from where the girls were being held, but Stepha, still with her acute elven sight, was able to see them clearly. Her expression told all as she waited for their approach.

"Well, Stephanatilantilis and Krirtie Wayward, we meet one more time. You know, your reoccurring persistence at causing me problems is becoming quite an annoyance."

"Greetings, King Starland," began Stepha, "but trust that I use the title loosely."

The dragon lord smiled. "Ah, yes, Stepha, charming to the end. Tell me, do you recognize my counterpart?" He raised Krirtie's sword, which he now held and pointed at the second figure, the same human appearance save for a long coiled reptilian tail appearing from his lower back.

They looked, and though the face appeared strikingly familiar, with all the subtle changes that had occurred with his transformation, she could not be sure. Krirtie, however, recognized the individual immediately. "He is William Meyer, once highly respected council member of Toopek and friend to my father."

William smiled. "Yes, Krirtie, I am pleased you remember. Also, let me extend my disgust at your brutal murder of Derik. Your father was always my friend."

The statement was directed to strike Krirtie a blow, but when she killed her father in the mountain elf village, she knew she was giving him what he most wanted. She had freed him from the dragons, and nothing said today would change that. "He is not your friend now. In fact, I suspect he sits with your son overlooking every horrible act you perform and feels nothing but hatred and, to use your word, disgust for what he sees."

"My son?" William's eyes took on an immediate look of surprise and then became fierce once again. "What lies do you now speak?"

Both girls were caught off guard by the response, but not as much as Keith Starland, the other dragon lord. The once King of Toopek frowned and firmly interjected, "There will be no more talk of the past. The future is what we hold. We have the weapons and the two prizes for our emperor. When he returns, we will crush the rebel forces in one stroke."

The strength and hatred in his words sent shivers down Stepha's spine. She glanced at Krirtie and knew the girl would no longer speak what she knew of William Meyer's son. The elf was not familiar with the situation surrounding him, but at her first opportunity, she aimed to find out. They had little to bargain with, but whatever Krirtie had struck on had cut the dragon lord deeply. It was not much, but it was something. Stepha did not feel this was the proper time to pursue the idea, but she was not one to be led into things she did not understand. She tried to pry into the dragon lord's plans. "You talk with large words and threats, but I can see your fear. You know Schram is still out there becoming stronger every day. You will never crush him."

Starland had begun to walk away but quickly turned and faced the elf. Liquid beads of water and lava-like drool fell between his lips, striking the ground with sizzling heat. Both girls watched the display in horror before the dragon lord opened into a deep laugh. "You are but a child in a world of men. Do you not see what your foolish endeavor has done? You have given Schram to us. How can he resist not to come rescue the two women he loves more than any others? You are nothing more than bait for another fool."

Stepha's head dropped while both dragon men continued their taunting laughter as they walked back in the direction they had come. Stepha took notice, however, when Starland stopped laughing abruptly and peered into the trees. He turned back to the girls and added, "Yes, Schram indeed will come." He then started another bellowing laugh before both dragon lords disappeared.

Stepha did not want to believe what he had said, but she knew it was the truth. This whole journey had been a mistake, and now it may have not only cost them their weapons and lives but ended the one chance they had at victory. They had sentenced Schram to be trapped as well.

Her large green eyes were red from the recent tears when the dark dwarf leader returned and untied them without a word spoken. His mood was pleasant, and the elf assumed he was to be well-rewarded for his work. To the elf he said, "We are to lead you through the caverns. When we arrive, you must swallow these." He handed two strange herbs to each woman. "They will cause you to sleep. There are many secrets to Draag you cannot be allowed to see. If you refuse, you will be forcibly dealt with until they are swallowed. Do you understand?"

Stepha nodded, and as they walked at sword tip behind the leader, she replayed the information to the stoic ears of Krirtie. The two dragon lords were no longer in sight, and since nothing had been said to them about remaining quiet, probably due to the leader's good cheer about his forthcoming wealth, the elf decided to seize the opportunity. She whispered, "Who is William Meyer and what is the situation surrounding his son?"

Krirtie glanced at the guards at her back and, seeing no notion from them at the start of conversation, she returned, also in a soft tone, "He is who I said he was, a high council member of Toopek. His son was someone I knew as a child. He was athletic, strong, and well-liked throughout the city. However, when the war started, he watched his father get taken by the globe, just as I did. I then escaped with Schram the following day whereas he stayed behind. When we returned to Toopek, I learned that his son, Billy, had been killed in the town square by a large black dragon. Following that, all the citizens who remained were stuffed into a deep storm shelter until the maneths and elves who fought to regain Toopek freed them. I believe the black dragon was Slayne, and by William's reaction, I do not think he knew his son was dead."

Stepha drew a brief aura of disappointment in the mention of his name, which Krirtie immediately nodded apologetically for. The elf then drew a soft smile and leaned closer to the human woman. "I think you are right, but what use this could be to us, I do not know."

The roaring rapids of the River Draag could be heard thundering above them. Eb-Brown led the way through the long tunnel, followed by Jermys and Fehr and then Dol-Teo bringing up the rear. Brown had instructed the others to remain silent because they never could be sure if any goblin armies would be near the tunnel exit. It was well-hidden, and due to the ferocious nature of the river at this area, the surrounding forest was not heavily patrolled. However, they had in the past run into a few isolated goblin parties, so caution was always observed.

Eb-Brown poked his head through some brush and motioned back for the others to do the same. After a brief moment of inspecting the area, all pulled back into the tunnel to talk.

Brown spoke first, to both of them but mainly facing Jermys. "You two are on your own now. You should not run into too much, if any, resistance approaching from this side, but you never know. Since you are but two individuals, you should hope that you do not. You are well south of the caverns and need to head only northward to come upon a rear entrance. Several trails are well marked, but I would stay off the paths if I were you. There will be a large force waiting at the other entrance of this tunnel if you require a retreat, but we would prefer that you do not give away this route unless your life depends on it. We will also have forces scattered throughout the Forgotten Forests, so if you can make it back across the river, there you will find allies. Last of all, good luck, and may Claudos travel with you."

The two shook hands, and the thought came to Jermys that it was probably the first time a dark dwarf and a mining dwarf had acted as such to each other. Besides the handshake and the leadership through the forest and tunnel, the reference to the dwarven god of travel showed the mining dwarf how similar the two really were. Jermys used the clasped hand to pull Brown forward and engulfed the dark brother in a tight hug. "Thank you for everything, cousin. I will not forget it."

After a similar exchange with Dol-Teo, Jermys motioned to Fehr that they should be off. The rat looked to the two dark dwarves and said, "I don't suppose you want to lay one of those hugs on me, do ya?"

They shook their heads but all could see a small smile curl under their beards. Dol-Teo looked back at both the rat and dwarf. "One thing at a time, rat. One thing at a time."

Fehr nodded, leaned forward, and whispered something to Teo and then, with a quick shuffle, skirted out through the brush.

Jermys smiled at the two and replied, "May Claudos travel with you, my friends." With that, he was off following Fehr's path.

Eb-Brown smiled, and after slapping Teo on the back with a chuckle, the two headed back to their camp.

Jermys caught the rat in moments. "What did you say to him?

"I told that no-good dark dwarf that if I make it out of this alive, I'll bet him two pouches of tobac he can never get my tail again."

Jermys laughed. "*Never* is an awfully long time to a dwarf."

The rat frowned. "It is an understood word."

"Yes, I know, my friend. But your understanding of time may be different." The rat shrugged as Jermys changed his tone. He looked around a bit and then added, "It will be morning soon. Let's get some sleep while we're in this relatively safe part of the forest."

Fehr nodded, and after they searched to find a thick patch of overgrown shrubs and trees to act as additional cover, the two sat down to rest. Fehr was to take first watch, but when he had relaxed for a short spell, he found himself fighting to keep his eyes open. Soon, his breaths became long and deep, displaying the rhythmic sounds of a bandicoot deep into an adventurous dream.

A distant voice broke across the wind, causing Jermys to rise and draw his hatchet in the same motion. He head was groggy, and since it was still before dawn, little could be seen. He surveyed every direction but could not see anything out of the ordinary. Then, he heard and eyed the sleeping rat. With a look of disgust and a few choice words, he turned his head away, frowning ear to ear, and took his position on watch.

The pre-morning air was soothing to the dwarf, and he let the feeling seduce his small frame. The tumbling waves of the rapids could still be heard through the gentle breeze, but from the distance they had taken from it, the sounds gave only a peaceful notion to the area. He stretched his arms out and replaced his ax before retaking his seat.

"Jermys," echoed a soft, faint voice through the air.

The dwarf leaped back to his feet, his face showing a ghostly white fear. He looked back to Fehr, who still remained motionless. The dwarf spun around, searching through the blackness for that which called his name.

"Jermys, are you there?" came the voice again, this time louder and clearer.

The dwarf was reaching a new level of anxiety. Twice now he had heard the voice, a soft female tone carried like music, but there was nobody around to issue it. Sweat began to bead down his face, and then he saw something. It was not anything clear or solid, but simply a discrepancy in the forest. It appeared as if a tiny cloud had fallen from the sky to rest among the trees. The dwarf stared at the space but was helpless even to approach it.

The haze around it began to swirl and change, and suddenly it took the shape of an elf. Then, with another breath from the wind, it swirled to form a beautiful human female. Long light-brown hair danced across soft delicately white skin. However, the shape was only present a moment and even then was partially transparent. "Jermys, I bring a gift from a friend." Then she vanished.

"You stupid ale-bellied river slug, it is your turn to take watch."

Jermys opened his eyes to greet the agitated stare of his counterpart. Sweat still beaded down his cheeks, and he quickly wiped it away as he swung his head over to where he had seen the cloud, or at least had thought he had seen the cloud. However, now only trees stood in their place. He turned back to the grimacing smirk of the rat. "You were asleep as well, troll bait."

Fehr looked stung. "I resent that. I may have dozed for a moment, but no one can sleep long with all your tossing, snoring, and rustling. You make more noise asleep than when you are awake."

His face went flat, and the tips of his ears started to turn red from anger. "Fine, I will take watch now. I doubt I could sleep more anyway."

"Fine," replied Fehr. "Try to stay awake this time."

Quickly he was back to his makeshift bed and in only moments was once again fast asleep. Jermys rose to his feet and paced around their camp area. He was not one to dream, especially a dream such as that. He did not like what had occurred, nor did he find any comfort in this forest that he originally had thought to be relatively safe. The sooner they would be on their way, the better. He looked toward the trees again and, feeling concern, grabbed for his hatchet. However, he nearly dropped it when he felt the lump now present in the helve. He lifted it up to reveal a small, diamond-shaped stone now cast into the wooden handle. The rock appeared to be nothing more than an ordinary piece of granite cut to form a three-dimensional diamond, but it had been placed in the wood as if done by the greatest elven carver. He stared at it, completely lost in what it meant, but certain it was not dark forces at work. His hatchet had many hidden qualities, one of which was to protect itself from evil. This stone, however, only caused the ax to take on a new level of peace. Seemingly soothed by the occurrence, Jermys relaxed and even laid his head down a moment to sleep.

Cindif

Schram stood beside Hawthorne as they looked across the vast expanse of the North Sea. Werner had moved ahead and entered a discussion with the five white canoks, who had moved to sit along the coast, wearing odd expressions. Schram stared questionably at the group, but then his eyes widened with amazement when he saw the surface begin to ripple and break.

At first it appeared that a huge sunken ship had lost its hold to the sea floor and was fighting to regain life above the surface. However, when the object dove, kicking up the huge tail as it descended, it was obvious that this was no manmade edifice but moreover some forgotten creature from the deep. A tremendous spray erupted from what appeared to be a crack in its head as it surfaced a second time. Schram turned to Hawthorne to see the woman was completely captivated by the sight. However, her face was lacking in the surprise and disbelief that was present on his. Hawthorne was focused on the creature like she was witnessing the return of a long lost friend. She began to take a step forward, and without turning her gaze, softly said, "Is it not truly amazing?"

She had moved several steps before Schram even began to form an answer for her question. He quickly realized no response was expected and took several quick paces to catch the woman's stride. Hawthorne did not even acknowledge his presence and only continued her path to join the canoks. The two met the group, and although Schram had many questions, when he saw the woman's calm demeanor and expression, he relaxed a bit and decided to hold his thoughts for now.

Once again, the smooth, almost glasslike surface of the water began to churn and bubble before the enormous deep-blue back of the sea creature emerged for a second time. Another spray fired upward, like the strongest of geysers, allowing the water to catch the breeze and shower those on shore. All smiled and relished in the cool water except Schram, who was too stunned to take notice. He stared blankly back into the huge, brown eyes of the magnificent beast before him.

Hawthorne noticed his gaze and smiled slightly. She placed her hand on the center of his back and softly whispered, "*Physeter catodon.*"

His jaw dropped and he turned down to her. "A physeter?"

A thundering voice burst through his head, cutting him off. The language was common tongue, but its intensity was unmeasured. He was not sure if he would be able to understand all the words, as his natural instincts worked to protect him against the incredible volume. "Who dares call me in this way?"

Werner moved forward. "I do, my old friend."

"You speak with language and mind of a race I have always known to be good. However, when I look upon you now, I only see shades of the creatures I once knew."

"I am Werner, canok and friend to all on Troyf and beyond. The nation you knew so long ago has faced the most powerful and dark evil, and only now has our divided family been able to counter and attack this evil that inflicted us."

"I recognize your heart, canok known as Werner, and I will welcome any relations you would have forthcoming. I am Khaled, leader of the lost colony of physeters"

Werner bowed. "I am pleased to meet you, and I too share your enthusiasm for our long lost relations."

Khaled's eyes narrowed. "Do not misinterpret my statements, one called Werner. My nation has dealt awful blows by those who live on land. Millions of my family were brutally stripped from these waters." Schram's face grew saddened as he listened, but he did not dare interrupt. "I would welcome the canok again as friends because they have never acted, nor do I believe ever would act, against us. We lost contact many years past by your measure. Only now, as I look upon your hardships, do I begin to understand why."

Again Werner nodded. "I too know of the evil and wrongdoings you have faced. Though we were acted on by different forces, perhaps now when we join, all could be made right."

Khaled dove briefly under the water and then resurfaced, wearing an expression that was completely devoid of pleasure. "I do not know to what you are referring, but if it would carry the chance of returning the physeters to the open sea, I will listen. Those with me for many years have been slowly dying. We have many times wished to strike against those who sentenced us to the life we now lead, but our nature would not allow it. However, as I continually watch those around me suffer, my peacefulness is slowly withered away."

"I feel your pain and have for many years." Werner said sadly and then slightly lifted his tone. "The best description I can give is to introduce those with me."

He began to name the whites who had controlled the calling but was cut off by the creature's powerful speech. "I feel the knowledge of those of your nation with you. Their hearts carry the same harmony as yours, the feelings of a family reunited." Khaled turned to look upon Hawthorne. "And you, fair one. I too know of your race and feel your heart. My trust is with you, as it has been since the beginning. I am pleased to once again feel your presence."

"And I yours," she replied softly. "I believed your race lost forever. Whatever magic has kept you alive beneath the sea is truly an act of good. Hopefully that good is about to envelop the world."

Khaled's eyes showed a brief moment of pleasure before he turned to Schram. His voice became hostile and cold, as if it were reaching out to draw the human into the water for one final war of vengeance. "You cannot hide behind the elven mask, human, I feel all that is in you"—he stopped and looked questionably toward

Hawthorne before continuing—"and it is your people who have nearly destroyed us. For over 200 years you were totally unprovoked when time and time again you slaughtered everything we were. I saw hundreds of those around me brutally murdered, filling our waters with our own blood. Any contact we attempted was greeted with spear tip. Had I the strength and ability to be free of the water for even a moment, I would spit on thee with my last breath."

Again the whale glanced toward Hawthorne, but now the woman only stared at Schram. His head had fallen into an adolescent bow but his eyes remained locked to carry his hidden strength. As Werner started to speak on Schram's behalf, the human rose his hand and cut him off. "One known as Khaled, I am not about to insult you with a bland apology for the horrendous hell humans dealt you. Nothing I say in words could ever make up for what has happened. However, I want you to be sure, as I am now king of the human city of Toopek, no further harm will ever come to you and those with you by human hands. As of this day, by my word as Schram, man and elf, the physeters are free to return to the seas. Upon my return all shall be made law and strictly enforced. I realize this is little payment for all that has happened, but hopefully it is a new beginning. Perhaps in time we shall learn to act with one another as friends. I only hope that today you look into my elven half and find the trust you value so dearly. Feel my heart, oh great one, for I feel yours."

Hawthorne smiled while all the canoks turned from the human to Khaled, Werner giving a pleading nod as he did so. The creature spent several minutes doing nothing but staring at the young man and then Hawthorne. Schram was intrigued by the attention the woman was getting, especially since he believed she too had to be at least part human herself, though her beauty exceeded that of any human woman. Khaled turned back to Schram and replied, "It is not your elven half which has earned it, but know that you do have my trust."

Schram bowed his head. "And know that your nation will soon be home again".

"I pray you are right, one known as Schram." He turned back to Werner. "Now tell me, friend. What is it of which you speak?"

The canok was surprised by the address but showed little sign of it in his voice. "A great evil has engulfed our land over the past 200 years. Its fingers have touched every creature on Troyf, whether in recent direct attacks or repercussions of those from the past. However, we have reached an apex where destruction of that evil is within our grasp. One black dragon, who is called Slayne, is at the heart of the progressive darkness. Schram has put fear in his eyes, and the dragon has fled to Cindif to recover the Rift Amulet. If Slayne is successful and the legend about the amulet is true, then the fate of every creature on Troyf could be in jeopardy. However, we can stop him if we can prevent his acquisition of the amulet, but to do that, we must have passage to Cindif at a pace that only the legendary *Physeter catodon* could achieve."

Khaled turned to survey the group, and then his eyes fell back to Werner. "The canoks have throughout time been our friends, and that action in itself will never be forgotten. If there is a chance that we may aid those who live free of the water's boundaries, then we will not hesitate to do so, for we recognize the symbiotic relationship we have. Should those on land not survive, then we shall eventually reach the same fate. There is no other creature in the sea that can move at the pace at which I will carry you, but if that should be faster than the wings of a dragon, I do not know."

Schram stepped forward. "Whatever we have is yours in return. I, and all who face that which we do, thank you, Khaled."

The creature's tone lightened. "If we are successful in our endeavor and the physeters can return to the sea, as you have implied, then all will be considered whole once again."

"It shall be as I have said. You have my word."

"I believe that to be of worth, one called Schram." Khaled moved to rest parallel to the nearest pier. "Now quickly, climb upon my back, for Cindif is a long journey. And if it is true that the dragon called Slayne has already begun his trek, then to waste further time would be foolish."

Werner bid the other canoks farewell and turned to Schram. "They will send word of our plans to those they judge the information pertinent. Those at Toopek, Elvinott, and most likely Feldschlosschen will be made aware of your journey. However, there have been strange reports coming from Antaag, and the situation must be evaluated there before the dwarves are fully trusted."

"Schram and Hawthorne joined the canok climbing onto Khaled's back, and after finding a safe position near the center and a quick enchantment to secure their seats, Schram looked questionably toward the canok. "What reports from Antaag?"

Werner shook his head. "The information is not authentic. King Kapmann has had frequent disappearances, which have suspicious circumstances surrounding them. There has been much talk of civil war throughout the Antaagian dwarves' mines. Whether it will occur or not and what is at its core are both unknown. However, if Kapmann has indeed turned to aid the dragon armies, specifically the dark dwarves, then it is certain that Antaag is in for some violent times. This would put Feldschlosschen in the no-win position of dividing its forces between defending its mines and trying to settle the disputes at Antaag. A divided nation is one which I understand fully, and to say it simply, they would be exposed."

"In any situation, the door would be wide open for a dragon attack," added Schram. "Perhaps Slayne is in a better position than I had thought."

"Yes," replied Hawthorne sadly. "It seems the times continue to get worse even as we make great strides forward." She stroked Werner's coat, which now showed many red streaks piercing through its blackness. The canok only nodded.

They broke through the water at an unbelievable pace, traveling what would take a ship three days in the first five hours. Frequently

Khaled would spray through his blowhole, dousing the group, and after repeated soakings, Schram erected a small magical barrier around the group. They seemed pleased with its effects and now found themselves relishing the amazing new environment they had never witnessed the likes of before. Schram used the first few hours drawing maps of the area, including any small island or rock outbreaking he saw. However, as they moved further into what was becoming an expanse many times the size of all the land he had ever traveled, the landmarks were very few and the usefulness of a map was lost in importance when compared to the stars.

Schram became consumed in thought as he stretched out on the back of the huge creature they were using as transport. His eyes stared across the vast expanse in the sky, and for the first time he began to realize how small and insignificant he really was. He folded the charts he had created and placed them into a pouch, resting his head back to fall across the tip of his staff. His long hair acted as a cushion, and while he lay motionless, his mind focused on his friends. Where were they and were they all right? He thought about Fehr and how pleased the rat would be with the maps he had begun to make. Then he thought of the dwarf, what troubles had infected the mines, and how Jermys would be involved. Next he remembered Krirtie. What had been different about her at Elvinott before he left? And Maldor, his fears were immeasurable. However, most of all he thought about the elf he loved. Was she all right? Suddenly, he leaped to his feet and hollered. "Werner!"

The canok, who was only a couple of paces away, nearly jumped from Khaled's back. With a worried gazed fixed on the human, he asked, "What is it, Schram?"

He saw the fear in his eyes and tried to relax to calm them both. Hawthorne had heard also and moved over beside the canok. "I am sorry to alarm you as such, but I have a question only you can answer."

Both Werner and Hawthorne appeared concerned but remained silent as Schram continued. "I have frequently perceived visions or dreams that were too vivid to be natural. Stepha told me that her father used to have similar visions, and she believed them to be messages sent between magic sources. Is this possible?"

The canok's face was long. "I believe it is, but I speak only from theory. Canoks naturally can use telepathy, but the receiver has to be within what would match a normal voice. Great distances are out of our abilities. However, I believe there is someone who might more be able to aid you." Without speaking further, the canok simply turned to the women next to him.

Her beautiful eyes and hair showed clearly even through the darkness of the night. Her concerned expression had changed slightly but still remained somber. She took a step closer to Schram and reached out her hand to place it on his shoulder. He felt power in her touch but still thought of her as some distant relation to human. He felt something strange within her but did not understand it. It was as if he knew something was there, but it was just out of his reach. However, he did sense something out of place with her, and he believed Werner too must feel it. When she spoke, her voice seemed to cause all suspicions to be cast aside, and a soothing song seduced the human magician. "Tell me, Schram, what brings this question now?"

He stared back toward her, taking her hand in his. "I was thinking about my friends, and I know something that will help them with what they have planned."

"What is this you know?" she asked softly.

"It came to me in a dream, or a vision, or something. It was when I was in Anbari's Dominion. I did not, at the time, know what it meant, but as I was lying here searching the stars, I saw it. I know where at Draag the dragons hide." He reached into one of his pouches and pulled out a long-forgotten artifact. "This diamond stone was given to me by Stepha's father in his life pouch. It is the key to Draag and the mirror room. I must send word to them if it is possible."

Hawthorne did not move or change expressions as she eyed the stone. It was almost as if she had been expecting it to be placed before her. Werner, on the other hand, stepped forward, inspecting the seemingly ordinary diamond rock with utmost scrutiny. Khaled went unnoticed through the conversation but rolled his eyes back to also look upon what Schram held so important.

Hawthorne replied, "It is well within your powers to send the message you wish. However, the forests surrounding Draag—if that is truly where they are—are also very powerful, and whether your message will reach its intended destination is another question. You may believe it does, when it really is received by a source with which you do not wish it to be."

"I must try. Tell me what do I do?"

"You already know, for you have attempted it before."

Schram's jaw dropped. "Who are you, Hawthorne?"

The question was completely out of place, but too many unusual inconsistencies had been occurring to allow it to go on unasked any longer. However, Hawthorne continued from her previous statement, leaving it unanswered just the same. "Take your staff, concentrate every fiber of your knowledge about the person through its power, and when you appear before them, say what you will."

He appeared displeased with her avoidance, but he would have time later to pursue the point, and the immediacy of the problem at hand had to take to precedence. He lifted his staff between both his hands, and as he began to concentrate, he could feel a sudden burst of power surging though him but centered on his fingertips. He felt like a child set free with no restrictions or limitations. He set his consciousness on every conception of Stepha he held within his mind. He saw and felt his environment begin to change, although he was certain his eyes were closed. The cool air blowing across the North Sea changed to the warmth of the southern boundaries of Troyf. He began to see shapes and forms giving him the impression of being in a forest. The trees he envisioned were not definite or crisp but held enough form to place himself somewhere near Draag. They were a darker variety, with twisted and contorted branches, which often appeared to be reaching out to grab those who passed.

Then the picture became blurry, and he began to move, though on Khaled's back he remained motionless to those watching. He was gripping his staff so tight that his knuckles began to crack and bleed. As he floated through the trees, a path began to show beneath him. He concentrated on the path, and almost magically various sounds and shapes began to appear.

Schram looked in horror as two dragon lords, one being his father, sat above Krirtie and Stepha, who appeared well but were bound together to a tree. They were speaking angrily to each other and a slew of dark dwarves looked on, possibly expecting the argument to end in the girl's immediate death. However, as the two lords turned away laughing, it was apparent both girls would be left unharmed, at least for the moment. Schram could use the current commotion to relay his message.

He remembered what Hawthorne had instructed him to do and he drew slightly closer to the girls and began to speak. As the first sound began to form, he felt a sharp pain in his sides and looked down to see the ghostly, almost transparent talons of a large dragon gripped tightly around him. The creature shrieked loud enough to shake the ground, but nobody in the area reacted except Keith Starland, Schram's father and dragon lord. He turned and looked straight toward them and then entered a deep laugh. The next thing Schram knew, he was being pulled through what appeared to be a vast red tube. The dragon was no longer present but its grip was, and Schram was helpless to break free.

He felt himself falling prey to the power which now held him. Pain shot through his wrists as new talons reached and fought to crush his hands and arms. However, he gripped his staff even tighter, knowing that to let go would leave him defenseless against what was trying to capture him. Suddenly there was a dragon screech louder than before, and Schram felt the grip around him loosen.

He pulled his staff close and concentrated on the only thought he believed could help him—Hawthorne.

There was a strange blurring sensation, and when he opened his eyes, he was greeted with nothing but darkness. As his elven sight quickly returned, he saw the outline of Werner standing over the motionless body of the woman. He was on his feet and next to them in only a moment more.

"She is fine," answered the canok to Schram's question his eyes must have asked. "Only exhaustion makes her sleep this moment. I am not exactly sure what took place, but near as I can tell, you owe her your life."

"I believe you are correct, but as with you, I do not understand why or how."

"Two problems," broke in Hawthorne's soft and seemingly tired voice, catching both Schram and Werner by surprise. "First, you must try to make contact when she is asleep or awaiting a message. You can alert her in the same way so she will be prepared for it, but if you only begin to speak, it could cause her to collapse from your presence suddenly entering her mind. This would be detrimental to you both. Second, the forest is enchanted to capture any magic sent into it. Probably after they were captured, it was made stronger in that area. Under normal circumstances, you should be able to break free on your own. You did well to hold true to your staff. It was the only thing which brought you back."

"What happened? All of a sudden the dragon released me?"

Hawthorne tried to show a small smile. "I was with you when you went through space. However, the magic that captured you did not know of my presence. I simply, as you would say, attacked from behind undetected with a simple spell. I had no desire to take on the entire force of the magic with you, only enable you an opportunity to break free. I am pleased to see it worked. Had you not attempted to return that instant, you would have been pulled into that environment as your reality"—she paused then added—"and the grip of the dragon could have been fatal to your mind, and thus to you."

"Do you mean he would have been transported to Draag?" asked Werner.

"Though it has never been achieved before, that is exactly what I mean. I cannot say whether you would have survived it or not."

Schram's face displayed grave worry and concern. "Did any of my messages get through?"

"No, the trap was designed to prevent exactly what you were trying to do. It seems that Slayne's plans are thorough."

There was a long pause while all speculated on their various choices. Each knew that their mission to Cindif to prevent Slayne's acquisition of the Rift Amulet must take precedence, but Schram also knew that without the knowledge he had learned from the diamond stone, his friends would never find their way through the Draag Caverns. Even Jermys, whose dwarven heritage should naturally lead him through any maze of twisting tunnels, in his first experience with Draag, had become confused and lost, only to end up where he had begun. The secret is with the diamond stone and the mirror room. "They must be informed," Schram continued his thought at loud.

Again there was a moment of silence until suddenly the human's expression changed. "If it is possible to capture me and transport me through, as the trap was designed to do, is it also therefore possible to transport the stone through?"

Hawthorne's eyes narrowed. "If the power controlling it and that person to receive it were both strong enough, perhaps then it could be done." She paused briefly then added, "Under normal circumstances, maybe, but Draag is not normal. Its magic would have to be accepting of it. You were going to be pulled through because it was designed to pull you through. It would not be designed to pull the stone through. Furthermore, neither Stepha, Krirtie, or Jermys would be blessed by enough magic to receive such a powerful spell."

Again his eyes fell, but only momentarily until he said, "The Hatchet of Claude. It could receive the stone."

An intrigued look grew across the woman's face. "I don't know. It might work, but it might not. Khaled, have you any knowledge regarding such a procedure?"

The whale-like creature twisted his head slightly, letting his large grey eyes fall back toward the group. His deep voice seemed powerful enough to further disrupt the sea but still landed gently upon their ears. "If the legend regarding the lost hatchet holds truth at its base, then it should prove adequate for such a transfer. However, it will take your combined power to perform it, and possibly that of mine and Werner's, to help guide you back. Further, I would test the area before attempting speech. The elaborate traps could prove too much for all of us if they expect another attempt. They know you were there once, and they now know you had help. It is my guess that Slayne did not anticipate one thing, the one called Hawthorne, to be present. Now that anticipation is present for him."

Hawthorne turned back to Schram. "His words are wise and should be considered as those of one who would know."

Schram nodded. "But then we will try—together."

"Yes, we shall," she replied. Her voice raised slightly. "Khaled, will you require any aid or special contact to join in our endeavor?"

"No," he replied gravely. "Simply instruct the one called Schram to keep his staff against my back. That should be enough to keep us together."

Schram nodded that he understood. Hawthorne added, "We too must stay joined. Your mind and power must get us to them while I remain in both places. However, if there is to be any word spoken, I will be the one to speak them only after I evaluate the enchantment we have entered. If there is any attack upon us, then center your thoughts toward Khaled and Werner and your staff, and they will guide you back. Keep hold on me only if it does not jeopardize your own secured return. Do you understand?"

Again Schram nodded.

"Good," continued Hawthorne as she moved behind him to place both hands in a tight grip around his waist. "Then concentrate every fiber you have on Jermys. If he is asleep when we appear before him, then we will act immediately, as I have discussed. If not, simply follow him watching over his trail. When he sleeps, we will fulfill our plans."

Werner bowed his head in a motion of praise, and Schram closed his eyes while pulling his staff against his body, resting its tip on the immense back of the whale. Each of their eyes became filled with a blank, entranced loneliness before closing tightly.

Schram's environment became cloudy and lost, as it had previously. Rarely could he make out any definite shapes, only seeing strange figures that made no sense, as his mind traveled through space. Gradually, faint light was seen among the clouds. It danced and spun as if it was being tossed like water over hot oil. With one final burst, he appeared to be floating over a roaring river. He surveyed the land on the north side of the rapids but could see no movement. He wanted to ask for what he should do, but as he felt for Hawthorne's hand, he realized he was alone.

With his mind, he moved from over the water to land at the much more conscious-pleasing position of standing on solid ground. As he stood on the embankment, he began to hear the sounds common to a forest under the controls of darkness. With each moment, the sensations were becoming stronger, almost as if he were being pulled into a deeper reality. Suddenly, he heard some stirring from nearby brush, and he about collapsed when his friends, the rat and dwarf, bounded out from a hidden tunnel to leap essentially right through his body. They were joking lightly and seemed to have no idea regarding Schram's presence.

Without delay, the two made their way into some thick brush and began to prepare a makeshift camp to catch some brief rest. It was when Jermys fell asleep that Schram realized he really had no idea what he was supposed to do. *How do you communicate with a hatchet?* he thought as he began to grow nervous and uncomfortable.

Gently, he felt two hands pushing against his sides. He did not need to look back to know Hawthorne was there with him.

Her touch gave him a power and confidence like he had never felt before. Slowly, he approached the sleeping dwarf. Like an angel singing, he heard the wind call out the dwarf's name. "Jermys, Jermys, are you there?"

When the dwarf rose, drawing his hatchet, Schram was struck by the appearance of two dwarves; one who lay sleeping peacefully in the same place as at his first sight, and another who stood hard, staring violently in every direction. However, he was drawn to the more striking oddity adjacent to him—a magnificent dragon with a green body and two large silver wings about twice human size peering back toward the human. It made no motion of attack, only stared with grandeur and excellence. Long moments seemed to pass where nothing was taking place. Schram searched his mind over and over again, and without hesitating further, he removed the diamond-shaped stone he carried and with one motion launched it at the beast before him.

There was a loud scream, and Schram felt two talon-like hands bite into his sides. He tried to turn and face what had grabbed him but did not have the strength to fight the unexpected attack. As his eyes move back toward Hawthorne, they dropped when he saw she was facing the same fate. He cursed himself for letting his guard down but knew their only chance for escape would be the staff and Khaled. He only hoped Hawthorne would be safe with him.

He cleared his mind and focused his power through the staff and Khaled. Immediately, the environment began to melt and reform. Darkness engulfed his mind, and he could feel strong hands trying told hold onto him. He began to be pulled back when with one mighty swipe, like a hand ripping down a sail before a storm, he was back on the North Sea.

He immediately swung his eyes. "Hawthorne!"

"Easy, son, I have her," echoed Khaled's slightly strained voice.

There was a burst of light, as if the air itself had just become charged, and then darkness again engulfed them. Where the energy had been now rested the still body of a woman. Schram ran to her side and placed his arm and staff against her. In moments, her eyes opened to reveal the softness and peace he had always seen carried within them. Her long hair fell against her back and onto that of the whale's as she threw her arms around the young man next to her. "You did well, even better than I would have believed. Your power was so strong." She rubbed one hand along Khaled's back. "Thank you for the guidance, my friend. You were truly my light to see by. I shall not forget."

Khaled's deep voice was filled with pleasure. "No thanks are necessary, for I have longed to be free to use my powers again. If I should die before this morn, what you have given me this night would justify my life. For too long the physeters have lived prisoners in a pocket beneath the sea. From this day on, that will change."

Schram pushed a short bit away from the tight embrace he was sharing but was not ready to completely lose contact either. He kept his hand tightly gripped around hers, letting her magical beauty flow through his body. "Were we successful?" he asked when their eyes fell to each other.

"Were we?" she replied back.

Schram shook his head, not knowing how to reply to her riddle. "Who was the dragon?"

She smiled as if a memory of one deeply loved was just recalled. "When you gave the diamond stone to the young, silver-winged green dragon, it was as if two children, almost brothers, had just realized their identities and began working together. That dragon is known as Cameron, and he is that who is the hatchet."

"The Hatchet of Claude is a dragon?"

Again she smiled. "No, the spirit and magic, which was a dragon, now resides within the hatchet."

Schram still showed disbelief, which was only matched by that of Werner. Both peered blankly back toward Hawthorne, who turned and took Schram's other hand in a tight grip. Rubbing her soft fingers across Schram's Ring of Joining (the ring he and Stepha shares) and the adjacent finger that once wore the Ring of Anbari, she answered, "Just as you are able to call on the powers of Ku carried within the ring, Jermys can call on the powers of Cameron."

Schram's face lightened with a notion of understanding. "Then who is Cameron, and what magic placed his spirit with the hatchet?"

Hawthorne appeared slightly worried but then calmed. "He is one of the sons of Anbari."

Werner's thick red eyebrows lifted while Schram sat frozen. There was pause of unknown but significant length before Schram forced his reply. "Then Anbari has four sons, each who have given their beings to the four weapons of the ring?"

"That is essentially accurate, though more simplistic that I have ever heard it defined."

Schram was somewhat displeased with her answer, wanting to not simply be provided ideas but truly understand the essence of what everything meant. "Please, Hawthorne, explain it to me. I must know more. I must understand."

Hawthorne placed her hand on his cheek and then moved it to his shoulder. "You are so young…" Her words were soft and fell off as she spoke. Then, seeing his expression, she gave a gentle sigh and fell back to rest in a more comfortable position. She began in a gentle voice, "Anbari is a great dragon. Often he has been called by enemy and friend the most powerful creature ever to walk Troyf. However, even with all his abilities, he never wished to rule or control any other creature. It was those around him who had the desires to use him to improve their stature. Ku, Claudos, Slayne, and uncountable others all used Anbari for their own benefits. He was trusting—too trusting—and by the time he realized what was happening, the damage was done. However, he is still wise and very powerful. He used his insight to undo what had been done. The weapons, his sons, even your birth and our trip to Cindif, all were given their initial push from Anbari."

The sun was beginning to break across the horizon and all could see the surprise on the young magician's face. Werner smiled a brief grin as he knew Schram's mind had focused on one statement—

your birth. Hawthorne paused a moment, giving all a chance to digest what they had heard. Schram only sat, staring blankly into space, with his wide green elven/human eyes seemingly locked on nothing but air. The woman was about to continue when Schram broke in. "How do you know all this?"

Her eyes softened. "At a time a long while in the past, a great, powerful, and also much younger silver dragon saved a small girl from a deadly encounter at a time where death was all around. She has remained with him since that day, and with every passing century, has felt nothing but a deeper and deeper love for the one known as Anbari."

There again was a long silence broken unexpectedly by the thundering voice from Khaled. "Anbari is the greatest creature to have ever walked upon Troyf. The physeter carry a heart equal to his own, and if there is ever a time when those in the sea may lend aid to him or those joined with him, then we will be at his call. If not, then I bid thee leave until our paths should cross again, for Cindif is upon us."

His comment snapped Schram and Werner from their trance, but Hawthorne had already risen and moved toward the huge creature's head. She knelt down, and after a moment Khaled closed his eyes and smiled. In a voice so soft it did not appear to be his own, he said, "And I thank you as well, great and most powerful one." He opened his eyes, and after a strange recitation that was foreign even to Schram, a magical bridge formed across the water to reach the shore. It was as Schram's eyes followed its reach that his eyes first caught site of the land before them.

He nearly fell over from the shock of the sight. A huge continent stretched as far as the eyes could see. Thick forests greeted the white sand beaches, and in the distance across the tree line, large purple mountains with white peaks spotted the skies. Schram's face showed only amazement when Werner said, "Il nok fal thalton."

"Aye, friend," replied Schram. "The lost country indeed."

Fehr and Maldor

"Get up, Fehr, you've been asleep all morning. If you had your way, you would enter another hibernation, and I would have to haul your sorry butt all around."

The rat's eyes grew with an appearance of a brain at work. Jermys frowned and added, "Don't even think it, or you will be a doormat in minutes."

Fehr smiled. "Oh, Jermys, you know I don't hibernate anymore. Lately we have had enough excitement to keep even a mining dwarf on his toes"—he paused then added—"but he probably still wouldn't get through his watch without falling asleep."

His laughter grew as he spoke, but when Jermys lifted his hatchet to reveal the diamond-shaped stone lodged in its helve, all noise ceased. "It came to me last night in a dream. I don't think it is evil, or my hatchet would act against it."

"It's not evil," replied the rat as he stared in disbelief. "It's from Schram. I saw it when I was going through his pouches"—he choked then finished—"I mean, when he dropped one of his pouches and I was helping him retrieve it."

"Are you sure it is from Schram?" asked the dwarf, ignoring the follow-up comment.

"Sure I'm sure. If I consider taking something, I always inspect it closely to be certain of its value. In this case, very little value I would guess," he added more to himself as Jermys was totally consumed by the new information.

"That blasted magician, he is always here when we need him." He turned to Fehr, who had begun to lose interest. "Come on. I don't know what it means, but the voice said it was a gift from a friend. Schram must have had a reason to attempt such a feat. I only hope when the time comes, I will know what to do."

Fehr trotted behind the dwarf with an intrigued look growing on his face. "What voice?"

"The voice that gave me the stone," replied Jermys angrily.

"I thought we just determined that Schram gave—" Fehr was silenced with a dwarven hand clasped over his mouth. Jermys lay on the ground next to him trying not to even breathe. The expression on the dwarf's face alone told the rat not to utter a sound. When Fehr blinked that he understood, Jermys removed his hand while both could already hear the voices.

"Run the brush for a raft," hollered a command in the butchered dwarven tongue common to dark brothers. "Lord Starland said there were intruders in the protective barriers. We are to find those responsible and bring them before the lords."

There was an onslaught of acknowledgements, and then the trees erupted with creatures. Most stayed on the paths, but a few more dedicated pushed through the thickest of cover. Jermys and Fehr remained motionless as a troll and dwarf stepped so near as to bend the grass under their feet and have that same grass strike the rat across the face. Fehr took the brunt of the strike without a sound, but when the troll's foot shifted and drove a thorn into his eye, the rat let out a shriek to rival a wounded swine. The troll and dwarf nearly fell over from the shock, which gave Fehr the chance he now deemed necessary. Without a word, he shoved off Jermys, pushing the dwarf deeper into their small brush cavern. Fehr let out another screech as he bounded in front of the troll heading directly toward the thickest cover he could find.

Within moments, the air was laden with arrows all striking in the wake of the rat's little feet. Trolls bounded with their misshapen bodies and swords hacking a furious path through the brush. Hollers were heard from nearly every direction behind Fehr, but their intent was lost in the air. All he was certain of was that he had to get as far from Jermys as he could and hope that the dwarf would not be fool enough to attempt to rescue him. Fehr knew from the beginning he would not be any tremendous help in their plight to free Maldor, but he never dreamed he would cause their capture. *Jermys had to remain free,* he thought, as a arrow struck a tree, grazing his forebrow as it passed.

With that, he veered left and headed for the river. There were fewer voices, and he was certain he could find a place to hide if he could lose the pursuit for even a moment. However, this luxury was one he quickly learned he would not be blessed with when four trolls crashed through some trees immediately at his heels. Fehr ducked through the last thicket quicker than they could manage, but this advantage only left him at the water's edge, trapped between the roughest rapids the river had to offer and perhaps twenty of the dragon army's finest.

Just as the first troll broke through the trees and the first dark dwarf arrow was lifted into flight, Fehr made a silent prayer to the only thing he believed to be god-like—Anbari—and then leaped into the water. He immediately disappeared beneath the surface only to burst through spitting up water several seconds and about a hundred feet later. Again arrows filled the air, including one troll who leaped in after the rat, but as the violent storm of the river roared, both disappeared, presumably never to resurface again.

"That damn rat! If I had half a brain I would have killed him the day we met," Jermys said to himself as he was tearing a path through the thick overgrowth, mumbling as he ran in the opposite direction Fehr had gone. His heart was telling him to turn back and help his friend, but his mind knew better. The only hope Fehr had would be his own natural skills alone. Jermys could do nothing against those numbers and Fehr had given him a chance to escape, though even his chances were low. The entire troll and dwarf force had followed the rat's noisy path toward the river. This left Jermys an opening that he would not have again. However, he was certain they would regroup soon and come to the realization that Fehr was not alone, and soon after, the dwarf's trail would be their focus.

The adrenaline pushed his concerns for his friend from his mind and drove the dwarf forward through some of the most dense ground cover he had ever seen. His priority at hand was to leave as many confusing counter trails as possible to do whatever he could to increase the distance between him and all those trying to locate him. He repeatedly retraced steps and broke branches along different trails to at least make any pursuit stop and question what direction to take. He was no elf, and he longed for Stepha's abilities, but he also took much of what she and Schram had taught him over their past journeys and knew that save him now it could. He knew he was only going to delay the inevitable unless he could construct a different plan. When he heard several shouts and hollers a good distance behind, he instantly slid into a panic state, knowing he was running out of time.

He held up his magical hatchet and stared longingly into the delicate diamond stone now set into its helve. "What would you have me do?" he asked, though there was no one around to answer. Yet, after he said it, the hatchet began to glow, and Jermys's mind calmed and relaxed. It was the most soothing feeling he had ever experienced. Issuing a long sigh, he almost fell to his knees.

Suddenly, his eyes grew wide and a large smile appeared across his lips. Without another moment lost, Jermys turned and ran at a full sprint back toward the pursuit. Their voices were growing louder at a constant rate, and he estimated that they were about 200 feet short of overtaking him. He quickly made several false trails and then examined the nearby trees. Replacing his hatchet and without making the slightest mark on the bark, he jumped up to a low-hanging branch and swung himself up. Within seconds, he was thirty feet off the ground watching the trail below him.

There was too much tree cover to locate the group by sight, but he could hear their shouts. It was then at this brief moment of safety that he realized the appearance of pursuit meant Fehr was dead. A deepened anger grew in his eyes and body, and his muscles became rigid. The appearance of the first troll beneath him caused the dwarf to wipe his eyes and set those emotions aside, for the time. He had to protect himself, or everything he and Fehr had worked for would be for nothing. Right now he was sitting on a large branch above a group of creatures that would as soon slit his throat than drink a pint of ale. The thought made the dwarf thirsty.

A group of ten goblins broke through the brush and joined the dark dwarves and trolls. Immediately the goblins seemed to place themselves as leaders over the entire group, causing the dwarves to draw weapons. After an ensuing exchange of jibes and a brief scuffle, leaving one of each group dead, all seemed to accept a substantiated equality. Jermys rolled his eyes and wondered how this scum even posed a threat, but as he remembered their numbers, he answered his own question.

"You bloody fools," hollered what appeared to be the lead goblin. "Here is his real trail. You have been searching down all his tricks. By the time you get your act together, this dwarf will be to the South Sea."

The thought of the South Sea did not appeal to Jermys, who remained amused at what was taking place below him. Luckily, however, the big goblin had actually found the right trail, so hopefully soon the entire group would be moving on. Assuming all goes as planned, they will trail him to where Jermys turned around and then backtrack a ways before giving up and blaming the others. Most likely that would end in another dispute and more duals to the death. "Maybe if I did this enough, I could make a real dent in their population," he said quietly to himself, smiling at the thought.

With a quiet thump, he landed on the ground and proceeded at a swift pace back to where they had first met the group. However, due to his quick exit, Jermys had lost some of his natural sense of direction. He knew that Fehr had darted out on a path heading upstream to give Jermys the clear shot to the rest of Draag, as they had planned, but now he knew Draag would be heavily guarded and alerted to his presence. Although Dol-Teo had advised avoiding the front face of the caverns because he knew them to be nearly impenetrable, it now appeared to Jermys that surprise at the front would be better than prepared to the rear. Furthermore, he believed Stepha and Krirtie were somewhere in this part of the forest, a comforting thought for the dwarf. He also knew they would not use the rear entrance because they did not know it existed.

Jermys pulled to a violent stop when he heard something out of the ordinary ahead of him—a faint rustling, as if someone was moving with the distinct effort of trying to hide their presence. Jermys drew his hatchet, though in his heart he knew who it was. He stared ahead and watched a large bush begin to slowly sway as if a gentle wind was lightly pushing its branches. However, the air was still, and no breeze was upon him. Slowly, two eyes appeared out of the bush, accompanied by some chanting, which even Jermys did not recognize. Suddenly, out leaped a small goblin, though it was somehow different from the goblins he had seen in the past. This one was unarmed, as far as he could tell, and his language, which he continued after his appearance, was as foreign as any he had heard. Jermys rose his hatchet to throw and realized he could barely move his arm. Just then a fierce pain shot up his leg as an arrow bit through tissue and bone.

Jermys doubled over, striking the ground hard as he was helpless to break his fall. He now recognized the goblin to be a magic user, but what good that knowledge would do him now was unknown. His muscles seemed locked. He was lying, as good as dead, powerless to move or even defend himself against the dark dwarf's laughter pouring across him. Blood was seeping from his wound, but for some reason, the pain was not as intense as he believed it should be. However, by the look in the dark brother's eyes, in a short while there would be little reason to worry about pain. The Hatchet of Claude was humming intensely, but Jermys realized he no longer held it. He cursed in his mind from dropping it. *What would Fehr think now?* he thought, remembering his friend as if he were still with him.

The dark dwarf walked over to where Jermys sat motionless while the goblin became intrigued with the hatchet which rested at his feet. His laughter had subsided slightly as he bent down and forcibly removed the arrow, not concerned in the least with the amount of blood and flesh he brought with it. Jermys winced in pain, but again it was not what it should be. He looked back to his Hatchet and then to the dark brother.

The dark dwarf appeared pleased with his distant cousin's anguish. "I am not the fool the others are, miner. I knew you would double back. You are as predictable as all stupid Feldschlosschen dwarves."

Jermys had begun to retain some mobility, and his disgust showed through his tone. "I can see by looking at the worn spots on the knees of your armor that the pathetic goblin"—the magic user glanced up, supporting a hideous grin—"is the brains behind your actions. You spend all your time kneeling to his authority." He paused then added smugly, "No Feldschlosschen dwarf would ever be servant to a goblin." Jermys filled his dry mouth with saliva and spit across the darkening face of his captor. "Imagine, a dwarf, a servant to a goblin. Yes, you can truly not be called a fool, for that would give you too much intelligence."

The dark dwarf's face was devoid of any emotion except hatred. His eyes formed balls of fire piercing beneath Jermys's skin. After wiping the spit from across his face, he removed his dagger from his side and, drawing a large smile across his face, plunged it into the dwarf's other leg.

This time the pain was profound and concentrated. Jermys tried to consciously calm his mind, but the agony was too intense. He felt his reality begin to melt and blur and knew that in moments, he would be unconscious. The last thing he remembered was a final bellowing laugh from the dark dwarf as he removed the knife and struck the butt across Jermys's face.

"Where are we?" asked Krirtie as she tried to sit up but quickly realized she was firmly tied to the ground.

"I'm not sure," Stepha replied. "Somewhere inside Draag Caverns. The last thing I remember is standing in the rain outside the entrance after taking those awful-tasting herbs."

She shook her head, now also remembering. "Did they carry us or wh—"

"SILENCE!" echoed a dwarven voice through an open doorway. Krirtie did not understand the language, but the message was clear in the tone. "Utter another word and it will be answered with a sword tip!"

The statement was followed by a series of chattering hollers depicting up to a dozen dark dwarves in the room. Both girls remained silent. Stepha signaled with her hand to not speak, knowing Krirtie had not understood the comments, but both girls continued to investigate their surroundings, pointing out various items to each other. The room they were being held in looked identical on the surface to the caverns Stepha had seen before, but there was something different, almost out of place. The walls were of the same jagged rock; however, they were too clean-cut and perfectly shaped. It was as if they were not natural.

Stepha turned her eyes to Krirtie and tried to relay what she was thinking. The look in her face told the elf that she too saw something she did not understand or could not define. Neither Stepha nor Krirtie really knew what had happened to them or even where they were for sure. As near as Stepha could tell, they were not in Draag Caverns, but they were being led to believe they were. Her thoughts were interrupted by footfalls approaching from a separate hallway far on the other side of the room. A dark arched doorway marked the passage, which appeared to be the only entrance or exit other than the adjacent room with the dwarf party inside.

"Greetings, Stephanatilantilis and Krirtie Wayward. I am pleased to see that you made the journey safely."

"You don't know how happy its makes us to please you, Starland, though there is little of that family name left within you now." Krirtie's words were exaggerated and sarcastic, catching both dragon lords and Stepha by surprise.

Dragon Lord Meyer replied, "Those are strong words from a dead girl. Would you not rather plead for your life while you can?" He did not give her time to answer and directed a deep and cold tone at her. "You should not have lied about my son. When you said he was dead, I had a brief period of loss. However, I have been led to understand that his death would have only occurred if he had directly attacked one of those trying to bring a unified peace to the land." He turned to Starland with a smile, then back to the girls, he added, "Further, he is not dead. With magic, I was allowed to see him through Starland's eyes." The once King of Toopek and now most powerful dragon lord smiled a cold, loathsome grin. "He argues even at this moment for the submission of Toopek to the dragon rule. He, much different from you, Krirtie, makes his father proud."

Krirtie's face reddened as each word from Meyer bit through her, but none more than the reference to her father. "You have been brainwashed by your own, Meyer." Her tone was hard and direct. She left no question about it. She paused and remembered what she knew. She had not actually seen his death because she had already fled with Schram and Kirven. However, many had spoken of the brutal unprovoked attack where one boy approached the great, black dragon who had landed in the city. A heartbeat later, the dragon had reduced him to ashes. Krirtie had visited the grave. She knew he was truly dead. The dragon lords had been reduced to using magic against their own. She was outraged and about ready to proclaim fraud when a pain like none she had ever felt before struck her side.

Beams of intense energy were projected from Lord Starland's outstretched hand, striking the helpless girl with an unmeasured brutal force. Stepha screamed as she watched Krirtie's completely secured body wildly convulse against the intense force. Sweat rolled with tears down her cheeks as every vein in her body began to appear through her skin. Blood oozed from several areas where her repeated jolts had allowed the rock floor beneath her to tear at her flesh. With one final burst of energy, all was silent.

Blood slid from her lips, ears, and even her eyes teared with red. Her body lie motionless and to Stepha, it appeared the woman was already dead. She prayed for Krirtie and her baby. Her motionless body coughed slightly, spilling more blood from her lips but giving Stepha a relief she had not felt in a long, long time. Her breathing was inconsistent and broken, but she was alive, at least for now.

Lord Starland stepped toward the girl, striking Stepha with his tail as he moved. The elf flinched a little, but the worry for her friend made the action go nearly unnoticed. He reached where Krirtie lay and leaned over her. "If you speak these lies again, your baby will not be the only thing you lose."

Krirtie was too far beyond consciousness to understand, but Stepha was not as her scream showed. "You knew, you bastard! If it is the last thing I do, I will end your reign of power being the hand at your death."

Starland turned, still wearing his smirk, his eyes depicting his total absence of emotion. "Now, is that how you should speak to your father-in-law?" He ran his finger along her face. "Maybe I should see what Schram has been enjoying all these years."

"Schram spat on you long ago, when he removed you from his family and Toopek, as did I. To him, you are already dead."

"The dragon lord frowned. "Then he will be given a rude awakening when I ride to Toopek to reclaim my city. It is he who is already dead, and I do not speak figuratively. There was a tremor in the barrier around Draag. Only he could have created it, but he was as foolish as always. He painted a trail for me to him. As we speak, that source is being annihilated. Your faith in him is as far-reached as your attempt to save the maneth. Now all of you are mine." He paused, "You will serve me, Stepha. In time you will."

His laughter, combined with that of Meyer's and the party of dark dwarves' who had come to watch, bit Stepha deeper than anything she had experienced before. With one final word before the two lords vanished into the hallway, the ropes binding them magically disappeared. "Take them to the dungeon, Whi-Tead."

The dark dwarf who had captured them in the forest moved out from the group. To Stepha, he said, "Carry the girl. If you cannot, she will be given to the goblins and trolls. My patience has grown thin with you, and I will tolerate nothing more than strict obedience."

She had crawled to her feet but her anger still was clouding her judgment. "What, are you certain enough of your status that you no longer require us? Or is it that you think you can go against the dragon lords without answering to them?"

Whi-Tead wiped the elven blood from the back of his hand before placing a dagger to the fallen elf's throat. "Another word, and your friend is given to the trolls while you watch." With a quick slash of his blade, a large clump of Stepha's hair fell to the ground. He reached down and scooped it up, tying it in a knot around his belt. "I need something to remember you by since never before has anyone ever left the dungeon, alive anyway."

He gave a motion which indicated that if she did not do as he said, his previous threats would hold true. Stepha struggled to her feet and, as gently as she could, lifted the battered woman into her arms. Krirtie's body was completely limp, and she was losing blood at an alarming rate. If she could not stop the bleeding, Stepha knew there would be little chance she would survive; not saying anything for her baby, a subject she found odd that Starland was aware of.

The guards led them through the small adjacent room where a large wooden wheel and a series of pulleys sat at the far side. With a gesture from Whi-Tead, Stepha moved onto a plank, which swayed as she stepped across it. The dark dwarf smiled, allowing a ball of drool to fall between his lips. "Only way in. Only way out."

Stepha said nothing as the other dwarves began to turn the huge wheel. It creaked loudly at first and, as it broke free from its rest, began to turn with surprising ease. The plank rocked back hard, bringing the elf to her knees, nearly dropping Krirtie as she fell. Small jeers and laughter filled their wake as they began to descend.

As they were lowered for what seemed to be an unimaginable distance, Stepha began to hear screams of an intensity beyond any pain and agony thought possible. The voice issuing them was male but sounded as if his vocal cords had been stretched to their limit. It was muffled and rough, but the torture was evident. Three successions took place before they suddenly silenced.

The lift struck ground in a room that had little to no light. Stepha's elven sight helped her but only to locate a doorway, which appeared to have a torch burning in the room beyond it. She glanced back up the rope and knew that the minute she was off it, the lift would immediately be pulled back. Her wings had been injured several times; and although she thought she may be able to fly herself out at some level, she could not do it holding Krirtie's full weight, at least not yet. Despite the issue with stepping off, she knew Krirtie's needs must take precedence and with that, she pushed herself up on her weakened legs and, with the girl still in her arms, began to move away from the lift. As she suspected, it jolted upward, nearly knocking her back over with her first step. She moved to the doorway cautiously, for she could still hear some odd movement occurring inside, the likes of which she could not place. As she slowly peered into the dimly lit room, she nearly dropped the woman at what crossed her eyes.

A small circular room made entirely of rock. Blue blood was scattered across nearly every corner stretching halfway up the wall as if violently sprayed there from some massive explosion. Lying in the center, violently tearing at what essentially was exposed leg bone, was a maneth. When he rolled over in one of the spastic fits Stepha had been hearing on her approach, she saw the outline of one she used to know to be a friend and companion. His free arm swung over, revealing the hand that had transformed around the Hammer of Anbari. The hammer appeared ordinary in every aspect and struck the ground hard as the maneth fought against the illusion.

"MALDOR!" screamed the elf as she laid Krirtie on the rock surface near the entry to the room. The maneth barely appeared to hear, but he did notice enough to look her way. When his eyes met hers, he screamed, his hoarse hollers sounded as if a dead creature had returned to life. He leaped to his feet. How he was standing, Stepha had no idea, but it was apparent that he was only living on pain now. It was also apparent that he had no recollection of her. His hammer swung back and forth in violent slashes, throwing what was left of his body into random stumbles.

Suddenly, he made an unpredictable lunge, which sent him crashing into the elf, sending them both to the ground. Stepha hit and slid on the rock floor, causing a surge of pain through her back. It was then she remembered her wing. With all the occurrences of late, she had forgotten to replace her makeshift bandages on her arrow-damaged wing. When she struck this time, she knew the wing was severely injured.

Maldor swung his hammer as if trying to kill his most hated enemy. However, due to his injuries, confusion, and weakened and panicked state of mind, his strike landed on the rock wall above Stepha's head. She shifted her weight and sent the maneth, who was over twice her size, to the side.

Both jumped back to their feet, their adrenaline allowing them to stand. "Maldor, it is me, Stepha, your old friend. Please hear me." She pleaded as she stared deep into his eyes, and for a moment, she saw the spark she knew from the past. But quickly, it was extinguished, and the terror and hatred once again took precedence. He swung his arm, bringing the attached hammer across as if he was chopping a tree. Slowly he stepped forward, Stepha matching his steps in reverse.

Nothing but fear was etched into his face. His jaw was torn and scratched with enough dried blood left unattended to make his flesh appear to be a sickly blue. Each step exuded enough pain to bring a normal creature to its knees. Yet Maldor pushed onward. What he saw attacking him was not clear. What he had seen over the period of his torture had changed his mind. Now all he saw was pain. Be it strength from the hammer or his own will to live, that power that drove him made Stepha realize that she had no hope of defeating him without killing him, if she could even do that.

She let out a soft scream and sigh as the wind was knocked from her chest as she tripped over a stone. Maldor seemed to thrive on the opportunity, pouncing down to straddle the elf with a speed common to their times together years before. He raised the Anbarian hammer above his head while holding the terrified and exhausted Stepha beneath him. His arm locked upward and Stepha saw cuts and raw flesh across nearly every exposed area of skin. She closed her eyes, knowing the pain he had experienced now controlled his actions. There was nothing she could do.

"Maldor, I forgive you." The elf began to cry through her words. "It is me, Stepha. We came to help you. Krirtie is with me, but she is not well."

The elf opened her eyes as the maneth's broken and cracked and bleeding lips began to tighten, and she knew he was about to strike his final strike. A tear fell from her large eyes and she thought about Schram. The maneth's arm flexed hard, but he simply stared at the woman, frozen, within a moment of taking the elf's life. Sweat appeared on his forebrow beneath his blood-matted mane. His free hand lifted from the elf's throat and moved to touch her face. He fought for several moments but then Stepha saw his mind release, and she knew he was about to give into the pain and strike.

"Stepha, are you here?"

The voice was soft and the words not well spoken, but instantly Maldor turned. The previously unobserved girl was moving slightly, but as he looked at her, Stepha saw a different expression on the big maneth. His eyes held compassion. His love for Krirtie was there, at least for the moment. The fear and terror carried throughout his muscles seemed to have vanished or at least lessened. She thought that if the hammer had not been attached, it would have fallen from his hand. *He recognized Krirtie's voice,* she said to herself.

"Yes, Krirtie, I am here."

"Krirtie?" whispered Maldor's rough voice.

There was a long silence before Stepha added, "Maldor is here, Krirtie. He is with us now."

The girl tried to look up but could not move. "Maldor? Are you truly here?"

The maneth let his arm with the hammer fall to his side and slowly rose, moving over to her. Stepha pushed herself up and went to kneel beside the girl. To Maldor, she said, "Krirtie is not well, and for that matter, neither are you. Do you understand?"

Maldor stared longingly at the elf. "Stepha?"

"Yes, Maldor, we are here," she replied, softly placing her hand on his shoulder. "Now, please lie down, and I will take care of both you and Krirtie."

Trees of Death San-Deene

The group descended onto the magical bridge, Hawthorne and Werner leading the way, followed by Schram. He was the only one who had not had any parting words with Khaled, for what he wished to say he preferred to say for Khaled's ears only to hear.

"Khaled, my new friend. As you know, my companions and I are traveling in unfriendly lands, which put us on a timetable out of our control. I wish you and those like you to be free in the waters, but I fear if you begin making your presence known before I return, greedy sea dogs with distant memories may see your race as a quick profit, as it was in the past. It is my will that you return to the seas peacefully, and although I am more than positive that the ability to crush an attacking human ship is well within your abilities, I sense you would as soon perish rather than bring about death as such, even in defense. Regardless, I cannot allow either situation to occur."

"I understand, one known as Schram. I will wait for your word before I, as you say, make my presence known."

Schram smiled. "No, there is another way. Go alone to the Toopekian waters. If you run into obstacles, do your best to get by them, harming few. Seek out the one called Geoff, a maneth. He has taken over ruling Toopek. He feels as I do and his word is law. As I say it now, soon you will be free again."

"Thank you, young Schram. I will do as you ask, and if all goes well, perhaps my assistance here you will desire."

"That would be very much appreciated, Khaled, though how much help you would be, being confined to the water, is unclear. However, safe passage back sounds appealing."

Khaled laughed, his deep voice carrying over the water. "No, a ride back is not what you may require from me, though I would be pleased if that were all." With a large flap of his tail, the whale turned and disappeared beneath the surface.

Schram glanced down to see that he was hovering above the tossing waves on a bridge that seemed fastened to the air. As he took a step toward the shore, the bridge behind gradually faded. He shook his head, with a smile, and then proceeded to join the others on the white sand beach of Cindif.

"Where to now?" he asked when he greeted the others.

Hawthorne replied, "Did you see the mountains as we approached?" He nodded as she continued. "If we follow the legend, we need to travel between the two largest peeks that rise up from the center of the chain. Beyond them, there should be a crystal pool known as Ice Lake where we will find a path that leads directly to the Realm of Darkness."

"Between the peaks, across the Ice Lake, and down the path to the Realm of Darkness—seems like something from Dora."

"What's Dora?"

"Nothing."

Schram then added, "The Realm of Darkness? Are you saying the guardians of the passage to the afterlife are who control the Rift Amulet?"

"Would it have made a difference if I told you that at the start?"

He shrugged knowing he did not actually answer the question but also knowing it would not have made a difference.

There was a pause before Werner asked, "Do you know how long of a journey it will be?"

She turned to the canok. "Like you, friend, I have never been here before, and we are following only a legend. I would guess two days by foot. I was hoping we might find another answer."

Schram wanted to ask what other answer she might be referring to, but after thinking about it a moment, he decided he would keep quiet. The fact that an enormous *Physeter catodon* from a wrinkle in the past took them an unknown distance overnight was enough to keep his mind occupied for a while. Without another word, Hawthorne gave a motion, and behind Werner's lead, she and Schram followed.

The air flowing off the water was cool and as fresh as any Schram had ever breathed. All too quickly they seemed to run out of clear land, and a thick forest opened its arms to invite them in. He took one look back across the water before descending into the trees, hoping that maybe the peace he felt at that moment may be carried on throughout their journey. However, in what seemed to be only moments, they were trudging through marshy wetlands that sucked their feet to the ground, making each step require added strength. The sun, which had shown brilliantly on the beach, was now absent, totally eclipsed by the tall tree cover. Schram even believed it to be raining due to the constant dew drips that fell from the leaves. The humidity drove beads of sweat down their faces, making Werner's thick red coat turn almost maroon and matted. Hawthorne seemed least affected by the marshy ground, but even she was showing the wear of the hot, heavy air.

They continued for the better part of a day before they decided to rest. Schram knelt down between the other two and spoke the first words since the beach. "It occurred to me a ways back, we have no provisions for food."

Hawthorne leaned forward. "I will not require anything for some time. I can gain enough nourishment from the vegetation until we are in a better area to gain food."

"Catl lac nuf," said Werner. Suddenly a strange haze formed on his back, which twisted the space into an array of colors before ending as a small pack. "I brought some food along to keep us going as well. Once we clear the marsh forest, there will be food available to us."

Schram was shocked by the appearance of the hidden pack but was more glad to have a bite of food. He was intrigued by the magic and wanted to inquire about it but knew this was not the time for such discussions. He also was caught by Werner's knowledge that they would be leaving the marsh area and further, that he knew that where they arrived to would be better and contain an abundance of food. Both thoughts held his mind while he reveled in his first few bites.

The three ate with relatively light conversation, speaking mainly about the legend of the Rift Amulet and how much of it they believed to be true. Basically, Schram learned nothing that he did not already know except about what they would encounter. The marsh forest would gradually become dryer and, at some point, the trees would thin, and they would reach the first mountains. After that, it was basic mountain traveling. They only hoped they would be able to determine the location of the two peeks without going too far into the mountains. Yet, they would cross that bridge when they came to it.

"Come on," said Werner. "We should be on our way."

"Sounds good, my friend," replied the human. I think we will make better time now as the marsh is not as thick and the tree line appears to have better pathways through it."

"I agree," added Hawthorne. "We should travel as best we can and gain any time possible."

The three proceeded forward, and as Hawthorne and Werner entered a conversation in the front, Schram held the rear and simply let his mind concentrate on his journey. He gripped his staff, and it provided some level of comfort that he still did not always understand. As he thought, strange and obscure visions came to his mind. He saw large dragons of every color and size roaming freely across open prairies and mountains, creatures from dwarves to minoks all sharing the same lands to live on, and human villages completely saturated with all forms of life. Then, as quickly as it had started, the vision changed. The land became desolate, almost desert-like. Every race of creatures lived as vagabonds, robbing and vandalizing other races and themselves. Several dragons could be seen soaring above the barren wastelands, but their disunion with the rest of the creatures made them appear foreigners to this world. Then Schram saw one dragon, large, green, and immaculate. She was female and alone. A moment later, she held a young blue in her arms. Suddenly his mind cleared, and all he saw was brilliant white light, which slowly faded into a dense forest.

"Schram, did you hear me?" repeated Werner.

He looked over toward the canok. "No, I am sorry. My mind had wandered."

Werner replied, "I said, 'Hawthorne says that someone is tracking us. She has moved ahead to check for a possible ambush.'"

Schram was instantly alert and ready. "I will slow my pace and see if I can get a glimpse of who is in our wake."

"No, Hawthorne wishes us to stay together. These forests are unknown to all of us, and we should not become too widespread. We will wait here for her return."

Schram was not pleased with the decision but saw the wisdom in it. He moved to stand beside Werner and asked, "Do you ever have visions of the past, or possibly the future? Visions in your mind as clear as if you were standing there as part of them."

"What brings this question, my friend?"

Schram looked down at the canok, surprised again by his response, but quickly realized how out of place his question was. "I am sorry. It is just that lately I have seen things in my mind, things which do not make sense and even contradict themselves at times."

Werner shook his head. "From the little I understand of your life, you have a gift which will take a lifetime to learn. I have always believed that a mind takes things in as soon as it is capable. In your case, I believe it is the opposite. Your mind lets knowledge out as soon as you are capable. Do you understand?"

"Yes, but there is so much in my mind I do not understand."

"Good, because there is very little I understand." He smiled and paused before continuing. "If you have questions about the magic you possess, Hawthorne is the one you should turn to for answers."

"Who is she, Werner?"

He shook his head. "You know as much as I do. To answer that question, it is up to Hawthorne to say." He paused then offered, "She arrived at my homeland only days before you. Her magic, much like yours, is totally protected, or maybe a better word is "hidden," from my understanding. When I look at her, I sense things I have never felt before in a human. My heart tells me two things: First, she is someone to be trusted, and second, her presence will have a tremendous bearing on the outcome of our war against Slayne."

Schram nodded, but all questions left unanswered in his mind showed in a strained expression across his face. Werner rose to his feet. "Do not worry yourself about such matters now, my friend. One thing I am certain of is that in time, you will understand all."

Schram stroked his thick red coat. "Thank you, Werner. Your words remind me of a friend from the past."

The canok smiled and walked to the path Hawthorne had followed. "She is returning."

A moment later, she burst through the trees, carrying a small hooded figure in her arms. She dropped the creature on the ground in the center of the clearing, causing its hood to be knocked off as it landed.

Once again Schram was speechless. As well traveled as he was, he had always believed that there were few things he had not seen. However, from gar to whale, this journey had never ceased to amaze him. Now, once again, a creature the likes of which developed in a nightmare sat motionless in front of him. It had what appeared to be only one eye, but its two long tentacles could have some optical activity. Set deep in its black, hair-covered face were two flat holes, most probably for scent. Its mouth was made up of hundreds of short hair-like projections functioning as tiny arms to pull food in. However, it was the rest of the body which Schram was more captivated by. Its structure was hidden under a robe, but little was left to the imagination. It appeared to be a large ball with approximately twelve thin, sticklike legs protruding from it. There were six on each side, which extended up above its head and then down to the rest on the ground. It also appeared to have incredible rejuvenating abilities, as one of its legs was severed as Hawthorne dropped it, only to be replaced almost immediately. Schram's eyes froze on the creature, making him not able to speak or move as he stared.

Hawthorne asked, "What interest have you in us?"

The creature's tentacles swung to the woman, its one eye pivoting around like it was on a swivel. When Schram took a closer look, he saw it could move its head completely around its body, enabling the creature to see all directions without moving. It stared at Hawthorne, not issuing any verbal words but acting as if it had understood hers.

She tilted her head in return. "I assure you we are not here as enemies. I am Hawthorne, and these are my friends, Werner and Schram. We are traveling to Ice Lake and would like to know the quickest route."

The creature cringed, cowering back. Schram glanced at Werner to see if he knew what was happening, but by his look, he appeared as lost as the human. Further time passed while no words were spoken except for some unspoken ones that seemed to be carried through the creature's actions. Hawthorne was the only one who understood and the only one who provided answers to the creature's questions.

After a short time, there seemed to be a break in the conversation, or whatever it was that Hawthorne and the creature were involved in. She smiled pleasantly and then entered in what appeared to be a strange greeting ritual. She stepped forward, and one by one took the creature's hands—or legs—in hers. Schram and Werner were both quite taken by the intensely passionate exchange but more surprised when Hawthorne parted and motioned to them to do the same.

Werner stepped forward as best as his four legs would allow, and the look across his face and in his eyes left Schram speechless and amazed. When the canok finished, all eyes fell toward the human.

Schram moved forward with as much confidence as he could muster; his arms nearly shaking, however, in anticipation and wonder. As his fingers made contact, his mind was bombarded with a flood of knowledge. However, it was not knowledge of any world of lifetime. It was simply a language. One moment he had no idea what it was, and the next, all was perfectly clear.

"I wish you luck on your journey, Schram of Toopek. I am Kuen, and I am pleased to make your acquaintance."

Schram replied a proper return, though he had no idea how he had done it. The words came as easily as his common tongue. The creature laughed slightly and then scurried off with a truly remarkable quickness. Schram turned to the others. "I do not have a clue what just took place, but I am truly amazed."

Werner added, "Aye, the same can be said for me. Never have I encountered one so adept at opening their mind but transferring only certain information. I felt a new great knowledge nearly within my grasp but just held out of reach; enough for me to know they are greater than I, but not allowing me to see exactly how much."

Hawthorne smiled. "You are correct, Werner. The spydigs do carry a great knowledge, but that is their only saving grace. They trust nobody who does not speak their language, and to know their language, one must be taught it. The only way to be taught is how we just were, through direct contact. However, to touch one who does not wish to be touched or to hold evil intensions to a spydig within your mind means death to most creatures. We were fortunate."

"How were you able to capture it?" Schram asked.

She smiled. "Dragons are impervious to their deadly touch. Anbari prepared me for what to expect should we encounter a colony. If he had not, in less than a mile, we would have entered a thick outcropping of trees, which we never would have exited from."

Both Werner and Schram glanced at each other, with the canok stepping forward. "Did you learn anything else about our quest?

She nodded. "Yes, and it is not all pleasant, beginning with the fact that we must continue as we talk." She turned and headed out of the glade on a course perpendicular to their previous direction. Schram and Werner fell in close behind, still listening to what she was saying. "It seems we are well south of Ice Lake, and traveling through the mountains would add several days to our journey. If we move parallel to the mountain chain for only a short while, then we can follow good trails that will cut between the mountains, leading right to the lake. I did not inform Kuen that our true destination was the Realm of Darkness, and if we should encounter any more creatures as such, I think we should continue on those lines. The realm is not a place the inhabitants here wish disturbed. I believe it would be detrimental to our cause to inform them of this."

Both nodded that they agreed and would oblige, but Werner still appeared concerned. "From what you have said, this is a much easier and shorter passage to take. What then is not pleasant, to use your words from earlier?"

"That is something I cannot answer for certain. Kuen was vague about it, but it was obvious that the topic was extremely sensitive to him. It seems that the area of the forest we are about to enter stretching all the way into the mountains has recently become what Kuen called the Trees of Death. Any creature that enters, never is heard from again. Over one-third of the spydigs have mysteriously vanished somewhere within its boundaries. They believe that a displeased god has brought an evil hand down from the Realm of Darkness and poisoned the land. They no longer even approach the forest, preferring to travel around its borders."

Schram's voice cracked a bit. "How wide is it?" "According to Kuen, his only word describing its length was vast. The trail of bodies has yet to definitely establish firm borders."

He replied more strongly now. "Am I then to believe we are going to pass through some of it?"

Hawthorne stopped and faced the two. "No, we are going to dissect its heart."

There was a short pause, which everyone felt, until Werner issued, "How long until we enter?"

Hawthorne turned back and continued on her pace as before. "At this rate, I believe we should reach it by nightfall."

Nobody added anything further, but all their minds were thinking the same thing—*What better time to reach something known as Trees of Death than at nightfall?*

<hr>

The sky thundered, sending sheets of water across all of Draag. The water splashing off his face woke Jermys to greet the barrage of pain he now felt. He did not move as his memory of the past events slowly filtered back into his mind. As near as he could tell, he was somewhere outside the caverns. Rain was falling profusely and, by the looks of the accumulation around him, had been doing so for some time. It was dark so he assumed whoever held him had stopped for the night. His legs were both well dressed, but it did little to hinder the pain he was feeling in them and in his head. He was certain he must have a lump the size of Fehr growing out of his forebrow, but as his hands were tightly bound to a tree, he was helpless to inspect it directly. Finally, he realized all his weapons, but most importantly the Hatchet of Claude, were gone.

A helpless feeling began to grow inside him, reaching its apex as his mind turned to the memory of his friend. *Surely Fehr was captured or killed,* he thought, and to himself he said, "For what? So I could be outsmarted by a fool dark dwarf and spell-weaving goblin. If it is the last thing I do, I will make that damn rat rue the day he ever got captured." He struggled with his bindings but became quickly aware that they were not of natural origin. Most likely some magical restraints, which only Schram might be able to crack. He let out a soft sigh, which drew the attention of a previously unseen dwarven guard.

"Ah, awake at last, miner. I have been waiting for you to stir."

Jermys frowned, "You can take your—" With a punishing thump again from the butt of his dagger, the dark dwarf knocked Jermys unconscious.

An unknown amount of time passed before he woke again. All he was certain of was that it was morning and his head throbbed. He felt worst than if he had drank two barrels of the strongest dwarven ale the night before. As he sat up, more pain shot through his body. Looking around, he saw he was now in a camp of about ten dwarves. The one who slugged him twice was on the far side of a large clearing, discussing something with a dwarf decked out in well-polished black armor bearing a dragon's head on the breastplate. As he gazed across the camp, he realized that all the dwarves, with the exception of the one who captured him, wore the same dragon head insignia on their armor. It was a new symbol, which made Jermys believe the dragon armies were becoming more unified.

He fought against his bindings, which this time did feel to be of real rope as the twine bit into his flesh as he struggled. Despite his grumbling and displeasure, none of the dwarves seemed to give him a second look. Perhaps they were certain he could not escape, or perhaps they knew even if he did, there would be no place for him to go, a fact he was beginning to realize firsthand. Whichever the case, he decided that he would let the dwarves make the next move. He would have to escape sometime regardless. If they took him under guard into Draag, one of his problems would already be solved. Then it would simply be a matter of breaking free. However, if he escaped now, he would still have to find his way into Draag.

Jermys leaned back, proud of his evaluation of the situation. He made a few more grunts and sighs to get the dwarves' attention, but once again they seemed not to care. His eyes fell back on the dwarf who had captured him. The goblin had joined his side and together they were both receiving two large sacks from the dark dwarf leader. With that, they turned to leave. The dwarf took one glance back toward Jermys and, seeing him awake, laughed and made a quick jester with his free hand, which any dwarf, whether miner or dark brother, knew meant only one thing. Jermys cringed and spit in the air, bringing further taunts from the dark dwarf before he disappeared in the trees behind the goblin.

The dark dwarf leader, who had handed the two the sacks, walked over toward Jermys when he noticed him awake. "I am San-Deene. I will have food brought over, as well as new dressings for your injuries. If you are well enough, I would prefer to leave by midday, but we will put your needs first for now."

Jermys gave a suspicious grin, cracking some of his dried blood from his cheek. "You must be a truly sad case to banter me so. If I could spit my last breath on thee, I would."

"Relax, dwarf. Though we are not friends, I hold to the belief that we are kin, no matter how distant. There will be no more beating, at least from this party."

He held his stare. "If you speak the truth, then I thank you. I am Jermys Ironshield of Feldschlosschen."

"Do not misinterpret my words, Jermys Ironshield. If you attempt any escape, you will be dealt with severely. Mark my words well, for you are still a prisoner to Draag, and whether you ever will see Feldschlosschen again is no longer your choice to make."

Jermys nodded that he understood, and San-Deene turned, issuing several orders to nearby dwarves. Moments later, guards returned with food and new cloth for bandages. They cut his bindings and when he reached his arms forward, shifting the weight under his legs, Jermys really experienced pain in its most primal form. Immediately the movement caused a new outburst of bleeding from both legs. He removed the blood-soaked rags that had been in place for an unknown amount of time to reveal two wounds, both pus-filled and green, secreting both blood and moisture. One of the guards turned away, either from the sight or the smell. Regardless, Jermys knew that without a healer's aid, his legs would have to be severed to keep the infection from spreading.

The commotion within the guards brought San-Deene back to the group. He glanced at the wounds only briefly and then back to Jermys, the mining dwarf's eyes showing fear for perhaps the first time in his life.

"I am sorry. I had no idea the wounds were as such. If I had, I would have changed the dressing myself as soon as I arrived."

Jermys said nothing and only looked on in horror. The pain he was feeling no longer occurred in his legs as much as his heart. A dwarf without legs was like a flyer without wings, a part of their life was gone. A dwarf's heritage took him to explore, mine, and live their extended life for every minute. The thought of ending it unable to do so and as a prisoner of the dragons turned his stomach.

San-Deene ordered the guards away and knelt down next to the dwarf who, for over 200 years, had cried only once—in the wake of his brother's death. But now he found himself fighting back the tears. The dark dwarf leaned forward. "I am truly sorry, Jermys, but we have no healers. If you wish to live, we must remove your legs."

Jermys felt his head beginning to spin and let his body fall back to lie flat on the ground. His thoughts went to his friends and his feelings of failure to them. He cringed when he heard the order from Deene. There was some shuffling of dwarves and then he heard two approach.

Deene's voice carried a sympathy he knew he would not have duplicated if the situation was reversed. For all his life, he had hated the DDs, and now in the last week he had seen a whole new side of the race, which his heritage was actually closest to. A deepened shame filled his mind. The dark dwarf said, "If you wish, I will strike your heart rather than your legs?"

Jermys looked up and replied sternly. "No, by approving as such I would be accepting suicide disguised in another's hand. Be that no different to me, and not an option."

"I understand," Deene replied. He handed him a bottle. "This is mathol taken straight off the surface of the ale barrels. It will help the pain."

Jermys took the bottle, but his mind had become focused on his last comment. He began to say something then refrained. Deene saw his discomfort and asked, "What, a mining dwarf that refuses a bit of spirits?"

A light laughter ensued from the surrounding guards but was quickly extinguished with the situation. Jermys, however, could not let the comment go unanswered. He opened the bottle and downed half of it in one gulp, a feat which would make most heave within moments. Jermys bit hard, concentrating on the pain in his legs to help ignore his trembling belly. With a large smile in its wake, he issued a deep and proud belch, bringing a certain nod of approval from the dwarven guard.

He cleared his throat and replied, "I would never insult such a kind host by refusing his drink." Again there was laughter, which even Jermys offered a smile toward.

It was probably the most ironic situation imaginable. A mining dwarf facing death needing to impress a group of dark dwarves holding him prisoner by drinking unsurpassable amounts of pure mathol. However, if serving no other purpose, it gave Jermys the confidence to ask for something he knew would be a futile suggestion. Not even dark dwarves would do it.

"Before removing my legs, will you please return the Hatchet of Claude to me? I will not attempt escape but it has guarded my well-being in the past. I believe it has healing within it."

The laughter stopped abruptly, and the two guards nearby even drew their weapons. San-Deene regarded Jermys with speculation but did not show it as much in his speech. "We have heard rumors of the hatchet's return but know nothing about its location, or being part of your possessions. Do not try to trick us, Jermys Ironshield, for we will only leave you here to die if that is the case."

Jermys was taken by the response, but as the mathol began to take effect, his rose-colored cheeks were all that this expression spoke of. His words, however becoming choppy, did get their point across. "That fool magic goblin kept it from you, aye. Stole it from me and hid it from you. He..."

Jermys continued into a rambling stupor, but San-Deene had heard all he needed to. He relayed orders, sending three of the dwarves out to bring back the dark dwarf who had captured Jermys and kill the goblin spell weaver on sight. He turned back to Jermys, who was still mumbling. "If I find out you do not speak the truth, my honor means I must kill you, but I don't suppose you find that altogether displeasing."

Jermys still comprehended enough to shed his disapproval of the idea. Dwarves, like all creatures who live through centuries, value life above all else. Although losing his legs may end the life his mind wants to live, he would choose that over losing his life in every situation. San-Deene nodded that he understood and left the dwarf to be alone.

The day seemed to crawl by. Jermys sat and could almost watch the condition of his legs deteriorate. It was clear that blood was no longer circulating to his feet, as their normal color had faded to a pale blue and their size had noticeably changed. There was mild talk from the remaining dark dwarves but none mentioned Jermys except by gestures with their eyes. Jermys was no longer bound, though no escape could take place anyway. The lack of binding was simply to allow him to sit as comfortably as possible.

Blood no longer flowed from the wounds. It had been replaced by massive amounts of a green slimy substance with an almost jelly-like consistency. He also felt no pain. In fact, all feelings in his legs had vanished. Jermys made no sounds of agony or pleads for help. He only lay motionless, having nothing left but to try to remain sane.

It was late in the afternoon when San-Deene rose and walked over to the nearly unconscious dwarf. "There has been no word from my guards. If we do not act now, it will be too late."

Jermys made no comment that showing understanding, and only took what was left of the bottle of mathol in one additional swallow.

San-Deene waved two guards over, and as one held the dwarf down at the shoulders, the other removed his ax. Its blade glistened in the evening light; and when he lifted it into the air, Jermys thought he saw a star bounce off its razored edge. That was his last memory before falling unconscious to the most intense pain of his life.

He was unsure how long he had been out, but when he woke, he saw nearly a half dozen empty mathol bottles and enough blood-soaked rags to change the color of a river. The sun had fallen, and torches provided the only light. He could not feel any pain in his legs but his upper thighs surged in an almost convulsive torture. His eyes teared under the anguish to join the sweat which beaded down his face. Jermys looked up from his demise to greet the stare of San-Deene sitting next to him.

The dark dwarf tried to force a smile. "I am pleased to see you are awake, or even alive for that matter. I have been worried."

Jermys attempted to sit up, but the pain was too intense, and his movement only caused the bleeding to begin again. "Have you been here the entire night?"

I have. We could not stop the bleeding. The cut was clean, but I never realized how much it would still bleed. You lost more blood in the first half of the night than I knew was in your body."

Jermys showed despair, and his voice was weak. "How long?"

"Just through nightfall. It will be dawn shortly."

"Did your scouts return?" He began to ask more, but a fit of coughing bringing blood up from his belly cut his words short.

"No, there has been no word yet. You rest now. We will not leave until I learn if what you claim is true, regardless of what the high command demand of me."

His final statement fell on deaf ears as Jermys had already fallen back unconscious. The dark brother shook his head and to himself added, "you are the toughest miner I have ever seen."

He awoke a second time to a mass of commotion occurring nearby. He was groggy and his vision blurred, but he was certain he saw the goblin spell weaver's body and its dark dwarf accomplice held at sword tip by San-Deene. There was some angry words being shouted back and forth, which were not understood by Jermys, but ended in two dwarves tearing cloaks from the dead goblin. A hush ensued as one of the dwarves removed and lifted the Hatchet of Claude into the air. San-Deene turned his attention from his new prisoner to behold the legendary hatchet. Taking the prize from his guard, a cheer echoed throughout the glade. He issued a final statement to one of the guards who quickly moved over and, with one swing, beheaded the dark dwarf who had originally captured Jermys. He nodded in some deep-held pleasure when he saw the body go limp.

San-Deene held the hatchet high, further enticing those around him to cheer greater than if they had just won a war. He then turned and approached Jermys, his camp falling in a semicircle behind him. "It seems you have spoken the truth, Jermys Ironshield, but to let such a treasure fall back into your possession is not for me to decide. Furthermore, it is too late for your reason for wanting it. I shall let the emperor decide your fate." His voice no longer carried concern for Jermys. Now only the pleasure of his find controlled his thoughts and tones. "We leave at first light tomorrow for Draag."

A slew of cheers followed as the group returned to their camp. By the looks of the sun, it was already past midday. The care for Jermys, which had been present the previous day, now fell victim to an ego-filled leader who saw himself sitting well in the emperor's eyes. One plate of food was tossed to Jermys, but it was mostly scraps, which he had to crawl about the distance of three paces to reach, causing extreme pain and further bleeding. The day moved slowly, which set the stage for a nighttime of eternity. To make matters worse, at nightfall, the dark dwarves bound him back to a tree, although they knew he was not in any condition to escape. However, as the first moon began to shine on the glade, Jermys felt a strange sensation in his wrists.

There was a tearing sound, and then his hands were free. Instantly he wanted to turn around, but the pain was too extensive and a blindfold was placed over his eyes to prevent it anyway. He felt a hand grab his and place an object in it.

Immediately, a warm peace began to seduce and comfort him. The pains throughout his body were replaced with a harmony sung by a magic beyond comparison. Though his eyes were covered, he was certain that his entire aura glowed. The individual who had helped him fell back, completely taken by what was occurring.

A bright light encompassed Jermys's body, becoming brighter as it reached his legs. The light stretched out, forming an outline around the limbs, which were no longer present. The humming grew louder, and the one watching glanced toward the main camp, worried that the dark dwarves may wake. Yet, they slept deeply, slowly allowing their bodies to wear off the ale from the past night's celebration.

Jermys said nothing, only displayed in his face the most intense inner peace that one could extend. Time seemed to completely stop over the next hour until with one strong motion, he leaped to his feet. Softly he whispered, "For whatever reason you have for requiring the blindfold, I will respect your desire to go nameless. Just know that my appreciation is something I will spend the rest of my life trying to repay."

There was no answer to his statement, but he did hear movement. Then, in his free hand, he felt a dagger being placed. The individual grabbed his arm up to where his elbow bent, taking a firm grip, not allowing any movement that he did not want. With a violent thrust, he forced Jermys's arm forward, forcing the dagger into his own belly. Jermys forced his arm back, but he could already feel the warm blood spilling across his hand.

A raspy, contorted voice said, "Now go. When I am found, they will hunt you down, and this time not to capture you but to kill you. I have just witnessed something amazing, and I therefore know I acted correctly."

With that, he heard the individual double over. Jermys's first inclination was to run, but he knew that he could not leave the one who had helped him so greatly alone to face the brutality of San-Deene and his guards when they woke. The dark dwarf leader had become seduced with his own self-interests, and whoever had risked everything to save him would certainly be faced with the most morbid death imaginable.

Jermys reached up and removed his blindfold. Looking down, terror grew in his eyes as he watched the blood spill onto the ground, but he did understand. With a silent thank you and nod, which went unnoticed, he turned to make his escape. Stopping abruptly, he spotted a small pack lying on the ground. He glanced back in disbelief and then scooped up the provisions and disappeared into the trees.

The Next Attack

"This is the darkest forest I have ever set foot in," said Schram after he had bumped into Werner.

Hawthorne added, "It only appears that way. The cloud cover is blocking out the moon, and the trees do not allow any free light to pass."

"Regardless of the reasons, it is dark, and with that, tense. To say it differently, I do not like it."

All found the description unsettling, but as they thought more about what he had said, they realized how accurate it really was. They were now well within the somewhat-obscured borders of the region known as the Trees of Death. Though they had come across nothing threatening since they entered, that fact in itself was a little disturbing. Not finding any animal life of any kind left the forest absent of a degree of nature. Furthermore, Schram had had the distinct feeling that someone or something was watching them, although his senses could not pinpoint how many, or in what direction. He frequently stopped and peered through the trees, but even with his elven sight as an aid, he could see nothing but dense forest cover. Each time issuing a long sigh, he would turn and walk at a quick pace to catch the others who had not bothered to stop.

Hawthorne looked back as he approached. "Do you feel it too, Schram?"

"If you are referring to a presence somewhere among the trees, then yes, I feel it too."

"Can you identify it?"

He looked annoyed. "Not only can I not identify it, I cannot be certain of its existence."

"Werner, do you have any idea what…"

"I also feel nothing definite," he replied. "Never have I experienced a sensation such as this."

Schram added, "What do you think, Hawthorne? Is there some foreign dark magic at work here?"

She shook her head, tossing her hair over her shoulders. "I think there is magic at work here, but I am not sure it is foreign or evil. I have felt this before, but I cannot place it."

Schram looked up. "Now that you say that, I have felt it before also. It was…"

"There is a party of five moving to cut us off," interrupted Werner.

"Yes," Hawthorne said. "I feel them too."

"There are at least that many, maybe more. They are moving in behind us." Schram turned and began incanting a spell."

Suddenly his hands became heavy and fell to his side. Just as quickly, magical bindings appeared and quickly fastened his arms behind him. He tried to call out, but a gag appeared and took its place about his head. Telepathically he sent the single word, *Ambush!* As quickly as everything set in, his mind became clouded, and he fell unconscious.

He woke in a small room to the gentle shaking of Hawthorne. She asked his condition, and he answered her with a simple affirmative nod. Slowly pushing himself up, he saw Werner standing to the side, and the two moved over to join him. They kept their voices low but felt more confident speaking outright rather than using telepathy.

Schram had an aching head, the origin of which he was not sure, but he was certain that it was related to where they were. "What happened?" he asked.

"We were made fools of," replied Hawthorne.

Werner then added, "They had been working a spell for some time to capture us. They covered it up but every once in a while making their presence felt so we would concentrate on locating them. By the time we realized what was occurring, it was too late.

Their spell was in place, and any magic we used against it was immediately reverted upon us. If you tried telepathy, which both Hawthorne and I did, you were instantly overtaken, sending your mind into darkness."

"I too tried telepathy," he added despairingly. All I accomplished was acquiring a beating headache." He paused and took a quick look around the small room, which appeared to have no exits. "Now my only questions are, Who are the *they* you were referring to, and what need do they have with us and my staff?"

Hawthorne had not noticed the missing staff but now appeared even more concerned. "We have no idea. The last thing I remember is seeing a robed figure, armed with a bow, drawing down on me, and approaching at a quick pace."

The canok nodded. "I don't even remember that much."

She continued, "I felt for sure we would be killed without question. If the rumors about this forest are correct, we should have been, but for some reason we were spared, possibly something to do with the staff. I should have realized its absence immediately. I will have to rethink our situation."

Each of their faces showed a different level of distress but none quite as much as Schram's. The pain in his head was growing more intense, and as every moment passed, it became more of a chore for him to just remain conscious. Hawthorne noticed his discomfort and moved toward him. Is the pain still there?"

"Yes, don't you feel it?" Sweat had begun beading down his face, and his large green eyes had become dull and faded.

Hawthorne glanced toward Werner. The canok shook his head. She smiled, trying to ease his pain. "Schram, I am going to enter your mind. It should not harm you, but if you feel any added pain, say something, and I will stop."

He nodded that he understood, and Hawthorne placed one hand on the side of his head, taking one of his hands in her other. There was a brief period of silence while she seemed to be fighting against something, causing both her and Schram to jerk in rapid and violent motions. Werner looked on with great concern, but he knew that he was helpless to offer aid. Any interference of two such joined could be detrimental for all involved.

Schram felt two hands caressing his mind, but the pain remained consistent. If anything, it returned stronger. Suddenly, the hands he had felt vanished, and an ear-piercing scream broke him from his trance. For a moment, he saw a huge dragon bearing down on him, then there was nothing, and the pain was gone.

He opened his eyes to see Werner standing over Hawthorne, her body resting motionless on the floor. "What happened? Is she all right?"

Werner looked up. "I do not know. One moment she was in contact with you, and the next she was screaming in agony." There was an odd look in the canok's eyes that made Schram believe he was not hearing the entire story. He began to move toward the two, but suddenly the space between them became obscured. He froze as the air began to take shape forming what Hawthorne had previously described perfectly—a dark, hooded figure.

The only noticeable characteristic on the figure was its two large round eyes, which reflected the slight light in the room like two green moons. The figure glanced at the woman on the floor and then approached Schram. Without a word, it reached an arm out toward the human, and upon first touch, both disappeared.

Jermys had run throughout the remainder of the night and been greeted with only a light rain as morning broke through the darkness. The woods had been surprisingly and suspiciously free of goblin and dark dwarf forces. He satisfied this absence by assuming that the threat to Draag had become minimal with his capture, and therefore the dragon army forces had been pulled back.

Although his theory may have worked to settle part of his anxieties, he still found little comfort in the fact that he was near the heart of the evil-occupied land and had little idea where he should head. He had spent the last three hours running blindly through the forest on his legs, the existence of which he did not understand. Now, well past dawn, he found himself wandering through dense trees, which gave little aid to determining his whereabouts.

He gripped his hatchet tightly as he walked, making his knuckles turn a bare white. Frequently he found himself swinging outward at low-hanging limbs and branches that blocked the path he was trying to follow, though calling it a path was a bit of a reach.

With one fierce chop just past midday, he found himself entering a small glade that he immediately knew he had been in before, though he was also certain that he had not left by way of the path he entered from now. He looked around the clearing and a chill slid down his spine as he saw burn marks. They most probably were left from his previous visit to this area with his companions during their first confrontation with Slayne, Kirven, and Almok, in which their escape had only occurred by Schram's recitation of words, which had magically been spoken to him. His incantation had called on the ancient powers left in the Ring of Ku, which he had received from the dragon Sabast only hours before. A moment later, they found themselves on the Dry Sea of Nakton to begin a trek back to Toopek, minus Schram who would leave on his own to follow a destiny understood best by only him.

Jermys issued a long sigh as he remembered the desperate situation from nearly two years ago. He wondered if the times had gotten better or worse. The one striking difference for him was constantly present every time he wanted to speak. Then, he had his companions to speak to. Now, he spoke only to himself for he was alone. All his friends, the rat included, had gotten mixed up in situations, which, for all he knew, had already brought their death. The dwarf pushed his lips together tightly, fighting to keep what composure he had left. He was determined to hold to the idea that all his friends were well and more than likely worried about him more than themselves. He was about to move further into the glade when suddenly the sun disappeared.

Jermys dove into the nearest brush, not hesitating to look at the sight he had grown to recognize so well. As quickly as it had vanished, the sun reappeared, and the dragon's shadow moved out across the trees. He stared to the sky to catch the sight of the creature just before his vision was blocked by the edge of the forest. It was a large blue, probably one of the oldest of the young dragons. It was traveling on a direct course toward what Jermys now knew to be the center of Draag Mountains. On its back was a large goblin, dressed in black armor, with some sort of insignia in place across its breastplate. At the speed they were heading away, Jermys was certain they had not noticed him. However, their velocity was obviously depictive of something important, and whether he was able to save Maldor or not, Jermys now had a second reason that he must infiltrate Draag. He had to discover what emergency would send a high-ranking dragon and goblin into such a frenzied flight. He gave a brief glance to be sure the rest of the sky was clear before starting at a soft jog up a path, which he had traveled in the other direction two years before. Despite the dangers involved with traveling through the evil forests around Draag, Jermys found comfort in knowing where he was and the idea that he might have accidentally stumbled on the safest place to enter the caverns, though perhaps also the most difficult.

It took him several hours of hard trudging, but by late afternoon, Jermys broke beyond the tree line and could see several hundred paces further ahead to the strange cutaway depicting the sky window to the mirror room of Draag Caverns. There seemed to be no activity in the area, but due to its openness, he thought it better to approach after sundown. Furthermore, he would need some items from the forest to make what he had planned possible.

He slid back into the tree cover and spent a short time rummaging through the pack, which had been prepared for his escape. He found a dagger, a normal dwarven battle ax, and most importantly, several days' provisions of food. He placed the dagger and ax opposite his hatchet and then broke off some bread and dried meat to eat. After finishing his short meal, he leaped to his feet to fulfill his other requirements.

Well past sundown, Jermys slowly crept up toward the sky window. Behind him he pulled a long vine, but whether it would be long enough to reach the cavern floor, he did not know.

What I would give to have Stepha here to fly me down, he thought to himself. "What I would give to have all my friends here," he now whispered softly. He shook off his emotions, trying to keep focused on what he had ahead of him. He had already made it further than he had expected to and now found himself roughly the distance of one hundred paces from being in the heart of Draag Caverns. However, these one hundred paces were not actual steps but the approximate distance he was above the cavern floor. He cringed as he peered into the dimly lit room below him. As he leaned his small frame further over the opening, a soft hum began to emit from his hatchet, sending a cold chill down the dwarf's back.

Jermys pulled back, immediately startled and confused. However, as soon as he was clear of the opening's face, the hum ceased and the night once again became ominously still. He grabbed his Hatchet and stared at it, taking notice of the peculiar diamond stone lodged into its helve. The hum this time had sounded slightly different, and his curiosity had become intrigued. He climbed back to his feet and peered over the edge, this time holding the hatchet behind him. There was no sound. Slowly he moved it forward until once again it crossed the plane of the opening. As if lighting a fire, it began to hum. Jermys stared at the magical weapon and saw what had previously gone unnoticed. The diamond stone was glowing with an unimaginable shine each time it drew over the sky window. He shook his head, totally clueless to what it meant but hoping that it was not a warning of upcoming evil. However, for where he was about to go, he was not about to believe he would be free of hindrance. He slapped his Hatchet back to his side and, after securing the vine to the support, began to lower himself downward.

The stone sang a constant song as he descended closer to the floor. It seemed to grow louder the lower he went. He was still about thirty to forty feet from the ground and felt that to leave the hanging vine would be a mistake. With a quick word to Claudos, he removed his battle ax and flung it spinning up toward the sky window. It impacted the framework with the blade, cutting through the vine as it struck. Jermys and the remaining piece of vine were sent at a free fall downward, striking the ground with enough force for dust and small rocks to break free from the wall and the giant mirror to vibrate abnormally.

He groggily raised his head to catch his reflection staring back at him. Once again, he was completely taken by the absolute perfection contained in the cut of the glass in the mirror. There was not a mark or scratch across it. If not for the constant hum from his hatchet, he possibly would have stared into it for days. However, when the intensity of the song bit his ears, his attention was quickly drawn to it if for no other reason than to attempt to silence it. Yet, all his efforts were useless. The sound continued, and its glow seemed to give light to the entire room. He knew if this continued, a blind troll would be able to find him.

He began scurrying around trying to carefully roll up the vine but not wasting too much time worrying about it. He had decided he would head down the same passageway he had his first time here, with the idea that he must have simply gotten turned around before. However, as he began to leave, he took one more gaze into the mirror. That was when he saw it.

Jermys's eyes widened, and he slowly stepped closer to the mirror, raising his magical hatchet as he moved. He stared a long time blankly into the reflection but nothing changed. The diamond stone, which was placed in the helve and glowed so brilliantly when he looked directly at it, was totally absent in the reflection. He gingerly reached forward, attempting to touch the absent diamond stone as it was seen in the mirror. However, as he did so, his finger felt only the smooth glass. Immediately upon the touch, however, the song and the glow stopped, and the stone now appeared in the reflection just as it did in the hatchet.

Jermys almost fell over. He spun around the room, but nothing else had changed. Turning back to the mirror, he again studied what he saw. Reaching his hand out as before, Jermys tried to touch the stone as it now appeared in the mirror. Again, immediately upon his touch, the humming began, and its reflection seemed to dissolve from existence.

He stepped back and confidently slapped his hatchet to his side. He threw the coiled vine over one shoulder and, bearing a large grin, moved toward the mirror. He believed he had just found the key that had opened Draag to him, and put his mind to rest as to how he could have gotten lost his last time here—the only time in his life he had ever been wrong in direction. Reaching out, he touched the mirror a third time, and once again the noise from the diamond stone ceased, and it returned to its original dull self. He only paused a moment before turning and heading down the cavern, which every icon of his rationality was telling him led back to the cave entrance. However, he knew it did not, and within a few hundred meters, he had found the proof he needed.

The tunnel he was in no longer appeared to be one carved through the existing rock. Its sides were smooth and made not of rock but some artificially molded stone-like material. He was certain only a powerful magic could have created such a hidden world. With this in mind, he also knew that he was definitely nearing Slayne's base. However, locating the black dragon was not part of his plans. He wanted to first discover what the dragon and goblin had been in such a hurry to report, and then second, locate his friend and escape. His idea to come here alone had steadily become clear to him to have been the most foolish thing he had ever attempted. It had almost cost him his life and had caused Fehr, who had become his closest friend, though he would never tell the rat as much, possibly the same. He let out a slight grumble but sucked it back in when several voices from ahead broke the silence of the halls.

Jermys crept down the corridor, and as he turned around a narrow bend, he saw from where the sounds originated. Two large doors left ajar filled this part of the hall with light. Due to the echoing acoustics, the room appeared to be very expansive. However, Jermys was not ready for what greeted him when he peered inside.

A chamber stretching as far as the eye could see with enough spots to seat several armies filled his eyes. At the front of the hall was probably the largest throne ever constructed. It reached twenty or more meters in length and possibly at least half as many in depth. Its cushions were not of some fine embroidered material. Moreover, they were dull and flat black, giving a truly ominous impression to whoever should look upon it. Between it and the first seats were three figures, two of which Jermys recognized for sure. The goblin he had seen riding the dragon only hours before was speaking with Lord Starland. The lord's hood was pulled down, but his scaly tail shown behind him. Next to Starland stood another dragon lord, whose identity was left well hidden. The only factor that revealed anything about him was the same dragon tail appearing through the back of his cloak.

Jermys could tell they were talking, but he could not be certain of their words. He knew he must move closer, but to do so would be extremely risky. Slowly he began to enter, crawling down the aisle until he could reach the safety of the back row of seats. He continued moving underneath until he was nearly halfway through the room and he could hear Starland's voice clearly.

"Then if the troops are in place, as you have said, it will only be a matter of time."

"They are as I have said, master," the goblin replied.

Starland turned to the other dragon lord and whispered something, which sent him with a nod out of the room. Returning to the goblin, he said, "Prepare those who shall ride the dragon forces. I will assemble all the young dragons, and we will leave at once to join the front. Then, at first light, we will crush Toopek."

The goblin issued some sort of salute before hurrying down the aisle through the back doors, never even pausing as he passed the crouched dwarf. Starland seemed to be drooling in pleasure as a starved tigon would when a thick slice of flesh was placed before it. He turned and knelt beneath the throne. After a short recitation, he stood, formed into a small ball of light, and then vanished.

Jermys sat frozen for several minutes, trembling from the knowledge he had just gained. Then he sat forward, using his strong will to regain his composure. He knew what he must do and that he must act swiftly if he was to be successful. It was too late to help Toopek, and he could only pray that the human city was prepared; but with the dragon forces concentrated in the attack, there would not be any better time to help Maldor.

Jermys took one more look toward the throne and then turned to slip out the back. However, as he moved, one object caught his attention. He stopped and looked back, trying to inspect it further. It was a large, delicately carved wooden box, but its presence itself was what ignited his curiosity. It was out of place with the rest of the room. The longer he stared at it, the more he realized that it had only recently been brought there.

He turned back to the throne and silently crept toward where the box rested. As he drew closer, he began to feel a strange warmth in his leg. He glanced down to see his hatchet beginning to faintly glow. The chest was not even locked, and as he lifted the lid, his eyes grew to wondrous balls. Krirtie's scimitar and Stepha's bow both rested peacefully inside its fitted case. They too seemed to begin to glow as he reached out to take them. Without hesitating, he placed the sword, which was nearly as long as he was tall, through a notch he had in his back armor. He tossed the bow over his shoulder and then, closing the chest, swiftly and silently darted from the room. Two things immediately struck him: First, he had no idea where to go, and second, what happened to Krirtie and Stepha that they no longer carried their weapons? Both thoughts seduced his mind only moments as he realized that as he stood loaded down with weapons in the cavern hall, he stuck out like a rat at a dark dwarf dinner.

"And that's a dinner I don't want to attend for a variety of reasons," he said to himself as he began to move forward in the only direction his gut told him to go.

Characters

Schram: King of the Human city of Toopek.

Stepha: Princess of the Flyer Elves

Krirtie: Human warrior. Friend to Schram.

Kirven: White Canok with black diamond spot. Friend to Schram.

Jermys: Twin Dwarf leader

Slayne: Black Dragon behind the evil attacks.

Fehr: Bandicoot rat. Friend of all the companions.

Madeiris: King of the Elves of Elvinott

Geoff: Leader of the Maneth.

Maldor: Head of the Batt Line of the Maneth. Was captured by Slayne.

Alan Grove: Human officer overseeing leadership of Toopek.

Anbari: Greatest dragon ever to live. Resides in the black pool of the South Sea.

Almok: Black Canok with white patch on forehead. Travels with Slayne.